"I *will* be a _____ Ethan said. "_____ be alone."

Lizzie pushed on a bright smile and ignored the pain that drummed against her heart.

Ethan Colton would be an amazing father to their child.

And that was all he'd be.

Shake it off, Lizzie-girl. Shake it off.

The fantasy she'd warned herself against over the past six months—ever since that night at the rodeo—curled against the corners of her mind with reaching fingers. Although she knew it for the emotional foolishness it was, that small, hopeful piece of her had wondered if there could be more with Ethan.

"That's a lot to take on, Ethan. Especially with all the issues I'm having back at home."

"Issues we'll face together."

She sensed him before she felt him, the light press of his fingers against her shoulder drawing her attention.

"Lizzie. I mean it. You're not alone."

"I'm always alone."

"I can only imagine how scared you've been," he said, "but we'll get to the bottom of it. No one's going to hurt you."

Except you.

* * *

We hope you enjoy this dramatic series:
The Coltons of Texas—Finding love and
buried family secrets in the Lone Star state...

COLTON'S SURPRISE HEIR

BY
ADDISON FOX

All rights reserved including the right of reproduction in whole or in part in any form. This edition is published by arrangement with Harlequin Books S.A.

This is a work of fiction. Names, characters, places, locations and incidents are purely fictional and bear no relationship to any real life individuals, living or dead, or to any actual places, business establishments, locations, events or incidents. Any resemblance is entirely coincidental.

This book is sold subject to the condition that it shall not, by way of trade or otherwise, be lent, resold, hired out or otherwise circulated without the prior consent of the publisher in any form of binding or cover other than that in which it is published and without a similar condition including this condition being imposed on the subsequent purchaser.

® and ™ are trademarks owned and used by the trademark owner and/or its licensee. Trademarks marked with ® are registered with the United Kingdom Patent Office and/or the Office for Harmonisation in the Internal Market and in other countries.

First Published in Great Britain 2016
By Mills & Boon, an imprint of HarperCollins*Publishers*
1 London Bridge Street, London, SE1 9GF

© 2016 Harlequin Books S.A.

Special thanks and acknowledgement to Addison Fox
for her contribution to The Coltons of Texas series.

ISBN: 978-0-263-91930-1

18-0216

Our policy is to use papers that are natural, renewable and recyclable products and made from wood grown in sustainable forests. The logging and manufacturing processes conform to the legal environmental regulations of the country of origin.

Printed and bound in Spain
by CPI, Barcelona

Texas transplant **Addison Fox** is a lifelong romance reader, addicted to happy-ever-after. There's nothing she enjoys more than penning novels about two strong-willed, exciting people on that magical fall into love. When she's not writing, she can be found spending time with family and friends, reading or enjoying a glass of wine.

Contact Addison at her website—www.addisonfox.com—or catch up with her on Facebook (addisonfoxauthor) and Twitter (@addisonfox).

For Martha & Larry and Danielle & Scott

Families are both born and made. I'm so grateful
you've made me one of yours.

Chapter 1

Stars winked like diamonds in a sky black as pitch, the cool Texas night buffeting him with a thick wind. Frost covered the ground, crunching under his feet, a sure sign winter wasn't yet done with them. Ethan Colton kept his head down and ignored nature's display as he trudged toward the barn and the pregnant horse one of his ranch hands had called him about.

"Boss! Glad you're here." Bill Peabody, his ranch foreman, waved him over to the last stall in the barn.

"Where's Doc Peters?"

"On his way."

Ethan nodded and took in the scene before him. His favorite filly, Dream, wasn't due to deliver for about six more weeks. But her heavy breathing and wide-eyed fright suggested her new foal wasn't prepared to wait for spring.

Ethan dropped to his knees beside Dream, his hands

gentle when he reached out to stroke her neck. "Hey, baby. Shh there, beautiful girl. It's okay."

His gaze drifted from the clear lines of pain that suffused her dark brown face on down over the sleek lines of her body. The filly's rib cage contracted hard with her labored breaths, and the distended belly—the telltale sign of her pregnancy—quivered almost of its own accord.

"Think we can stop her from delivering?"

"Doc told me to keep her comfortable and as still as possible until he got here." Bill paced next to the stall. "Says he'll know better after he looks at her."

Bill's words kicked up an odd twist of memory—absolutely unbidden—of another night long ago. But with an outcome that had no hope of ending well.

Those memories had become more frequent of late, his brother's recent tussle with their father stirring it all to the fore. With the iron will he'd honed through the years, he pushed the ever-clear memory away and focused on Dream.

She was his pride and joy, along with the rest of the horses in his stable. The years of hard work, building something that was his own. That no one could taint.

He'd be damned if he'd sit by and let her suffer. Or see to it he didn't do everything he could do to make sure she had a healthy foal.

Bill worked with him in silence as they followed the vet's instructions, keeping Dream as calm as possible while they waited for help. He was pleased to see her breathing even out a bit as they settled a blanket beneath her head and several more to support the long length of her back.

"Babies are a tough thing. They're natural but not normal." Doc Peters bustled in, his cheery smile at odds with the still-sleepy eyes and tufts of gray hair that stuck out all over his head.

"Not normal?" Ethan kept his voice low, not wanting to spook Dream, but he couldn't keep from questioning the vet.

"Of course. Pregnancy is a natural state, but it's hard on the body." Doc Peters dropped to his knees, his lithe form belying what had to be at least forty years of caring for large animals. "But we'll take care of Dream here, won't we, sweetheart."

Ethan kept a calming hand on Dream's neck but said nothing more, allowing the doctor to do his work. The vet inspected the horse, his hands following all the places Ethan's own gaze had roamed for the past twenty minutes. After several endless moments of inspection and even more checks with the stethoscope, Doc Peters got to his feet.

"You ready for a long night?"

Ethan stared up at the doc's slim figure, standing over his horse. "She's having the foal tonight?"

"Not if we can help it. But we do have to get him turned around. There are two pairs of long, long legs pointing exactly where they don't belong."

Ethan took solace that the doctor seemed in control of the situation and nodded his head. "Tell us what to do."

The frigid night had given way to a cold crisp morning, and Ethan breathed in deep as he headed for the ranch house. He'd spent hours worrying they wouldn't be able to help Dream, but Doc Peters had been a pro. Bit by bit, he'd managed to turn Dream's foal back into position. Ethan knew they were out of the woods now, but he hadn't missed the concern that had stamped itself deep in the grooves on Peters's face around four that morning.

Things had been more than touch and go for a while, and Ethan had barely dared to believe things could end well, convinced he needed to brace himself for the worst. For the inevitable.

Yet the doc had done it. Dream was on her feet and happily grazing on a fresh batch of oats Bill had poured just for her when Ethan finished washing up in the sinks in the barn.

Now all he could think about was a hot shower and roughly a gallon of coffee. He might even manage something beyond the breakfast sandwiches he typically microwaved each morning. In fact, he thought he remembered seeing a rasher of bacon in the fridge the last time Bill's wife, Joyce, did a shopping order.

The back door swung open under his hand and he caught himself. Hadn't he locked it when he headed out?

The smell of coffee accosted him and the mystery of the back door vanished as he imagined Joyce over here, putting on a pot for when he got back. That woman was gold, and he'd have to remember to thank her later.

He dragged off his boots in the mudroom and turned for the kitchen. The distinct scent of bacon assailed him just before the soft, subtle hum of a popular country song followed.

But it was the woman who stood before his stove that had Ethan going still.

"What the hell are you doing here?"

Elizabeth Marie Conner—Lizzie to the few who knew and loved her—already knew she was pushing beyond acceptable boundaries by coming here in the first place.

Since she figured she had to get this over with, she might as well add bacon to the mix.

Men *loved* bacon. Heck, there were whole websites devoted to the very best part of the pig. And based on what Joyce had said when she'd let her in, Ethan had just spent a hard night.

She was smart enough to know the bacon wouldn't go all that far to soften the blow she was about to deliver, but she was hungry as a horse all the time, and it would make *her* feel better.

"That's some welcome."

The man had the sense to look contrite, and she took it as a good sign. But when a quick shot of something warm and hungry flitted through his gaze before those rich hazel depths turned cold once more, Lizzie pressed a firm hand to her fluttering stomach beneath the oversize sweatshirt she'd tugged on for the visit.

Ethan Colton was anything but cold.

And she'd had six months of very warm memories reminding her of that fact.

"You can imagine my surprise to find a woman cooking me breakfast."

Lizzie did her best to keep her body facing the stove, only turning to eye Ethan over her shoulder. "Joyce let me in. Said you were having a tough night with one of your horses. How is she?"

"Good. Fine." Talk of his horse seemed to mellow him a bit more, and he crossed to the pot of coffee. "Want some?"

"No, thanks. I'm not a coffee girl. No one at work can understand it but—" She broke off, the reality that there was no work any longer more bitter than she'd expected.

"But what?"

"Nothing."

Ethan poured his coffee and, after doctoring it with a sugar and some creamer from the fridge, moved to the long island counter at her back. "Look. I'm sorry for my greeting. I'm tired and I didn't expect anyone to be in here when I got back. And—"

He stilled, a small smile edging his lips. "And that's lame. I'm sorry for my greeting. How are you, Lizzie?"

She'd thought she was prepared. Had believed she could keep her emotions in check and her mind clear for all that was still to come between them.

Oh, how wrong she'd been.

Those hazel eyes—the ones that were an amazing mix of green and brown and several spots of gray—drew her in and touched something deep inside she couldn't quite define.

Need? Yes.

Desire? Yes.

Love? She was so *not* going there.

Even if she had harbored feelings for him since she was young. He was the big brother of her best friend in foster care. As a lifelong foster child, she'd known full well that getting attached was a bad idea, but she'd gone and done it anyway. Josie Colton had been her best friend, and her older brother Ethan… Oh, how Lizzie had looked forward to those visits he'd made three times a year to see his sister.

Until it had all ended with nothing but empty promises and long, lonely days without her best friend.

So when he'd appeared like a dream six months ago at a rodeo they were both attending, she couldn't shake off the chance to see him again and spend some time together.

"Lizzie? How are you?"

She pulled herself back from the thick morass of memories and unfulfilled wants. "Good. I'm good."

"You look good—" He broke off before he added, "But you always look good. No one I've ever met has green eyes quite like yours."

She stilled, the bacon popping and crackling, as she braced herself for what she had to do. Flipping off the stove, she moved the bacon to the back burner and turned around and looked her fill.

Her gaze roamed, hungry, over the sandy-brown hair she knew was the texture of unrefined cotton. On down over the broad shoulders that seemed custom-made for a woman's hands. And then over the broad chest that was banded in thick sinew, from the hard swath of his pectorals on down to the ridges of muscle that framed his stomach.

The man was a vision, and the sweet boy she'd had a crush on had grown into a formidable man.

Get it together, Elizabeth Marie. Stop ogling him and tell the man the reason you're here.

Yet even as that steely voice—the one that had pushed her through college and on into becoming the youngest loan officer at her bank—whispered to her to just come out with it, she couldn't help but indulge the woman's need that had her stopping for a moment. It was rude to stare—hadn't one of her foster mothers taught her that?—but she couldn't quite help herself.

She'd look her fill, because after this morning things would never again be the same.

And as Ethan's gaze traveled its own path, over her face, a tentative smile quirking his lips, she knew the moment when something else registered.

Knew the moment that smile faltered when he caught

sight of the very clear bump that had replaced her normally flat stomach.

"Lizzie? What—"

A loud popping sound pulled her from the moment and Lizzie turned on a hard exhalation. "Oh, no!"

Even though she'd moved it off the heat, the bacon had continued cooking in the oil and had gone crisp to the point of burning.

"Let me." Ethan moved into her space, gently pushing her aside as he grabbed the thick cast iron off the stove. He tilted the pan over a pie plate she'd already set aside, layered with paper towels to absorb the grease.

And as she watched the bacon slide from the skillet, the grease that had cooked out sliding along with it, Lizzie felt the bottom drop out of her stomach.

Clamping a hand over her mouth, she ran toward the mudroom and prayed she'd make it to the back door in time.

One moment he was staring into eyes of the most vivid green, fresh as a spring day, and imagining things he most definitely should *not* be imagining. Then his mind had taken an entirely different tack as his gaze settled on her stomach.

And then Ethan was watching Lizzie Conner race out of his kitchen as though Satan's hounds were nipping at her heels.

He slammed the skillet back on the stove, then raced after her. What in the blazing hell was going on?

Ethan heard the hard slam of the back screen door and the distinctive sounds of retching just as he came upon the entryway. As clear as a bell, Doc Peters's words screamed through his mind.

Babies are a tough thing. They're natural but not normal.

"Lizzie!" He pushed through the door, his mind whirling with a thousand thoughts, all louder than the cicadas in August.

But the thought that screamed the loudest was to get to her.

He closed the short distance between the door and the bushes that rimmed his back patio and wrapped his arm around her shoulders, holding her as she leaned forward once more. He kept one hand on her arm while the other gathered the thick, curly strands of her hair into a firm hold.

"Shh. It's all right."

Heat suffused her cheeks, and he felt the same warmth radiating from her slim shoulders as he pulled her close. "Are you okay?"

"Oh, no." The words came out in a mix of half squeak and half moan as she straightened. "Oh, Ethan. I'm so sorry."

"It's fine."

Those slim shoulders straightened right up and she pulled out of his hold. The soft strands of her hair slipped through his fingers, and he was surprised at how bereft he felt when nothing but cold morning air took their place.

"What's going on, Lizzie?"

Pregnancy is a natural state, but it's hard on the body.

Those damn words continued to taunt him, the unspoken truth hovering between them more powerful than the tornadoes that whipped through Texas in spring.

"Can we go back inside?" Her lips quivered, and he

quickly shrugged out of the old sweatshirt he'd shoved on the night before.

"Layer up. It's only February."

He took her hand and pulled her toward the house. Something in his chest turned over when she dragged the ratty old Dallas Cowboys sweatshirt on over her head, her stomach pressed against the material of the sweatshirt she already wore. She was a slender thing, tall and willowy, but even with another thick layer of material covering her torso, her stomach still bore a definitive bump.

It was no trick of the morning light through his back windows. Nor was it some fanciful play of imagination after a long night without sleep.

The flat stomach he'd explored on a sensual journey one lonely night was nowhere in evidence. And after living with a head full of erotic visions for six agonizing months, he knew damn well his memory wasn't the least bit faulty.

He'd explored every inch of Lizzie Conner's body. Had tasted every soft dip and expanse of her skin. Had buried himself deep inside her, allowing every one of the long, lonely years they'd held in common to fade away in the joy of being together.

Ethan stopped himself, pushing away the sharp tang of awareness that made him want things he had resolved never to have.

The scent of bacon still lit up the kitchen, and he shot a concerned glance at her. "Do you need me to throw out breakfast?"

"No!" She shook her head before wrapping her hands tight around herself. "No, I'm fine now."

"Why don't we go into the living room. It'll keep for a few more minutes."

"Drain it first. Please. It was—" She broke off, swallowing hard. "The grease was what turned my stomach. If you don't drain it, we can't eat it later. I just need to slip to your powder room for a quick minute."

He directed her down the hall, then did as she'd asked with breakfast. He snatched up one of the slices as he patted the rest dry with paper towels, knowing full well he needed a heck of a lot more fortification than a few pieces of bacon.

But a man took what he could get.

And braced himself for the news he was going to be a father.

Lizzie ignored the pale face that stared back at her from the mirror and deftly swished her mouth out with water. She'd thought she was past tossing her cookies after the first trimester, but there were still some things with food that sneaked up and caught her unawares.

Now bacon grease, she mentally chastised herself, adding to the growing list that also included raw chicken, onions and pudding.

"Oh, and don't forget facing the father of your child," she muttered to herself as she did a quick hunt for mouthwash in the medicine cabinet. She came up empty on the rinse but did find a small tube of toothpaste in its stead.

Mouth clean once more, Lizzie squared her shoulders. She'd put this off long enough—it was time to tell Ethan the truth. She slipped off the sweatshirt, loath to remove the soft cotton that smelled of him—a mix of the outdoors and something raw and wholly *male*—and folded it as she walked.

He stood before the large fireplace, the thick stone like a frame. He was a hard man, she knew, harder even than the slate at his back. He'd shown signs of it even as a young boy—and who wouldn't after what he and his siblings had lived through?

But Ethan had suffered more than the rest of them.

At the age of seven he'd discovered his mother lying murdered out behind the family's farmhouse. A red bull's-eye was painted on her forehead in Magic Marker, the clear mark of his father, one of Texas's most notorious serial killers.

"Lizzie, are you okay?"

"I'm fine."

She pushed away the images that assailed her at the very thought of what he'd discovered and focused on the here and now.

And what she had to share with him.

"I have something to tell you."

Ethan nodded, his face resigned, but he held his position before the fireplace. "I think I might have an idea."

"I'm pregnant."

He nodded again, and whether it was in acknowledgment of her words or the response of someone dumbfounded and searching for something to say, she wasn't sure. After all, she'd had almost six months to get used to the idea.

And he'd had none.

"What took you so long to tell me?"

"I didn't—" She hesitated, even though she'd prepared for this question. "I know how you feel about children. You were honest with me. That night and even when we were kids, you'd mentioned it a few times. That you don't want children. That you're afraid to pass on—"

She broke off again, heat creeping up her neck and into her cheeks.

Damn. She so didn't want to go there.

Ethan had told her of his fears. That he believed his

father's psychopathic tendencies ran in his blood, and for that reason, he'd never have children. She'd tried to tell him it was a load of bullshit, but he wouldn't be put off. And if Lizzie were fair, she knew the roots of his fear were all too real.

She'd grown up in foster care, too, her parents a non-existent memory. Who gave up their child, leaving them to the care of strangers? She hadn't even been good enough for adoption. Oh, no, instead she'd gone from foster home to foster home, cared for by people who by and large were kind but overworked, overextended with the number of children in their care and unwilling to allow themselves to get too attached.

"You're right. I made a vow, and I believe in my reasons. None of it changes the reality that there is a child on its way that, by your presence, I assume is mine."

"Of course!"

The question beneath his words was a slap, but she stood tall. Although she wasn't an innocent, she wasn't a woman who would pass off the child of another man. And she hadn't had sex in some time, all her relationships seeming to end after a date or two, before things got intimate or too serious.

"I'm sorry." He shook his head. "That was out of line. I know you. And I've known you for a long time. I just didn't think— I mean, we used protection."

"Which I thought was effective. I did ask my doctor about it, and she said that while usually effective, there's a reason the box comes with a warning. We're the one percent where the condom didn't work."

"I guess we are." A harsh laugh escaped his lips. "I've spent my entire damn life avoiding slips outside the lines. Clearly I'm not trying hard enough."

His words were like icicles against her skin, but

she stood strong, refusing to cower. She wanted to be angry—to accuse him of being a heartless bastard—but she knew all about trying to live a good life. A *perfect* life. And she knew what that quest for perfection did to a person.

That bone-deep fear that you'd never be enough, just as you were.

She'd spent years working through the lingering pain of being a foster child, and she knew there were no easy answers. After she'd got her job with the bank, the benefits had allowed her to seek out counseling, and she'd willingly gone to a therapist, eager to talk through the self-doubt that had plagued her through much of her life.

Although she'd instinctively known the choice to abandon her was the fault of those nameless, faceless parents, working with someone had helped bring things into focus. Had helped her believe in herself and her dreams for her future.

So she marched on. And on the days when the doubt demons spoke too loudly, she practiced the techniques Dr. Johansen had given her to stay afloat.

"Yes, I'm having a baby. And yes, it's yours."

"Is it a boy or a girl?"

"I—" She broke off, surprise filling her at the simple question. "I don't know. I haven't wanted to know."

His hazel eyes had gone nearly as gray as the wall of slate behind him. "I deserved to know, Lizzie."

He *did* deserve to know. And while she'd had her reasons for waiting—namely his lifelong feelings on fatherhood—it didn't change the fact that she'd cheated him of the knowledge he was going to be a parent.

"I didn't want to burden you with this. I know how you feel about…about children."

"So you thought I'd rather stay in the dark than accept my responsibilities?" His voice was quiet—too quiet—but the power of his words ricocheted around the room with all the force of gunshots.

Head high, she drew on every reserve she had. "I know how to accept *my* responsibilities. And I can take care of myself and my child."

"Our child."

Our child. *Our.*

She only nodded, the truth that had needled her since discovering her pregnancy blossoming into full-blown guilt. "Yes. Our child."

"So what changed?"

"I've had some problems at work."

Whatever else he'd been about to say faded as he stared at her. "What sort of problems?"

The fear that had dogged her for the past few months gripped her in tight fingers, rattling her spine until a line of shivers worked its way through her body. "Notes. Flowers. And recently, someone broke into my house."

"Do you know who?"

"No." Something in his gaze had her going still and words clogged in her throat.

He finally moved, dragging her close, his arms wrapping tight around her. "You don't have any idea? None at all?"

"I can't think of anyone." She kept her arms at her sides, unwilling to get too close to the delicious heat that was Ethan Colton. Too afraid to draw on the strength to be found in his arms. "But the incidents began after I announced my pregnancy at work."

"Tell me about them." His arms stayed wrapped around her, but his hand drifted to her lower back, rubbing in small circles. Heat filled her everywhere their bodies touched, but it was that simple gesture of comfort that was nearly her undoing.

Tears gripped her throat in a hard fist and she swallowed around it, unwilling to finally let the dam break on her emotions.

"The notes are bad. And they've escalated. The last one was the worst. It was wrapped around a rattle in the crib I'd set up in the baby's room."

Ethan's arms tightened around her while his body stiffened into implacable lines. "What did it say?"

"It said—" Lizzie winced at the hitch that caught in her throat, but pressed on anyway. "The note said, 'I'll be a great daddy. You'll see.'"

Chapter 2

Ethan gritted his teeth, his jaw so tight it was a wonder it didn't lock.

I'll be a great daddy.

Taunting notes from a cowardly bastard, determined to scare Lizzie. Or worse.

Although he'd avoided police work like the plague, growing up with five of his siblings in various branches of law enforcement had given him a better sense of the criminal mind than the average person. Add on his upbringing and he could practically teach a damn class on the criminal mind.

But it was the "You'll see" signing off the note that had him the most concerned. Escalating behavior that by her own assessment had grown worse over the past few months. And taunting notes that now accompanied a B&E.

He maintained his hold on her arms, but moved them

both to the couch. "Why don't we start from the beginning. Tell me everything."

"I need to get something out of the way first."

Those large green eyes remained steady on his, her spine arrow straight. Despite the fatigue that had dogged him since heading out to the barn the night before, something he couldn't quite hold back sparked deep inside.

Damn, but she was a looker. And just as forthright and honest as she'd been when she was ten.

He could still picture those days. The sanctioned foster visits from the home he had been placed in to his kid sister, Josie, and the time he'd spent with her and her best friend, Lizzie. Josie had made it a point to include the gangly, awkward girl, whispering to Ethan that Lizzie had no one and he needed to be nice.

Not that he'd have ever been anything else. His father might have set a poor example, but his mother had drilled into him and his siblings the proper way to behave. And how to treat others.

Shaking off the ancient thoughts, he focused again on Lizzie. The gangly preteen had given way to an incredibly beautiful woman. She was tall—he'd estimate five-nine to his six-two—and slim. Refined. The child who'd delighted in mud pies and tree climbing had given way to an elegant young woman with a sophisticated tumble of soft brown curls that framed her face, ambition flaring high and bright in her gaze.

"Okay. What is it?"

"I didn't do this—" She stared down at her stomach. "I didn't get pregnant on purpose."

"Okay."

"That's it?"

"Are you telling me the truth?"

"Of course."

"Then okay."

Ethan wasn't a man who smiled often, but her puzzled expression nearly had him laughing. "I'm a straight talker, Lizzie. You know that."

"Yes, but—"

"But what?"

"I didn't expect such easy acceptance. Not about this."

A small voice kept beating against his skull that bringing a child into the world was a bad idea, but it was increasingly outshouted by the image of a tiny infant, snuggled warm and safe in her arms. His child.

Their child.

The panic he'd have expected at the news swarmed through his bloodstream but never seemed to land anywhere. Never seemed to settle.

Ethan wanted to be angry—hell, he expected *that* reaction—but no matter how he turned the raw play of emotions threatening to swamp him, he couldn't quite manage to hang on to a single one.

Except need.

A sort of bone-deep desperation that simply cut a man off at the knees.

A strange reality settled over them, charging the quiet air with sparks of electricity.

Chemistry.

They'd had it, even as children. His sister needn't have bothered with her admonishments to be nice and friendly. He'd always had a soft spot for Lizzie Conner. And long after the visits to see Josie at her foster home had stopped, he'd had fond memories of the endless, carefree days they'd played hide-and-seek and tag and dodgeball.

He hadn't had many carefree days in his life, and he cherished the memories.

"I'll figure out the acceptance part later. Right now, let's focus on what's happening. You're having a baby. *My* baby."

The fierce possession that fired his blood was even more surprising than the visions of a tiny infant wrapped in her arms.

He was going to be a father.

And despite the piss-poor example he'd been given, he would do everything in his power to do right by his child.

Lizzie's gaze lifted to meet his once more, and something he couldn't quite define lit up those verdant green depths. It was too soft to be anger, yet too mild to be anything near acceptance. "This is my child, and there is nothing I won't do to protect him. Or her."

"Likewise."

"Good." She laid her hands over her belly, and he wondered if she even realized the gesture of protection for what it was. The tightness in his gut ever since he saw the bump beneath her sweatshirt loosened another few degrees, and he latched on to something a bit easier to handle.

"You really don't know if it's a boy or girl?"

"I wanted it to be a surprise."

"But you've decorated?"

"A few things. Just some of the basics, really. The rest will come."

The hands that had cradled her stomach settled in her lap, twisting over each other. That small show of nerves released another layer of tension, and he had to admit it had taken real courage for her to come to him this morning.

"I don't want to rehash old territory, but you made it clear to me you didn't want children. What's changed your mind?"

Reality.

That lone word screamed through his mind, but he remembered their conversation, too, that night at the rodeo. His harsh implacability, even when she'd dared to suggest he'd make a wonderful father.

"I—" She hesitated before pressing on. "I understand your reasons, Ethan."

He'd made it a personal policy never to talk about his father. And then he'd run into Lizzie, both of them attending the rodeo on lone tickets. He'd gone on impulse, the desire to escape roiling emotions he had no interest in feeling pushing him toward an evening of mindless entertainment.

And then he'd found her, standing at will call picking up a ticket she'd arranged earlier that afternoon.

Polite conversation and a shared tub of popcorn had given way to an evening together. The local stock association had made a night of it, adding a lit tent for dancing after the rodeo out in the large field adjacent to the event center. They'd talked and danced, the conversation flowing as easy as the beer.

Something had changed that night. Matthew Colton's sins had always suffocated him, the emotional equivalent of a wool blanket in July, but that night he'd let some of it go. They'd talked, their shared history giving way to a sense of intimacy he rarely allowed himself.

He had shared with her his attitude on marriage and fatherhood. While he wasn't averse to marriage, he knew children would be a natural expectation of his wife, and he wasn't willing to saddle anyone with the risk.

His father's blood beat in his veins.

Matthew Colton was one of Texas's most notorious serial killers, currently serving out several life terms for a shocking string of murders, the last of which was his wife. The state had tried repeatedly for the death penalty, but the old man had managed to dodge the proverbial noose. And now he was dying of cancer.

Ethan had got the cancer news the same day as the rodeo. It was the only reason he'd been able to give himself as to why he'd been so honest with Lizzie. He was human, after all. And no matter how much he wanted to bottle up the endless sea of hatred he held for the old man, even the deepest waters sometimes washed up on shore.

Lizzie knew him and his family. Their background. She was safe. And he'd shared more with her than he'd ever shared with anyone.

He'd thought about calling her since then, more than once. Although they hadn't shared personal information, he could have found her. Hell, he knew damn well it wouldn't have taken more than a quick computer search to discover some way to get in contact. Or he could simply reverse that hour-long drive back to her home clear across the county.

But he'd held back, torturing himself with the heated memories of the hours they'd shared together, convinced she deserved so much more than he could give her.

Yet here he sat, six agonizing months later, in the crosshairs of a sobering truth. The very thing he'd spent his adult life running from had finally caught up with him.

Ethan stared at her, her large eyes solemn as she held his gaze. With gentle fingers, he reached out and brushed a soft curl behind her ear.

"My reasons don't matter anymore. From this moment on, we discuss our child. We make decisions for our child. Together."

There were those words again. *Our child.* As if Ethan Colton was an anxious, expectant father, excited to finally welcome his son or daughter into the world.

Don't get attached, Lizzie girl. It never ends well.

Shaking off the reality of her life along with the warmth of his touch, she stood. She couldn't allow herself to become dependent.

Or to need him too much.

"I haven't told you everything yet."

That tough demeanor had returned to his gaze as Ethan stood, matching her toe to toe. "You mean the notes."

She nodded, then took a deep breath. She'd practiced on the car ride here, working through how she'd tell him.

Calm. Cool. Controlled.

She'd imagined those words, then imagined what they'd feel like, willing her emotions to match.

So how mortifying to feel the sting of tears pricking her eyes.

"Come on, Lizzie." He took her hand and pulled her to the couch. "We'll deal with it. Whatever it is."

She wanted to fight the delicious warmth of his hand wrapped around hers, but it felt so good. And so safe. The endless days of thinking herself in the throes of some pregnant mania had given way to a sobering reality, and it felt good to have some support, even if it would ultimately be fleeting.

So she kept her hand in his and launched into her story.

"I think you know I'm a loan officer for a bank, in their corporate office. We have responsibility for about thirty counties in Texas and a sister office in Austin that covers the southern portion of the state. It's a sizable territory, and there are about eighty of us."

"It sounds like a good job."

Was a good job, Lizzie lamented to herself before she pressed on. "It is. I was well respected and getting more responsibility. I made it clear to my boss that this is my career and I'm committed to it."

"And they got upset when you announced your pregnancy?"

"That's what was odd. Not only was my boss excited, she wanted to throw me a shower. Said this was happy news and that I'd make a great mother."

She saw the confusion stamped on Ethan's face and knew it was a match for her own. The conversation she'd dreaded from the moment she'd discovered her pregnancy had instead confirmed she'd been working for the right employer. The office consistently preached work-life balance and family values, and their reaction had only confirmed that ethos.

They were happy for her.

"So what's with the notes? It doesn't sound like anyone has an ax to grind."

"A few weeks after my pregnancy became office news, the notes started. I'd waited until I'd passed my first trimester, but you can only hide the proof for so long." A small laugh bubbled up at that, the maternity clothes she'd purchased early on a giveaway of her condition, even to the few who hadn't heard the news. "As I said, my boss was excited, and once I gave her the okay to mention it, all she could talk about was baby clothes and a shower and stuffed animals."

"Is it possible someone at the office got jealous? Maybe someone who couldn't have a child? Joy in others often makes what we can't have even worse."

"I don't think so. I mean, we're a relatively young staff and several other coworkers have had babies or the fathers have taken paternity leave. There's nothing out of the ordinary in being pregnant."

"Did you keep the notes?"

"Not right away. The first couple I threw away. I know it was stupid, but I didn't want to give them any credence or an ounce of my time. But after I got a few more I took them to the police."

"Did they put someone on your case? Someone who could watch out for you?"

"For a few days, but when nothing else manifested they had to prioritize something more important."

"That's a load of bull. You were obviously threatened."

"And they tried. A detective came to work and asked questions, and several officers drove by my home. But what were they supposed to do, Ethan? The threats stopped for a while, but they can't watch out for me indefinitely."

"What about the flowers? Did the detective follow that lead?"

"Yes, and it was a dead end. The florist was questioned, but the payment was in cash and the name given for the sender ended up being fake."

Ethan snorted at that, his disgust palpable. While she was inclined to agree with him—especially staring down a series of creepy notes—she also knew the police had to deal with real cases.

Real victims.

Until the last one.

"They've called several times since to check on me, but once the rattle came I'd had enough."

"What did the good detective say about that one?"

"It was hard for him to say anything."

"Why's that? You had evidence. Something that likely had prints."

"I'm sure it didn't. The few notes they analyzed had no fingerprints. Whoever's doing this has been careful. Besides, it didn't matter." A hard shiver gripped her despite the warmth of the room. "The rattle disappeared."

"What? When?"

"Two nights ago. When I got home from work. I didn't know what to do with it, so I left it on my kitchen counter, but when I got home it was gone."

"Do you have a security system?"

His simple, direct questions calmed her, and she focused on his words. On answering each query instead of on the reality of what she was dealing with. A monster.

"I never saw the point. I don't live in anything extravagant."

"You're a woman alone. You should have protection."

"I realize that now. But I quit the next morning and packed up my stuff. I can't afford to leave my job, but I can't stay. I can't, Ethan. I can't."

The panic she'd managed to hold at bay reached up to swamp her, the shivers turning into coarse waves of terror.

Someone wanted to harm her baby.

And they had no problem going through her to reach their goal.

Erica Morgan dug her keys out of her purse and hot-footed it through the crisp early morning air. Why did the parking lot of the Granite Gulch Saloon always look so forlorn and empty in the daylight?

Even with the vivid blue sky overhead, the gray gravel parking lot seemed to suck up Mother Nature's attempts at brightening the day.

A wicked gust of wind kicked up and she ignored a hard shudder as she stuck the key into the lock of her old pickup. Wow, was it freaking cold. February had been a bitch so far, and the weather reports suggested they were in for at least another week of the bone-chilling cold. All she wanted was her bed and the thriller whose pages still beckoned from her bedside table.

She could have been wrapped up in her grandmother's old quilt already if she hadn't volunteered to do inventory after closing. But the owner paid well for the overtime, and besides the thriller, it wasn't as if she had much else to do.

Of course, she hadn't meant to fall asleep in the back office, either. The sound of crunching gravel outside the window had finally woken her up and it had taken her several moments to figure out where the heck she was with her cheek stuck to a clipboard.

Erica shook her head and stuffed a free hand in her pocket while she jiggled the lock. Stupid truck.

The lock finally flipped open, and she jumped into the cab that was nearly as cold as the outside temperature. The only saving grace was the absence of wind. The engine turned over a few times before finally catching, and she slammed the heat on high, not even remotely hopeful her old beater would be warm by the time she pulled into her spot in front of her apartment.

She gave the truck a moment to warm up and considered the noise that had finally brought her awake. What was outside Hal's office at eight in the morning? Unwilling to stick around and make an introduction to some Texas wildlife, she'd left Hal a note to check her numbers on the new keg orders and headed out. She'd have to remember to tell him about whatever it was sneaking around—coyotes, probably—she thought as she put the pickup into Drive.

The early morning sun caught on something in the distance, and she hit the brake. Leaning forward over the steering wheel, she tried to make sense of the flash she'd seen.

A mirror?

The light flashed once more, and she had the vague sense of a pair of binoculars before it vanished.

Without stopping to question why, Erica slammed her hand over her door lock and peeled out of the parking lot. She just needed to get home.

And once she did—once she was wrapped up in Nana's quilt—she'd think about what she saw.

And then she'd tell Hal there was someone creeping around outside the Granite Gulch Saloon.

Chapter 3

Ethan shoved his feet back into his work boots, his conversation with Lizzie louder than crashing cymbals in his head.

A stalker had threatened her. The police were about as helpful as they usually were. And he was going to be a father.

"It's certainly been a hell of a morning, Colton."

He finished tying off his laces and got to his feet, embarrassed to be caught talking to himself when he saw Lizzie standing at the entry to the kitchen. "Did you hear that?"

"Yes."

"Sorry."

"For speaking the truth? I can hardly blame you for that, Ethan."

"I don't usually do that." He wasn't crazy, and he hated anything that might make him appear as if he was.

"I talk to myself all the time. Most of the time I'm better company than the majority of people I know."

Ethan couldn't quite resist her wry grin and once again was struck by how enticing she was. Sunlight spilled through the mudroom, highlighting her features. She was too tall to be considered delicate, yet there was something ethereal about her. As if she were made of spun sugar and would float away at the slightest touch.

Since he already knew she tasted better than an entire bag of cotton candy, he shook off the fanciful notion and pointed toward the back door. "I need to go check on Dream."

"Your horse? Joyce mentioned she was having some issues when she let me in."

The reminder that his foreman's wife had already met Lizzie—and no doubt hadn't missed the pregnancy bump—only made what they'd shared that much more real. Joyce wasn't a gossip, but she would be beside herself at the news there was a baby on the way.

"She had a rough night, but the vet thinks she's back on track."

"May I go with you? To see her?"

He'd been raised with six siblings, none of whom loved animals with quite the same bone-deep affection he had. On the rare occasions they got together, his siblings were forever teasing him about his preference for a barn instead of a party.

"You really want to?"

"Oh, yes." Color ran high on her cheeks, and her enthusiasm was contagious.

"Bundle up. The barn is cold."

She slipped into a large puffy coat and Ethan watched, fascinated, as the material stretched across her stomach. He didn't want to be caught staring, but he couldn't quite hide the continued mix of shock and satisfaction that gripped him. That bump was *his* child, warm and safe, protected by Lizzie's body.

Since that thought quickly led to how the child had got there, he pushed aside the primitive thoughts and gestured her out the door.

"Winter's been colder than usual." Several puffs of breath punctuated her comment.

"It's always a crapshoot in this part of the state, but we've definitely got our fair share. Reports keep saying we're due for at least two more storms before the month's out." Ethan took her arm to help her over the dented dirt path that led to the barn and made a mental note to fill in several of the larger divots.

They walked the rest of the way in silence, their breathing the only sound between them. Ethan opened the door of the barn and gestured her through, then followed her down the long corridor that held stalls branching off on both sides.

From behind he couldn't see any difference in her shape, and a strange—and altogether unexpected— thought popped into his head. His sister Annabel had mentioned a friend who "carried high" and claimed it was a boy.

Was Lizzie carrying his son?

Ethan had always wondered at the people who seemed desperate to have one sex over the other. Wasn't a healthy child the goal?

But the prospect—old wives' tale or not—that the child might be a boy struck with a hard slap. Boys grew into men. And just like that, images of his father and all the man had been capable of rooted him to the ground as if he were wearing cement shoes.

It wasn't possible, was it? The idea he'd pass his father's blood on to a child had always filled him with fear. But *now*.

Now that there was a real baby…

"What is it?"

Ethan hadn't even realized he'd stopped until Lizzie turned around and waved him forward. "Nothing."

"You sure? You look like you've seen a cross between the ghost of Christmas past and the Headless Horseman."

Her tease was light and airy, but the concern underneath the words was hard to miss. "I'm good."

Ethan flung off whatever had momentarily gripped him. He needed to deal in facts. And in reality. He was going to be a father, and now that he knew that, he'd do whatever it took to care for his child. To see that he or she grew into a healthy, well-adjusted adult. He'd give everything he possessed to make that a reality.

He stalked the rest of the way to Dream's stall, pleased to see his filly's eyes bright and devoid of pain. "Hello, beautiful girl."

Dream nuzzled his hand, her soft movements full of the trusting bond they shared. Ethan spent several long minutes stroking the horse's neck before turning toward Lizzie. "This is Dream."

"She's gorgeous."

Lizzie stepped up, her hand already extended before Ethan stilled the movement. "Why don't you sweeten the deal a bit?"

He dug an ever-present sugar cube from his coat pocket and handed it over. "It's always nice to bring a gift for a brand-new introduction."

Something warm raced up his arm as their fingers touched, the simple gesture of handing over the sugar cube suddenly fraught with electricity and meaning. Her green siren's eyes widened before something needy and deeply primitive flashed there.

Attraction. Want. Desire.

The force of it nearly took him to his knees, and he ran his index finger over her open palm, the flesh soft and pliant.

"Thanks for the sugar." Her gaze dropped to where their hands were still tentatively joined, and he sensed the deepest regret when she pulled her palm away. "I hope she likes me."

He couldn't quite find his voice, the thick croak when he did finally speak gruff and hoarse. "She'll like you fine."

"We'll see." Without hesitation, Lizzie stuck her hand out, her reach steady. "Hello again, sweet girl. How are you?"

The sugar cube vanished in an instant, but it was enough to break the ice. Dream lightly pressed her nose to Lizzie's palm before bending her head slightly. They spent several moments like that, Lizzie running her hands over Dream's nose, cheeks and neck and Dream accepting the simple gestures of affection.

Ethan stood back to give them a moment, struck by the odd awareness they were both pregnant. He knew it wasn't the same—a woman and a horse—yet he couldn't deny there was something both deeply present and mysteriously ancient about their mutual situation.

Lizzie turned from her ministrations, her hand still lingering on the mane of her new friend. "What was wrong this morning? She seems absolutely fine. She's such a sweet thing."

"Her foal needed to be turned around."

"She's pregnant?"

"Yep. If things stay on track, we'll have a new foal next month."

Lizzie wasn't sure why the fact Ethan had spent the night in the barn with a pregnant horse struck her with such force, but the symbolism lanced through her with all the finesse of a battering ram.

A sign.

She couldn't deny the sweet joy and relief that swept through her at the silly acknowledgment.

Although she considered herself far too practical to engage in things beyond her control, she'd spent her life paying attention to the small signs that seemed like a direction, pointing the way. A small patch of pink tulips that bloomed the day she received her college acceptance letter. The same colored blooms planted around the entrance to her office the day she interviewed for her job.

Those and so many others made up a series of memories that told her she was pushing in the proper direction.

Finding out Ethan Colton's prize horse was pregnant, too, felt like that patch of tulips.

Important.

The hum of voices echoed from the far end of the barn. Lizzie had nearly turned, ready to let Ethan know she'd leave him to his work for a while, when a comment by one of his ranch hands had her going still.

"They say it's another serial killer, right here in Blackthorn County. Being steered from prison by Matthew Colton."

"No way, Gus. Colton's locked up good and tight. It's a copycat out for attention."

The two men came to a halt when they realized there were others in the barn, and both quickly doffed their hats. "Good morning, ma'am. Mr. Colton."

Ethan had gone so still he could have been carved in glass, and Lizzie didn't even realize she'd been holding her breath until he spoke.

"Morning, Gus. Trey. Bill will be in a bit late. We had some midnight excitement with Dream here."

She waited while Ethan talked to his men, their attention focused on the list of tasks as he described them. Both nodded their heads and seemed eager to get to work.

Lizzie waited until the men went off to their tasks before turning toward Ethan. She wanted to cringe at her overly bright voice but pressed on. "Why don't I let you get back to things? It sounds like a busy morning. I can take care of our breakfast dishes and get out of your hair for a bit."

"You're not in my hair." He tugged at a few strands of his short sandy-brown hair. "See. Empty."

"Ethan—"

It was a silly joke, and she almost laughed, solely to keep that delicate balance of normal, when he moved up into her space, a short curse spilling from his lips. "I'm sorry you had to hear that."

"I'm not. I read the paper. Watch the news. I know what's been going on in Blackthorn County."

And she did know. A series of copycat killings were happening in their backyard, all of them leaving the victims with the distinctive red bull's-eye that had been Matthew Colton's trademark.

The Alphabet Killer, as the press had dubbed the perpetrator, was increasingly gaining national coverage. With both the bull's-eye marking and a penchant for killing women in alphabetical order, the murderer's notoriety was building. The murders had been all her coworkers could talk about, and now that the killer was up to *D*, it was all the nation could talk about, too.

"My father is in prison. He's not making an outreach to anyone. He can't be behind this again. We've all made sure of that."

His use of the word *again* tore at something deep within her, but she kept her attention firm. Unyielding. His younger sister, Josie, had been her best friend, and after their initial days getting to know each other, they'd become confidantes.

She could still remember Josie's frustration when talking about her father.

People look at you with such pity, as if they can somehow wish it all away. It's like if they don't mention him or all he's done, he's not some deranged psychotic killer.

But he is.

"People do some terrible things for attention. There are those who look to convicted criminals as inspiration."

"My father's a monster."

"Yet to some, he's a hero."

Although she was aware of the crimes, the story had taken a backseat to her own problems. Now that she was here, Lizzie finally understood the problem wasn't so distant to Ethan.

"Your brother Sam's a cop, right? What does he think about it?"

Ethan glanced over his shoulder in the direction of his stable hands before taking her arm once more. "Let's go back in the house."

"Of course."

In a matter of minutes, she was once again seated on his couch, a fire blazing to chase away the cold. Ethan sat beside her, but even with the fire so close, it couldn't chase away the cold shadow that seemed to hover around him.

"You want to talk about it?"

"Not really."

"Let me rephrase that. Why don't you tell me what you know. What does Sam think about a copycat killer on the loose?"

Based on his reticence to discuss the murders, Lizzie braced herself for a cold, clinical retelling of whatever information he had.

The fierce grip on her hands told an entirely different tale.

"Sam thinks—" Ethan broke off on a hard shudder before shifting gears. "Lizzie. Don't you see? That's what lives inside me. What now lives inside our child. I've passed it on to an innocent."

His gaze dropped to her stomach, and she'd have had to be blind to miss the fierce protection she saw in the hazel depths. Whatever he believed, she knew she had to convince him otherwise. "It's not genetics, Ethan. It's a sick and twisted reaction to life. To living. You're not your father, and our child won't be, either."

"How can you say that?"

"I know it. To the very depths of my soul, I *know*."

Ethan dropped the hold on her hands and leaped up as if singed. He paced the length of the room, his strides long. Powerful. "He's my father. And he went on a killing spree twenty years ago to avenge his issues with his brother. His own damn flesh and blood. How can you say that's not personal? That it's not based on something sick and twisted inside him?"

While she knew he'd never physically hurt her, Lizzie was shocked at the grief that burrowed into the deepest part of her. Staring into Ethan Colton's eyes, she saw a layer of pain and heartbreak and sheer agony she could never have imagined.

She knew the story of his father. You'd be hard-pressed to find a soul in the entire state of Texas who didn't. Matthew Colton had hated his older brother, Big J, and all the man's wealth and influence. In some sick, twisted need for retribution, he had murdered a series of men who all looked like his brother, leaving each and every one with a bull's-eye on his forehead, drawn with a thick red marker.

Despite the heinous crimes, she'd never believed he'd passed that on. She'd known Matthew's children from a young age. They were good, decent individuals. She knew it so many years ago and she knew it now. All seven siblings had gone on to rise above their father's legacy, the equivalent of a family of phoenixes. Law enforcement. Ranching. Even Josie, who had disappeared, had been a dear, dear friend to her.

Ethan might struggle with lingering fear over his father's actions, but she didn't.

Nor had she considered—for even the briefest of moments—her child might be tainted by that. "We make our own choices in life, for good or for bad. You and I are living proof of that."

"I'm the child of a bad person. A killer, Lizzie. You can't compare that to a couple of people who felt they couldn't handle a kid."

The truth she'd spent her life dealing with stung and he must have seen something on her face.

"I'm sorry." The fierce light that filled his eyes at

the mention of his father faded, the apology more than evident in his narrowed gaze. "That was clumsy of me."

"No, it's honest. There's a difference." And regardless of their reason, in the end her parents' actions were just as he said. People who'd been unable to care for a child.

Pushing it aside, Lizzie pressed on. But oh, how did she reach him? For the first time, the beliefs she'd carried all the way to his front door wavered before her eyes. How did she make him understand this?

Standing, she moved to stand toe to toe. She reached for him, gripping the solid length of his forearm, willing the power of touch to maybe break through his resistance.

"Don't you see? Even with how we were raised, we're both good, honest, decent human beings. People who know right from wrong. People who believe the world can be a better place. Our child will have genetics, yes. But he or she will also have love. And a mother and father to teach right and wrong."

"How can you be so naive?"

She dropped his arm and stepped back. The heat of his words branded her, but it was the disillusionment that painted his gaze in a dim wash of gray that had something sinking to the very bottom of her stomach.

"It's hardly naive to believe in my future. To believe in my child's future."

The briefest acknowledgment flitted through his gaze before those hazel depths went flat once more. "I've done everything right. You've done everything right. Yet here we are, smack in the middle of it happening all over again. The threatening notes. The baby rattle. Even another serial killer on the loose."

Lizzie dropped down onto the couch again, his words

pinging through her mind with all the power of a hailstorm.

Maybe she had been naive. Worse, she'd finally allowed herself to hope. To believe she had a bright future ahead.

And instead, she had to face the reality. She was about to bring a child into a world that was dark and bleak and very, very cold.

Chapter 4

Ethan busied himself with a series of mundane chores, the act of mucking stalls and working through several small fix-it projects designed to keep his mind off the woman currently taking a nap several hundred yards away in his house. It was only when he hammered the last nail into a sagging door frame that he finally admitted the truth.

He'd failed miserably.

His mind was full of Lizzie, and no amount of physical labor had removed her from the center of his thoughts. He even had a bruise on his knuckles from when he wasn't paying attention to prove it.

Although he was far from comfortable with it, he was beginning to get used to the idea of being a father. What he hadn't quite conquered was the bone-shuddering need that had swept through him at the sight of his child's mother.

She was pregnant, for heaven's sake. He shouldn't be looking at her as if he wanted to devour her. She deserved his respect. And gentleness. And a man who wasn't thinking about long sultry nights wrapped up in each other.

He'd have thought the sight of her pregnant belly would take his mind off the sensual thoughts. So it was more than a little unsettling to realize her softly rounded stomach drew out the need to protect as well as a base sexuality he'd never have imagined.

She was carrying his *baby*.

Tossing his hammer into his toolbox, Ethan let out a low curse and went to check on Dream. He might have no clue how to deal with a woman—or the sea of emotions one woman in particular managed to whip up—but he knew what to do with animals. Quiet and more than willing to share their affection, with them he always knew where he stood.

Dream nudged his shoulder the moment he was within distance of her stall, her sweet head bump going a long way toward uncoiling the tension wrapping his shoulders. "You want out for a walk, baby?"

Anticipation lit her dark eyes, and Ethan made quick work of her lead. In moments, he had her in the paddock, watching as she pranced in happy circles. He briefly thought about calling the doctor to confirm she wouldn't injure her foal, but knew he was being overly cautious. Doc Peters had said Dream could resume regular activity. In fact, he'd made it an imperative.

So he trusted the animal knew what was best for her and stood back to watch.

The late afternoon quiet wrapped around him. Several hands had the other horses out, exercising and riding the land, while another crew had gone out to mend a patch of fence. He'd wanted to go with them—knew he *should* be with them—but he found himself loath to go too far from the house.

Roiling emotions aside, he couldn't shake the fear that something terrible was hovering out there, waiting for them. He cursed again and fought to keep his focus firmly on fact. He'd spent his childhood living in fear, and the moment he had some control over his life, he'd sworn off continuing to live that way. He would handle this.

Whatever *this* was.

He had means. And he had a damn good head on his shoulders. If neither worked, he had a loaded shotgun in his closet that could help seal the deal.

At the image of the gun, Ethan quickly made a mental note to purchase a gun safe. There was no way he was keeping an unlocked gun around a small child. One who would be in his house all too soon.

"Those are some heavy thoughts."

Ethan turned at the soft words and came face-to-face with Lizzie. The afternoon sun had warmed things and she stood there in her sweatshirt and an old vest he kept hanging in his mudroom. The image of her in his things shot another arrow of need through him, and he turned toward the paddock and away from the tempting sight. "Just giving Dream a run. She needed some fresh air."

Lizzie took a spot next to him on the rail, her booted foot propped up on the bottom rung. Color ran high on her cheeks as she pointed toward the far side of the ring. "She looks well."

"Doc Peters is amazing."

"He may be, but it looks like you've got a pretty amazing horse, too."

Ethan felt the scrutiny—Lizzie wasn't subtle—and

marveled at the frank honesty. Even when she was a small child, she'd had that gaze. Bright green eyes that could size you up and tease you in one fell swoop.

Unwilling to keep his gaze diverted, he turned to stare into the familiar. And had to admit the wide-eyed innocence of the child had given way to the knowledge of a grown woman.

"Dream's perfect."

"You always wanted a barn full of horses. I remember how you used to talk of the ranch you'd have. I could see it, too." Lizzie stepped back from the paddock rail and turned slowly, making a full circle, before she turned back toward him. "It's just as you'd said it would be."

"I knew what I wanted."

"Yes, you did. And now you have it. That must be satisfying."

Satisfying, yes. But a bit empty.

The thought caught him completely unaware, and Ethan scrambled to reorganize the odd impressions swirling through his mind.

Empty? When had that idea settled in and taken root?

Even as the confusion whirled around in his thoughts like a dust storm, Ethan knew. That weekend after he and Lizzie had shared time at the rodeo, he'd walked the land and wondered why the vastness he'd always welcomed suddenly seemed oppressive.

The ranch was *his*. This corner of Texas, so open and wide, had become his own. He'd put every ounce of himself into the place since he was nineteen. First as a hand, then as foreman and then—finally—as his own after his old boss wanted out of the business.

The ranch was his life. It was as much a part of him as his heart and soul.

So when had it stopped being enough?

"Ethan?"

"Sorry. Long day."

She let his polite lie pass and turned back to the paddock. "I'll give her credit. She certainly has more energy than I do."

"Are you okay?" He had one hand on her back and the other covering her hand before he could even think to check his movements. "Do you need to lie down?"

Her shoulders stiffened beneath his hands before relaxing, and she moved a heartbeat closer. "I'm fine. I just tire easier, even with an afternoon spent lazing around like a cat."

"The benefit of moving on four legs instead of two?"

Lizzie laughed at that, her smile wide and open. "Maybe that's it."

"You've had a lot on your mind."

Those delicate shoulders stiffened once more and he cursed himself for bringing such unpleasantness into their conversation.

"Yes. I have."

"Well, one thing to take off it is me."

Her gaze changed, shifted. The bright smile she'd worn while watching Dream was nowhere in evidence. "How so?"

"This is my child. You have my commitment that I will help you and stand by you. Both."

"That's comforting."

"It's fact. You won't face this alone. I will be a father to my child."

Lizzie pushed on a bright smile and ignored the pain that drummed against her heart with all the finesse of a blunt instrument.

Ethan Colton would be an amazing father to their child.

And that was all he'd be.

Shake it off, Lizzie girl. Shake it off.

The fantasy she'd warned herself against over the past six months—ever since that night at the rodeo—curled against the corners of her mind with reaching fingers. Although she knew it for the emotional foolishness it was, that small, hopeful piece of her had wondered if there could be more with Ethan.

With her gaze on the horse, she kept her voice level. "That's a lot to take on. Especially with all the issues I'm having back at home."

"Issues we'll face together." She sensed him before she felt him, the light press of his fingers against her shoulder drawing her attention. "Lizzie. I mean it. You're not alone."

"I'm always alone."

The words were out before she could censor them. She hated playing the abandonment card—it suggested a weakness she refused to feel. She was proud of how hard she'd worked to overcome her childhood so she could focus on a bright future full of love and laughter.

So why was it so easy to drift back to that place?

The therapist she'd found after she started at the bank had been gentle, urging her to put voice to the feelings she'd lived with her whole life instead of keeping them locked inside. How humbling, then, to realize just how easy it was to regress.

He lifted his hand from her shoulder, but instead of breaking contact, he moved his fingers lightly over the length of her arm, coming to rest just above her wrist. Although she'd believed her sweatshirt was warm enough to battle the February afternoon chill, she'd had no idea the movement of the worn cotton over her skin could feel so sensual. So erotic.

She'd read the pregnancy books and knew her hormones were to blame for the immediate response to his touch, but deep down Lizzie wondered if it was something more.

Something that went far deeper than she'd admit, even to herself.

"I can only imagine how scared you've been, but we'll get to the bottom of it. No one's going to hurt you."

Except you.

She laid her hand over his and gave in to the urge to look at him. Really look at him. Although the afternoon was comfortable, a light wind had filled his cheeks with ruddy color. The pinkish-red hue was a match for his lips, the firm, strong lines of his mouth drawing her attention.

He was a beautiful man, almost startlingly so, with thick lips and a firm jawline she itched to trace. To soften. He rarely smiled, instead facing the world with a stoic facade that tugged at something deep inside her.

It had always been that way, even when they were young. He'd seen so much—had lived with the image of finding his dead mother—and it sat heavy on his shoulders.

Lizzie knew what an impact parents had on their children—whether present or not—but Ethan's life had been defined by his parents even more than most. Yet even with those ghosts—or demons, as a more apt description of Matthew Colton—Ethan had still made something of himself.

He was so strong. Capable. And so quintessentially *male*. Thick with muscle, he appeared comfortable in a body that was used to hard work and long days. But it was his face. Long lashes that were a dusty goldish brown framed those rich hazel eyes that had seen so much. There was a haunted quality to Ethan Colton, and she had no idea if he even realized it.

Shadows lurked in those hazel depths, and she desperately wanted to be the one to chase them away.

The hand that covered her forearm tightened, and Lizzie became conscious of the seconds ticking by. Of the sound of their breathing, rising in tempo, matched in rhythm. She couldn't want this. She had her child to think of, and he or she needed to be her full focus right now.

But heaven help her, she couldn't look away.

And then there was no choice as Ethan lowered his head, his mouth barely touching hers. Her breath lodged in her chest as her entire body went still.

Did she dare?

And then her arms were around his neck and she couldn't have pulled away if the barn had risen in flames behind them.

Ethan's hands shifted to her hips, turning her fully from the fence rails to stand flush against his body. Their child pressed between them, a vivid, tangible reminder that they'd created life.

The past months faded away as his lips met hers. Every ounce of pent-up longing and need seemed to shudder through her as Lizzie gave herself over to the moment. The man she'd dreamed of through more years than she wanted to count was here.

And she was in his arms.

A soft sigh drifted up her throat, the unconscious exhalation an interpretation of all that was in her heart. That sigh seemed to say: *Finally*.

His tongue met the barrier of her lips and she opened

for him, the act of possession unmistakable as he slipped inside. His fingers clutched at her hips, pulling her even more tightly against him, and even with their child between them, she could feel the need that tightened his body with the same driving force that consumed her.

Lizzie lost all sense of her surroundings as her world narrowed and expanded all at once. All she could feel was Ethan. All she could think was Ethan.

All she wanted was Ethan.

The boy she remembered had become a hard man, tough and strong, his body as unyielding as the land that was his.

Yet just like the vivid blooms that found a way to flourish, even in the hardest earth, Ethan had made something of himself. Had followed his dream and his love of animals to create a life for himself.

A home.

Lizzie clung to him a bit tighter, allowing him to deepen the kiss even further, as one thought thundered louder than all else.

She wanted that home with him.

It was that truth that finally had her pulling away. With determined steps, she tore herself away from the only force on earth that made her forget herself.

"Lizzie—" His lips were wet, his hazel eyes almost black with the heavy dilation of his pupils as he stared at her.

"I—" She broke off, the question in his eyes almost powerful enough to have her moving right back into those strong arms.

Almost.

The baby chose that moment to kick, the swift punch of a tiny foot under her rib cage enough to break her fully out of Ethan's thrall. Her hands went to her stomach, and she winced as their child aimed one more field goal toward her ribs.

"What is it?"

"It must be three o'clock."

"What? Why?"

"The baby's active. He starts like clockwork every day at the same time."

"He?"

She offered up a rueful smile. "Yesterday I called it a she all day. I trade off every day."

His gaze drifted down over her stomach, and she saw something cross his face before he took a firm step back.

"What is it?"

"I… I mean, do you mind if I—" He extended a hand, and she gripped his palm firmly in hers before he gave himself a chance to pull away.

Shifting away the material of his thick vest, she placed Ethan's hand high over her abdomen and was rewarded with another kick. His fingers flexed against her skin, the wide press of his palm nearly covering half the width of her as a look of sheer awe had his mouth widening into a smile.

"I think we've got a UT football scholarship in our future." He tightened his hand once more as the baby shot out another foot jab. "Feel that kick."

"Or a Rockette." She smiled as the image of thick football pads faded into a sequined dance outfit. Lizzie knew their comments were steeped in society's views on girls and boys, and she'd had several months to admit to herself she wasn't fully immune to the ingrained pull of baby culture. Everything she looked at in the stores was pink or blue, a wave of color determined to stamp identity from the very earliest age.

Conscious of that, she couldn't resist poking at whatever image had settled in Ethan's mind. "Maybe we'll have the first girl kicker at UT."

He smiled down at her. "Or a cowboy–slash–ballet dancer who wows them on the New York stage."

She welcomed her child's interests, whatever they might be, but hadn't realized how relieved she was to hear his unspoken agreement. "You'd be okay with that?"

"My child can be whatever he or she wants to be. I'll be proud." His hand cradled her stomach as his gaze settled on hers, intense and unwavering. "Always."

Lizzie nodded, not sure what to say. She'd thought to tease out any inherent bias and instead had her game turned on her in the most impactful of ways. While she had no doubt Ethan Colton would be an amazing father, to actually hear the pride that already filled his voice left her with the insane urge to start bawling right there in the middle of his ranch.

Unwilling to analyze those emotions too closely, she closed them up and vowed not to take them back out until she was alone. She already knew her attraction to Ethan hovered way too close to the surface. She did *not* need to add hormones and the urge to weep every five minutes to her list of emotional sins where Ethan Colton was concerned.

He removed his hand from her stomach, a gentle reluctance painting his features before he put a few additional steps between them. He shifted on the balls of his feet, his gaze drifting out over the paddock. The fierce conviction that had painted his features as he made promises for their child's future faded as his gaze followed Dream's easy progression around the practice ring.

Their quiet moments drifted off on the light afternoon breeze. The strong, gentle man who had been so present and in the moment with her had gone, leaving the hard, stoic face he showed the world standing in his place.

Lizzie wanted to bring that other Ethan back—wanted to pull him away from the cloud of memories that seemed to perpetually hang around him, no matter what the situation—but she kept her distance.

It wasn't her place.

And while it nearly killed her to acknowledge that fact, carrying his child didn't change anything. She and Ethan Colton didn't have a relationship. For her own emotional protection, she'd do well to remember that a baby couldn't banish the demons he carried inside.

"There are storm clouds in your eyes, Lizzie."

The quiet observation pulled her from her own thoughts, and she stared up at him. The questions in her mind fought to come to light, but she held them back, offering up a small shrug instead.

"It's nothing but a trick of the light."

The woman stood in the distance and stared at Ethan Colton and Lizzie Conner. Damn stubborn fools. It didn't take the high-powered binoculars in her hand to see the connection that snapped between them like Texas heat lightning.

What would it be like to be filled with an attraction that intense? The thought filled her with a shot of something so powerful her knees actually trembled from the force.

And now there would be a baby.

The first Colton grandchild.

Matthew would be beside himself when he found out. Despite his absolute inability to control the horrible urges that lived beneath his skin, he valued family above all else. It shaped him, like clay molded from the earth, and had driven his every action since childhood.

He even attributed his need to kill to his family.

The terrible jealousy Matthew had felt for Big J Colton had driven him down the darkest and most twisted path a human could travel. His need to kill—or maybe it was simply the excuse he'd settled on—had all been tied to the brother who'd never loved him or cared for him.

And it was a legacy that haunted them all.

Chapter 5

Lizzie smoothed the purse on her lap, a motion that was going to wear a hole in the leather if she didn't stop. She'd thought to spend the day in her room in an attempt to give Ethan space as he tried to come to grips with the impending change she'd thrust upon his life. So it was more than a little surprising to wake up to a home-cooked breakfast, a hot cup of herbal tea and the announcement they were going to investigate her house.

"We really don't need to do this."

They'd nearly traversed the length of Blackthorn County, and she could see the familiar landmarks that made up the last two miles to her home.

"That's the fourth time you've said that."

"Have not."

"Yes, you have. First you asked me if I had better things to do today. Then you suggested I might want to turn around and stay home to keep an eye on Dream.

And about ten miles back you told me your house was a mess and you're embarrassed to bring anyone into it."

Okay, maybe she'd exaggerated about the house, Lizzie thought as she pictured the cleaning she'd done before she left. But she hadn't got to the kitchen floors and *that* was an embarrassment. "I don't want to put you out."

"I get that. What I don't understand is why you don't want me to see your place."

"You have seen my place."

Flashes of the night they'd shared sprang to the fore-front of her thoughts, vivid memories full of passion and heat. She'd invited him home after the rodeo, and Ethan had followed behind in his truck. She'd spent the entire drive convinced he'd take the gentlemanly way out and tell her he couldn't come in after thinking it over. Yet she'd worried for nothing when they'd practically fallen out of their cars, barely making it across her small front yard to the door, their hands full of each other.

"Why don't you want me to see your place today?"

The question pulled her from the haze of memories, and Lizzie swallowed hard around her suddenly dry throat. "It's not that I don't want you to see my place. You're always welcome in my home."

She fought the traitorous voice that whispered through her mind, taunting her with the truth. She *did* want Ethan to see her place. Often.

Forever.

Shaking it off, Lizzie ignored the temptation to hope and instead acknowledged the inevitable: he wasn't turning the car around. She forced optimism into her tone and pasted on a small, determined smile. "I'm just sorry I've dragged you into this."

Ethan's gaze remained fixed on the road ahead, but

it was impossible to miss the hard flex of his jaw or the sparks that lit up his gaze. "You have nothing to be sorry about. Someone's been intent on scaring you. Worse, they've taken advantage of a terribly vulnerable time in your life. I'm here to help."

"I know. And I thank you more than I can ever say."

His jaw remained stiff, and Lizzie wasn't sure if her gratitude irritated or frustrated. She felt both emotions and a host of others she hadn't even figured out yet.

Although she hadn't wanted to keep the baby a total secret from him, she knew Ethan's feelings on children. After the initial shock of discovering her pregnancy, she'd consoled herself with the idea that she'd tell him after she'd adjusted to motherhood. She and the baby would get into a routine. Make a life together. And then she'd figure out a way to tell him.

Instead, some creepy jerk had forced her hand and put a very dark mark on that future.

She directed Ethan to the turn for her small subdivision, a townhome community that sat about a mile off Main Street. When he only nodded his head and murmured a husky "I remember," she turned her gaze to the window, another one of those nameless emotions bubbling to the surface.

The February weather had been colder than usual, so the trees that lined the entry to her development were still bare. Even without the pretty shades of green that had canopied the neighborhood on his last visit, Ethan took each turn like a pro.

He *did* remember.

Which did nothing to help her internal argument to stay cool, calm and distant toward Ethan Colton.

An unbearable heaviness threatened to pull her under at the realization, and she rubbed a slow, soothing hand over her belly. The baby was in one of its quiet periods and had settled down during the drive. Over the past few months, every time she'd begun to feel any anxiety, Lizzie had focused on the life she carried. Staying calm for the baby was essential to its well-being, and she was determined to avoid as much stress as possible.

Or at least the self-induced kind, Lizzie admitted with a quick eye roll that reflected back at her from the window of Ethan's truck.

Oblivious to her thoughts, Ethan turned in to her driveway and cut the engine. His gaze roamed over the brick facing before he turned toward her with a smile. "What a great place. I thought so before, and it's only more true in the light of day."

"I love it. I've loved this place from the first moment I saw it." The baby gave a sharp kick as if to punctuate the point, and Lizzie laid a firm hand over her stomach.

"You okay?"

"Field-goal practice has begun once more."

"Do you need to sit for a moment?"

"No. Walking will help move her a bit." She was already reaching for the door handle when long, strong fingers came down over her hand.

"Wait. I'll come around." The strength that lined his features softened as his gaze drifted to her stomach. "So the baby's a girl today?"

"I told you. I like to trade off each day."

"So you did." His hand lifted from hers to settle over the large mound of her belly. "But she's still kicking field goals?"

Her voice came out on a husky croak, her throat desert dry. "Like a champ."

"Which means you definitely need a bit of pampering. I'll come around to get you."

The tender moment of connection ended, the crackle of electricity that seemed to flow between them effortlessly fizzling in the cool air that blew in through his open door. Lizzie kept her hand on the door handle but followed Ethan's command to stay put.

It was nice to have the help and the extra bit of attention. Even if she put aside the feelings for Ethan that never seemed to fully go away, it was just nice to have someone to talk to about the baby. Her coworkers had been excited for her, and she'd made a few friends since she'd started at the bank, but they weren't with her in her more private moments. Decorating the baby's room or picking out some items at the store had been all her own doing.

"Why don't you give me your keys and I'll go in ahead of you?"

"I know you're worried, but it's not that bad. This is my house."

One eyebrow rose. "Humor me."

Lizzie stilled from where she worked her way out of the seat belt. "You use that look to get whatever you want, Colton?"

"Did it work?"

"Sadly, yes."

One of those rare smiles lit up his face. "Then consider it an effective tactic."

Lizzie allowed Ethan to help her from the elevated passenger seat of his truck, then handed over her keys. "I'll stay behind you."

She stayed true to her word but couldn't fully eliminate the seeds of resentment that took root as she followed him to her front door. This was her home. She'd worked and saved and had been so proud when she'd qualified for the mortgage on her own. All her hard work and dedication, focus and goal setting, had paid off. And ten months ago, she'd signed the papers and moved in.

Now she had to face the fact that someone had threatened all she'd worked for. Worse, they'd threatened the fragile life she protected within her.

"Come on in." Ethan gestured her through her open front door. "I'll look around, but everything looks like it's in place."

"Everything's where it should be. The curse of the foster child."

"Oh?"

The curious "Oh" had gone straight over her head, but the question beneath his question didn't. Lizzie glanced up from her focused perusal of the front living area. "Sure. Keep things neat as a pin so you don't give them a reason to get rid of you."

"You said that without a trace of bitterness."

"Because I'm not bitter. Not at all." When he only continued to stare at her, Lizzie pressed on. "I had wonderful people who took care of me. They did the best they could and they did love me."

"I hear a *but* there."

"But I was the stubborn teenager who kept my distance from them. They weren't my real parents, and I never let them forget it."

"You sound sad about that."

"More than you can know. Roy and Rhonda Carlton were my last foster family and they cared for me. They gave me a home, and I didn't appreciate them nearly enough."

"My brother Chris mentioned their passing several years back. We thought they might have known—"

Lizzie's attention sharpened on all Ethan didn't say. "Thought what?"

"It's nothing."

She leveled her own stare on him and knew the well-practiced gesture had a similar effect as his lone eyebrow. Nor did she miss the resigned look or the small exhalation as Ethan paced through her living room, his large frame at odds with the delicate furniture she'd selected.

"Chris is a PI, and he looked into them a bit when we were trying to find out more about Josie. To see if they knew anything. That was about a year after she disappeared and—" his large shoulders rose and fell in a simple shrug "—he discovered they died in a car accident."

"A hit-and-run on a night full of storms," she affirmed. "It was a terrible tragedy, but I've always taken comfort that they were together."

"Did they have other foster children at the time?"

"No. After Josie ran away they didn't seem to have the heart for it any longer. She and I were the last fosters they had."

"What about you?"

"What about me?"

"Didn't you miss Josie?"

Pain she'd long buried speared through her midsection at the direct mention of his sister. Although she was a year and a half older, Josie had been her best friend, and the two of them had been as close as sisters.

Until the day they weren't.

"Of course I did. The Carltons practically raised both of us. But she and I had grown apart and then one day she just disappeared."

"She did that to us, too." Ethan continued to drift around the room, his restless energy as raw as an impending storm. "Grew apart. Stopped wanting to see us for our court-sanctioned visits. Until the day she just vanished."

"Did you ever find out where she went?"

"No." He picked up a small crystal giraffe from her coffee table and turned it over in his hands. Although his gaze was ostensibly on the small piece, Lizzie could tell he was a million miles away. "And no amount of digging by my law-steeped siblings has provided any information."

As she watched him, another thought hit Lizzie, as powerful as the proverbial storms she saw in Ethan. Curious, she pushed them in a different direction. "You don't believe the nonsense some asinine journalists have begun spouting about her. The ridiculous notion that she's taken up your father's torch and is the Alphabet Killer."

Ethan stiffened at her words, his normally stoic facade going to granite. "It's not just the journalists."

"Who, then?"

"Forget I mentioned it." Ethan glanced down at the object he had gripped tight in his hands before gently settling it back on the coffee table.

"Come on, Ethan. You can't tell me you really believe it. I realize none of us knew Josie as well as we thought, but I do know her well enough to know she's not a killer."

"No. I don't believe—"

His words vanished into the air as a hard thud echoed from overhead. Ethan looked up, his gaze sharp. "What room is that? Above us?"

"The baby's room."

Another thud sounded above them and Ethan leaped

from the room, the heavy tread of his footsteps already echoing as he raced up her stairs.

"Call 911!"

Ethan was torn between staying with Lizzie downstairs and heading after the intruder in her home, but every instinct screamed to take the option that might end this here and now.

More noise echoed from the upstairs hall and Ethan headed in the direction of the sound, quickly catching his bearings as he ascended to the second-floor landing. A door at the far end of the hall slammed closed and he had no doubt it was now locked as well.

As he moved determinedly toward the door, Ethan mentally cataloged what he knew of the house. It was relatively new and Lizzie was only the second owner, which meant the builder had likely left skeleton keys in the event someone was locked in.

A large quilted giraffe hung from the door and Ethan lifted his hand to the lintel, satisfied when his fingers brushed the thin piece of metal. He had the key in the lock and the door open in moments.

Only to find his rush was in vain.

The empty room's lone window was already open, its bright pastel-colored curtains blowing in the afternoon breeze.

He crossed the small space in a matter of steps and caught sight of a figure racing across the back of the development. It briefly crossed his mind to follow, but he knew it for a fool's errand.

"Did you—" Lizzie broke off, her voice heavy and out of breath as she came through the door.

"He's gone."

"He?"

"I thought." Ethan stopped and turned back toward the window. The figure had vanished, but he conjured up the image in his mind. "He was wearing a thick sweatshirt with the hood up, so I guess it could be anyone. They were too far away to get a sense of height."

"The police will ask what color."

"It was nondescript navy blue." Ethan glanced down at his own sweatshirt, tossed on that morning from a stack of similar clothes in the bottom of his drawer. "Just like I'm wearing. Hell, like half the population wears every weekend."

"It's still something."

Lizzie stood framed inside the doorway, long, curly waves of hair framing her face, and he stilled. Since he'd seen her the morning before, his emotions had roller-coastered through the ups and downs of his new reality.

Yet here she was. Standing in the doorway of their child's room, a warrior goddess prepared to do battle to protect her home. He saw no fear. Instead, all he saw was a ripe, righteous anger, spilling from her in hard, deep breaths.

"Maybe you should sit down?"

"I'm too mad to sit."

"Once again, I'm forced to ask the obvious. Humor me."

He reached for the window, but she stopped him. "Leave it. It's not that cold, and maybe there are fingerprints."

Although he had no doubt the perp had left nothing behind, Ethan did as she requested. She'd already taken a seat in the rocking chair in the corner, and he felt his knees buckle at the image that rose up to replace her in his mind's eye.

Lizzie, rocking in that same chair, their child nestled in her arms, suckling at her breast.

The shock of emotion that burrowed beneath his heart raced through him, and Ethan fought to keep any trace of it from showing. How could he feel so much joy at something so unexpected?

At something he'd never wanted?

He'd grappled with that fact from the very first moments with Lizzie the morning before in his kitchen and had yet to find any answer.

Yes, she carried his child. And yes, that had raised a protective instinct he never knew he possessed. But it was something more. Something deeper.

He'd spent his entire adult life avoiding entanglements, so the depth of how far he and Lizzie were now entwined should have been a concern. So how come he wasn't feeling more restrained? He should feel as if he had a noose notched against his throat, but instead, these weird moments of excitement broke over him, swamping him in a confusing mix of protectiveness and desire.

The sound of sirens broke through his thoughts, and he grasped at the intrusion like a lifeline. He needed to get out of his head and focus on the issue at hand.

Lizzie was in danger.

The anger that had ridden her cheeks had faded, leaving her face pale, her green eyes wide. She was scared— more than she'd likely admit—and it broke his heart that she had to deal with something like this.

"Rest a minute. I'll go meet them at the door."

A lifetime spent around law-enforcement professionals had given Ethan a wary level of respect for them. Anyone who put their life on the line for the safety of others would always have his admiration.

But he sure as hell didn't trust them.

Cops saw too much. Listened too much. And, at times, drew conclusions where there were none. The two cops currently sitting at Lizzie's kitchen table fell firmly in the latter category.

After a quick look in the baby's room and a series of innocuous questions, Officer McNulty dived in. Ethan pegged him for about a quarter century on the force and a know-it-all, and he wasn't disappointed.

"Miss Conner. How long have these incidents been going on?"

"They started a few months ago at work. I gave all these details to Detective Bell when I filed a complaint a few weeks ago."

McNulty kept his smile broad, but his implacable tone never wavered. "And we appreciate that. But Officer Warren and I would like to get a sense for ourselves."

Lizzie walked through the same details she'd provided Ethan with the day before. By the time she got to the rattle incident, she was visibly shaken.

Ethan laid a hand over hers and didn't miss McNulty's pointed stare at the protective gesture. He leveled one of his own on the cop and was pleased to see the man look away first.

He might have an appreciation for the law, but he refused to be cowed by it.

McNulty turned things over to his partner, and the broad smile indicated Officer Warren was clearly playing good cop today. He took a softer tack, starting with nice, easy questions about the baby and when it was due. Sweet comments designed to put Lizzie at ease. From the hard flex of her hand beneath his fingers, Ethan knew the officer's questions had done anything but.

"You say these incidents have been going on about two months now?"

"Yes."

"That's also about the time the Alphabet Killer began his rampage." Warren lobbed that bomb across the table, and Ethan picked it up without a second thought.

"Granite Gulch is clear across Blackthorn County."

"Yes, Mr. Colton." Warren's smile sharpened, a wolf under those sheep's clothes. "A place your family is well acquainted with."

"Granite Gulch is my home. My family's home."

"It was your father's home, too."

The barb hit its mark, and Ethan fought showing any response beyond irritated boredom. "My father's home is a maximum-security prison, Officer. What's your point?"

"I'm sure you know."

"And I'm quite sure I don't."

Officer McNulty chose that moment to step in. "Surely you're well aware of the rumors about your sister, Mr. Colton."

"The ones that claim my youngest sister has taken up my father's mantle, killing victims with his same pattern? That rumor, Officer?"

"One and the same."

"Josie's innocent!" The words spilled from Lizzie's lips, her cry echoing around the kitchen and startling them all from the impasse that was quickly brewing.

"Do you know something, Miss Conner? Something that can help the police find whoever is responsible for these murders?"

Lizzie set her jaw, conviction shining from the very depths of her eyes. "Only that it's not Josie. I know it's not. She's not capable of it."

"People are capable of any number of things, Miss Conner," Officer McNulty said before standing.

"You're leaving?"

"Yes, ma'am. Thank you for the coffee. Officer Warren and I will be in touch."

Ethan squeezed Lizzie's hand, a silent order to stay put, and walked the officers to her front door. "Thank you for coming."

Officer McNulty took one last glance around the living room before turning his direct stare on Ethan. As the action was meant to intimidate, Ethan simply stood taller, the scrutiny something he'd lived with his entire life.

"Keep an eye on her, Mr. Colton." McNulty touched the tip of his hat.

The surprising shot of compassion when he'd only expected censure had Ethan nodding, his voice gruff. "Count on it."

The two officers stepped through the door and Ethan closed it firmly behind them, flipping the locks. Their discussion with the cops continued to roll through his mind on a loop, and he struggled with the way the conversation had shifted from a faceless intruder to his sister.

Josie had been gone for so long. They'd all looked for her, unwilling to give up hope they'd find her, but after repeated disappointment he and his siblings had made a pact to do their best to preserve their sanity. Her disappearance had taken another piece of each of them, carving away what emotional protection each had created after their mother's death and Matthew's conviction.

It had been Annabel who'd finally suggested they drop the focused search. They loved their baby sister, but looking for her remained an open wound none of them could heal from. Ethan knew Trevor perpetually kept an FBI file open and followed small leads every now and again. And Sam's position in the Granite Gulch PD gave him access to the records room, which he hunted through every now and again. Beyond that, they'd all done their best to move on after Josie Colton had vanished at the age of seventeen, seemingly into thin air.

So how had her name now become synonymous with the Alphabet Killer?

"That was fun." Lizzie stood at the opposite end of the hallway, in front of the kitchen, a half-drunk pot of coffee in her hands.

Her words pulled him from his musings, and Ethan closed the short distance down the hall. "I'm sorry if they upset you."

"Nothing like feeling like a suspect in your own home."

"Did the detective assigned to your case make you feel that way?"

"No." She poured the remaining coffee into his cup before turning toward the sink. "He's been very kind and understanding. I do think he's doing his best with limited information."

"If today's events are any indication, I don't think he's doing enough." Ethan picked up his mug, the events of the past hour swirling through his mind. In addition to the interrogation, McNulty and Warren had called in a field unit to do a quick dusting of the windowsill for prints. When they'd turned up nothing on the sill, Lizzie had opted to avoid ruining the rest of the room with the mess the powder would make.

"You haven't met him, Ethan. He's a good guy. And after that Keystone Cops routine, I'm more than tempted to call Detective Bell. How dare those officers come in here and make it look like we're criminals?"

"Coltons are an easy target. I'm sorry you got dragged in for fun."

She slammed a dish towel against the kitchen sink and whirled on him. "Oh, that's a load of BS and you know it."

"Oh, really?" Ethan heard the spark in her voice and allowed it to roll over the lingering anger he'd carried all afternoon, igniting like a match to gasoline. He hadn't intended to say another word about his sister, yet the words spilled out before he could even think to draw them back. "How was this anything but an interrogation of Matthew Colton's son and a fishing expedition to see if his daughter is a killer?"

"Josie didn't do it."

"Tell that to the court of public opinion."

Lizzie stilled. "Do you think your sister's the one responsible for the murders?"

"I—" His hand trembled against the handle of his mug, and Ethan left the cup on the table. "No, I don't."

"So what is it? If you don't think Josie's involved in the murders, what has you so upset?"

"How can you ask me that? We're here because some faceless bastard is trying to hurt you and the baby. Hell, he was here while we were in the house!"

Lizzie moved toward the table, standing near him but not touching. "I'm upset, too, but I don't see how these situations are related. The officers were wrong to try and make a connection between what's happening with the Alphabet Killer and some creepy jerk who's trying to make my life a living hell."

"Don't you see it?"

He didn't want to scare her—that was the furthest

thing from his mind—but how was Lizzie unable to see what was so obvious?

"See what? I realize the murders are on the top of everyone's mind, especially with a twenty-four–seven news cycle, but what does that have to do with some creep who's been writing me notes?"

Ethan reached out, unable to keep his distance. But as his hand closed over hers, the flesh beneath his palm soft and warm, he regretted the words that came next.

"Your name begins with an *E*, Lizzie. Elizabeth is your given name."

Chapter 6

Ethan's words struck deep, and Lizzie took a seat at the table, no longer sure her legs could hold her. Ethan tightened his hold on her hand, as if to confirm she was okay, before releasing their clasped fingers.

The offered warmth was welcome, but it couldn't do anything to chase away the cold that whistled over her bones.

Had she missed the obvious?

While she didn't believe—nor would she believe—that Josie Colton was killing women in alphabetical order in Granite Gulch, she couldn't deny the strange coincidence between the start of the murders and the beginning of her own problems.

"You can't possibly think the killer's targeted me. I live nearly an hour away from Granite Gulch. And every correspondence from this jerk has been focused on the baby. On this weird obsession with us being a family."

Lizzie searched her mind for some proof, no mat-

ter how feeble, that would reinforce her point. Yes, she
was scared, but nothing in the notes she'd received had
indicated she was in the crosshairs of a serial killer.

It wasn't possible.

"The rattle. And the letters. Were the other women
taunted like that?"

"No. But that doesn't mean the pattern can't change.
Killers can and do escalate their styles."

"What do your brothers say?"

"Trevor's closest to it all, especially now that the FBI's
involved."

"And? Has he shared details that the press doesn't
have?"

"Nothing substantial. They've held back a few small
details, but nothing that would keep people from pro-
tecting themselves."

Lizzie knew she was grasping at straws, but she
wanted something—anything—that would tell her she
wasn't dealing with a serial killer.

A psycho, yes. But a killer bent on making her his
next victim? No way.

Ethan continued, acknowledging her question. "The
killer hasn't played with his victims. Nor has he terror-
ized them before killing them. The rattle and the notes
would break pattern."

"You said 'he.' So why would the cops possibly think
it's your sister?"

"Pronoun choice, nothing more. But the piece that
hasn't been released to the public is that some of the
crime-scene information suggests a woman may be involved."

Lizzie mentally cataloged all of the news stories she'd
watched so far on the Alphabet Killer. Reporters had
confirmed the same killer was believed to be respon-

sible for each of the murders, but their reports also assumed the killer was male.

Until the recent speculation around Josie's involvement.

She'd been angry the first time she'd heard it, the idea of her childhood friend dragged through the mud more hurtful than she could have imagined. Even though they'd lost touch, she had loved Josie like a sister.

"How do they know that? There's been no DNA evidence from the news reports."

"Angles. Stress points on the body. Different heights and body strength would cause different bruising patterns on the victims. The bullets would enter the body at different angles of trajectory. It's a working theory right now, according to Trev. They don't have anything definitive because there's nothing that says it couldn't be a small man, either."

Lizzie's head spun with the implications. Although she'd been too young to remember, Matthew Colton's killing spree across Blackthorn County had captured the country's imagination over two decades before. And even with the knowledge Matthew was still safely locked up, Lizzie couldn't quite grasp the idea that it was happening all over again.

"What is it?" Ethan's voice was gentle, that husky tone as patient with her as he must be with his prize horses.

"Nothing. It's nothing."

"Don't hold out on me."

"It's just—" She broke off, their conversation so many months ago after the rodeo filling her mind.

"I don't talk about him. I've done everything in my power to put him out of my mind."

"But he's your father, Ethan. Surely it can't be healthy to repress it all?"

"Talking about it won't change what he did to my mother. To so many other innocents. It won't change what he is."

"So why are you telling me?"

"I'm not sure." Those hazel eyes that had captivated her since she was small held her in an unwavering thrall before he shook his head. "That's not true. I'm talking to you because I can. You listen and you know my family, so you won't judge. You'll just listen."

"Always."

That play of color across his irises darkened, the golden brown rising to the fore. "My father's dying. I found out today the old man's got cancer and a few months to live. He claims he wants to see each of us. Wants a chance to talk to each of his children before he goes."

"Will you go?"

"Hell, no. For twenty years he's refused to tell us where he buried my mother after I found her and ran to get help. I won't give the bastard the satisfaction."

Ethan tapped a finger on the back of her hand. The gesture was simple, so small as to be almost nothing, yet Lizzie could have sworn she felt it all the way down to the tips of her toes.

"What did you want to say?"

"Is it possible your father's engineering this entire thing from prison?"

Erica Morgan nuzzled underneath her grandmother's quilt, half-asleep with a recent thriller dangling from her fingertips. She'd spent what was left of her day off staying up half the night reading about her favorite secret agent's latest exploits and hadn't done much since the sun came up except catnap and devour more chapters.

A heavy scrape outside the sliding glass door that ran along the back of her apartment had her coming fully awake, sitting straight up on the couch.

Ice lit up her spine, and her granny's warm quilt was no match for the shot of pure adrenaline that pumped through her heart. It was self-preservation, she knew.

And something that felt a lot like fear.

That weird sensation she'd had when leaving the bar filled her mind's eye once more, and even though she knew the reaction was stupid, she was hard-pressed to argue with her body's fear response.

Irritated she'd even given the matter another thought, she threw the blanket off and stood, muttering to herself, "Shake it off and quit being such a baby."

Erica had nearly convinced herself it was nothing more than late-night book adventures driving her jittery thoughts when that scraping noise came again, flush against the house.

She kicked the blanket away from her feet and moved to the wall, keeping it to her back as she inched toward the sliding door. She'd never wanted a gun—had believed them dangerous—and had a shot of regret at the possibly hasty decision.

On a deep breath, her gaze caught on her cell phone across the room. She debated leaving it in favor of investigating and shooing off whoever or whatever was out there, but gave in to common sense. It was nothing but a few moments to race across the living room and snatch her phone from the end table.

The reassuring press of metal met her palm, and

she raced back into position, her back to the wall. With shaking fingers she dialed 911, waiting to press Send.

And then she moved.

She dragged hard on the thick, floor-length curtain that covered the sliding door, whipping it out of the way as her fingers scrabbled for the lock on the door. The imagined bogeyman on the other side of the glass was nowhere in evidence as her gaze roamed over the gravel parking lot that backed her apartment.

With a hard tug on the handle, she popped the thick door free, sliding it along the tracks, and stepped onto the concrete slab that made up her back patio. The cool air slapped into her, fresh and clean and totally at odds with the hard fear that still coursed through her in choppy waves.

Again, she scanned the distance, unable to see anything or anyone that could have been responsible for the noise at her door. Abstractly aware of the phone gripped tight in her hands, Erica pulled it close to cancel the numbers she'd dialed in preparation.

And as she bent her head to erase the intended call, her gaze lit on a thick, shapeless black mound on the patio. A scream worked its way up her throat as she took in the size and familiar outline.

A bird, its neck clearly broken by a human hand, lay at her feet.

Lizzie wiped down the windowsill in the baby's room, the black powder the cops had used to dust for fingerprints a fine residue that had resisted her attempts to fully erase it. She'd already been through several antibacterial wipes and popped out another to make one final pass.

The cleaning was meant to serve two purposes—

the beautiful room she'd so carefully decorated was a dusty mess, and she wanted nothing more than to remove all traces of the intruder in her child's space. The activity also gave Ethan a bit of space after her question about his father.

Had she made a mistake?

Ethan hadn't dismissed her question about Matthew completely out of hand, but he hadn't agreed with her, either. Instead, he'd shifted the conversation back to his frustration with the cops and his desire to ask his brother Chris to put his private-investigation skills to good use and do some nosing around on the local PD.

While she appreciated the extra eyes and ears, she suspected Chris's PI skills wouldn't turn up any more information than the professionals. Whoever was after her had been careful. And frighteningly thorough.

But she did agree to let Chris in on what was happening in her life.

She tossed the dirty wipe into the small plastic bag she'd brought upstairs with her and snagged a fresh one from the canister. Ethan's voice drifted up the stairs in small snatches and she was tempted to listen at the door, but no matter how curious she was, he deserved his privacy. Even with their separation on different floors, she had caught the mention of Josie, the creep who'd run from her house and the thoroughly unhelpful cops. At the mention of McNulty and Warren, she reconsidered Ethan's suggestion that Detective Bell wasn't doing all he could.

The man had come to her office and to her home. He'd reviewed the letters she'd kept and listened carefully when she explained the discovery of the rattle and its subsequent disappearance. He'd been sincere and genuine and she trusted him.

Yet the creepy note sender had still found a way into her home.

Lizzie took comfort that she'd had Ethan with her when the intruder had been inside her home, but what if she'd been alone? Her stalker had no way of knowing she'd gone to Ethan's for the weekend or that they'd come back together.

Thoughts she'd resolutely tamped down for the past few months swelled over her in a crashing wave.

What if Ethan hadn't been here with her? And what if the stalker really was escalating? Or worse, what if the stalker actually was the Alphabet Killer?

Tears pricked the backs of her eyes and she tossed the cleaning rags into the trash. Cradling her belly, she dropped into the rocking chair and gave the fears a moment to crest through her system.

Acknowledge.

Assess.

Manage.

She'd worked through every problem in her life the same way and knew she needed to treat this one no differently. Yes, she was scared. But she'd do whatever was necessary to protect her child. She could run. Move away and start a new life. She could even take a new identity. It wasn't impossible to go off the grid, and she'd find a way if that meant they'd be safe.

Her thoughts pounded so heavily through her mind she didn't hear Ethan come up the stairs. It was only when he crouched down in front of her, his hands gripping hers and his voice sharp, that she surfaced from her whirling thoughts.

"Lizzie!"

Thoughts of driving to a remote area of California

or Maine still clouded her mind as Ethan's voice pulled her back to her baby's room in the middle of Texas.

"Talk to me, Lizzie. Please."

"I—" She swallowed hard. "I can't believe he was here. Inside the room. I was cleaning up the fingerprint powder and thinking about the cops and then realized I don't know what I'd have done if you weren't here." The tears that had threatened to spill over did, on a hard sob. "What if you weren't here?"

"Shh." One hand remained over hers in a tight hold while the other drifted toward her cheek. The warmth of his palm covered her jaw as he kept her head still, his gaze boring into hers. "Shh, now. It's nothing but what-ifs. Whatever you're thinking didn't happen. It's not real. You're safe. The baby's safe."

His calm tone drifted over her, and she had the abstract understanding of why he was so good with animals. His voice was deep and calm and powerfully soothing. Lizzie settled into his touch, the adrenaline rush fading as she leaned into him, secure in his arms.

He was safe. And she was safe with him.

They stayed like that for several minutes until Ethan shifted from the balls of his feet where he'd crouched before her to his knees.

Lizzie surfaced from the moment, pulling her hands from beneath his to settle on his shoulders. "You can't be comfortable like that. I'm okay now. Come on. Stand up."

She tightened her hold on his shoulders, but the force was just enough with his unbalanced position to knock him backward. One moment they were wrapped in each other and the next he was flat on his butt, his long legs folded up like a pretzel before him.

The moment was so ridiculous—and his position so clearly uncomfortable—a giggle rose up in her throat.

"Are you laughing at me?" Injured pride painted his face as he grunted, trying to crab walk backward from his contorted position against the rocking chair.

His affronted dignity and the awkward movements of his large body only made her laugh harder as she tried to catch her breath. "Yes…yes. I am."

He finally regained his feet, his shoulders still stiff. She only laughed harder, the boyish petulance painting his features reminding her of a day years ago when she and Josie had pushed him into a local watering hole not far from the Carltons'.

Her giggles faded, but she couldn't erase the humor under her words. "I've seen that look, you know."

"What look?"

"That stubborn Ethan Colton pride look."

"I don't have an Ethan Colton look."

"Actually, you've got several." She was round but not yet uncomfortable and got to her feet with ease. "Come here."

She pointed him toward the mirror she had hanging over the baby's dressing table. "Look right there. See how your brow's furrowed and the little line that's as straight as an arrow between your eyebrows."

"I see it."

"*That's* the stubborn pride look."

He smoothed the line with his finger before turning his back to the mirror. Although his affront hadn't fully faded, she could sense the humor lurking underneath his gruff voice. "You've made a study of my faces?"

"I've been looking at you for most of my life. Yes, I know your faces."

All trace of humor vanished as his features morphed

once more. For a man who she suspected believed he held a poker face in all circumstances, he'd likely be surprised to know how easily she could read him.

And what she saw nearly stole her breath.

Need and longing and an affection she'd dared not hope for painted his features, from the lazy heaviness in his eyes to the hard pulse visible at his neck.

"You look at me, Lizzie?"

When she'd made the decision to go to Ethan with her problems, she'd sworn to herself she wasn't going to get in over her head. Yet here she was, a mere day later, ready to tumble as fast as she could into his arms. Her problems hadn't gone anywhere, and no matter how kind and caring, Ethan wasn't in love with her. He hadn't even made an outreach after their night together.

Did she really think a few longing glances and shared memories would change that?

Despite all that, she refused to be dishonest. "Of course I look at you. I've always looked at you."

"No, you don't."

"I do."

He didn't move, yet she couldn't hide the shiver that raced across her skin as his gaze traveled over her face, then over her body, before following the path straight back to her eyes. "You're one of the few who sees me."

Memories long forgotten surfaced, and she recalled a comment Chris made once on a family visit to see Josie. Her foster mother, Rhonda, had commented on how high-spirited the Colton brothers were, all except for Ethan. Chris, a talker even then, had confirmed Ethan had always been quiet, more content to play with the family dog or the neighbor's barn cats than shouting and playing their endless games of cops and robbers.

"Your family sees you. Your brothers and sisters care about you very much."

"They also see me through a filter."

"A filter of love."

"And grief. They're all convinced I'm one tenuous thread away from snapping."

"That's absurd."

"Cowboys can't live on the edge?"

"Of course they can. Anyone can. But you're not. You've taken what's happened to you in life and exorcised it, becoming stronger in the process."

"How do you know that?"

"Because I know you."

"Up until six months ago, we hadn't seen each other in several years."

"It doesn't change the fact that I know you. I've known you for most of my life. And I've seen you with your animals. You could never care for a living creature the way you do if you were broken. The animals trust you and they respond to your quiet strength and understanding."

And so do I.

The words were nearly out before she pulled them back. This wasn't a conversation about her, no matter how many feelings Ethan Colton had managed to stir up.

"Which only proves my point." He reached out a hand, his fingers trailing over the edge of her cheek before dropping to his side. "You see me."

The powerful compliment crumpled her resistance, crushing it to dust. The truth was, she *did* see Ethan. Long before she understood the feelings as attraction, she'd wanted to know him. Had wanted to understand him.

As she got older, she was better able to put words

like *attraction* and *desire* to her feelings. By the time she understood her feelings, Josie was gone and the Colton family had stopped their court-sanctioned visits, all of the children grown into adults with their own lives. Their chance meeting at the rodeo had been an accident, nothing more.

Yet every time she tried to frame it as "nothing more" in her mind, she couldn't quite manage to believe herself.

Ethan had come back into her life for a reason. The baby obviously sat at the top of the list, but increasingly, she wondered if there was something else.

The quiet man who shared little with anyone had shared himself with her that night. He'd given her the gift of their child, but he'd also shared his thoughts. The horror at what his father had done. The pain of losing his mother that had never faded, no matter how many seasons passed. He'd even shared his strange, unaccountable anger at his father for dying.

Their child might not have been planned or expected, but he'd been conceived in mutual attraction and understanding, comfort and need.

On a hard sigh, the words she'd tried to find spilled out. "I was going to tell you. After the baby came."

The soft light that filtered through the room seemed to shift at her words—or maybe it was just the way he looked at her. Something warm and achy settled in behind that hazel gaze and her legs wobbled slightly at the intensity she saw there.

"You were?"

"Yes." Her throat tightened, but she pressed on. "It's important you know that. I needed to adjust. To become a mother first. But I had every intention of telling you. I know that sounds empty now, but I wanted you to know."

He said nothing more, just continued to stare at her with that intensity that clogged her breath in her chest.

She'd never considered herself bold. Ambitious and determined, yes. Thoughtful, even. But bold wasn't in her repertoire. So it was with no small measure of surprise that her body acted before she could check herself or think through all the angles.

Laying her hands on his shoulders, she moved in and pressed her lips against his throat. The pulse she'd seen a few moments before lay beneath her lips, the hard beats proof he wasn't unaffected. With a light flick of her tongue, she tasted the salty tang of his skin and reveled in the heat of his body.

Ethan shifted, exposing more of his neck to her teasing lips. She took full advantage, the stubble on his chin slightly rough against her lips as she traced the line of his jaw. She moved her hands over his shoulders, tightening her fingers on the hard tension of his muscles while her lips continued to explore the angles and planes of his face.

The roiling thoughts that had kept her company for the past months quieted in the reality of Ethan. Here, with him, she was safe.

As if recognizing that fact, her mind took the moment of quiet to tease her with something new. Steady as his heartbeat, one idea began to thrum, loud and urgent in her mind.

Be bold, Elizabeth Marie. Be bold.

Chapter 7

Lizzie pressed her lips to Ethan's, the aggressor in a battle he'd already consigned himself to lose. He wanted her. And no matter how many different reasons he gave himself that giving in was a bad idea, Ethan couldn't walk away. She hadn't been far from his thoughts in six months, and even before then, he'd think of her from time to time, curious as to how she was or how to even contact her.

He'd consider it for a few days, finally opting to let it slide. His rational side knew she was a woman who wanted more out of her life than a fling with a cowboy. And he'd never seen himself able to offer anything more.

Yet fate had found a way after all, their attraction to each other holding a strangely powerful magnetism.

In some dim corner of his mind, Ethan tried to figure out why he wasn't fighting that a bit more. Physically, he was strung out like a teenager, layered with the wants and desires of an adult. The tightly coiled need that had gripped him the moment he walked into his kitchen the day before and saw Lizzie Conner standing at his stove was rational. Normal. A man's desire for a woman as beautiful on the inside as she was out.

But emotionally?

Why was he willing to tell her the things he told no one else? And how did she seem to innately understand the things he couldn't even put into words?

Although he'd been content to let her play the aggressor, Ethan grew anxious to turn the tables. He lifted his hands to her neck, brushing a long flood of wavy hair over her shoulder. Her hair was so soft, lush with the thick curls he'd loved since he was a boy, and he couldn't resist the temptation to make a fist in all that softness.

Lizzie pressed closer, her mouth never leaving his. He could feel the press of her belly against his jeans and marveled he could feel so protective and so attracted to her all at once. She carried his child—a life they'd made together—and that simple fact was as erotic as it was profound.

He remembered every moment of conceiving their child. And while the outcome was unexpected, it was increasingly welcome.

The ring of his phone interrupted the moment, and Ethan nearly let it go until he remembered his conversation with Chris and his brother's promised follow-up. Reluctantly, he pulled away from the warm, willing woman in his arms. "I need to get this."

"Of course."

He allowed his hand to trail down her hair, the tips of his fingers caressing those soft curls, before lifting his phone to his ear. "Colton."

As he'd promised, Chris already had a line on the local police. McNulty and Warren had strong reputations and were considered good cops. Chris's nosing on Detective Bell had turned up similar feedback.

"They don't have eyes in the back of their heads, Ethan. Even good cops can't be everywhere."

An idea that had taken shape through the weekend solidified in his mind as he watched Lizzie finish tidying the room. Chris was right. The cops couldn't be everywhere.

But he could.

"Thanks, Chris. I'll call you tomorrow."

"Ethan. Don't forget—Trev wants to talk to you about visiting Dad."

"Yeah."

"Ethan—"

"I got it." He knew the hard snap in his tone spoke volumes about his current resistance to visiting the old man, and he wasn't ready to look too closely at that one. Softening his tone, he added, "I'll follow up with him."

"Your brother was fast." Lizzie finished folding a small quilt imprinted with various animals from Noah's Ark, then folded it over the side rail of the crib. "Did he find anything out about the policemen who came here?"

"They're good men. Chris even listed out a few commendations each has received."

"And the detective?" She traced the pattern on the quilt, her gaze on the blanket instead of him.

"Same. You've got good people working your case."

Her focus shifted, that soft green gaze unyielding. "Then why do you look so upset?"

"My brother has that effect on me."

Before she could press him on the reasons why, Ethan

pushed forward with his own agenda. "I'd like you to pack a bag. I want you to stay with me."

"I am with you. I've got my overnight bag."

"Something larger. I'd like you to stay with me until we can get this figured out."

Her gaze darted around the room before settling back on the crib. "I can't just move out. I need to finish setting up for the baby and—"

"This looks pretty settled to me. Besides, he or she will sleep in a small bassinet in your room for the first few months anyway."

"And I need to look for a job."

"You were seriously planning on job hunting in the last trimester of pregnancy?"

"No… I mean, I—" She broke off before catching her breath. "I have a life here. And I need to be living it. You don't need a guest in your home."

"You're the mother of my child, Lizzie. That makes you far more than just a guest."

Although they weren't words of love, Lizzie couldn't quite stop the flood of emotion that filled her at Ethan's words.

Not a guest.

Her entire life, she'd felt a guest in others' homes. Even with the Carltons, who'd loved her and wanted the best for her, she'd felt like an outsider. An interloper.

"Come on. You know it's the right thing."

"But I have a life. I can't just hole up at your place indefinitely."

"Why not?"

"You saw what happened today. What if he comes back? Or does something to my home? I can't just abandon my home to some psycho."

"Better your house than you and the baby."

The blanket she'd smoothed before laying it across the baby's crib had crumpled in her hands. "Why are you so insistent on this?"

"Why are you being so stubborn?"

"I'm not—"

A grin played about his lips—wholly un-Ethan-like—and Lizzie narrowed her eyes. "What's that look for?"

"I was just curious what 'Ethan Colton look' I was giving you now."

"That's not funny. We're talking about our lives here."

"Exactly. Our lives. And the life of our child."

"That's not fair."

"I'm not trying to play fair." Ethan glanced around the room before extending a hand toward the door. "Come on. Let's get moving, unless you want me to help you pack."

Whether it was the threat of help or lack of a sound argument to rebut him, Lizzie didn't know. But here she was, almost an hour later, with a full suitcase and a growing case of nerves.

Since the officers had promised to continue driving past the house on rounds for the next several days, Ethan had agreed to make a run to the hardware store while she finished up with her things. She knew he was downstairs even now fitting each of her doors with new locks, and his closeness had only added to the unsettled nerves.

Lizzie wanted to be mad at how easily he'd handled her. She'd even worked up a fair head of steam after he'd left, wondering how he could simply order her around as though she had no say in her life. But logic and the shoots of fear that had taken root deep inside since the threats had begun had counterbalanced the mad with quiet gratitude.

She was afraid. And the baby's safety came first, no question.

But how was she going to spend every day in close proximity to Ethan Colton? Her lips still tingled from their kiss, and she could swear her hips still bore the brand of his fingertips.

And then there was the conversation with his brother. Ethan might not have wanted to discuss it, but she'd heard Chris's voice through the phone. She'd not meant to eavesdrop, but the baby's room wasn't that big.

His brother wanted him to visit their father?

She pulled the zipper closed on her large suitcase and nearly had it lifted off the bed when a voice rang out. "Don't lift that!"

Ethan strode across the room, his gaze dark. "You can't lift that."

"Why not? I'm pregnant, not helpless."

"It's heavy."

"So am I, as of late. It doesn't change the fact that my arms work perfectly fine."

"Humor me." Ethan dragged the suitcase off the bed. She hadn't packed light, but he moved the oversize case as if it weighed nothing.

"Seems I'm doing a lot of that today." Lizzie heard the petulant tone and actually reveled in the sour words. She did appreciate the help, but she'd been on her own for so long, she wasn't used to anyone ordering her around.

And she certainly hadn't ever pictured herself as a ward in Ethan Colton's home.

"I know this is an upheaval, but I promise I'm not that bad to live with."

She had no doubt he was wonderful to live with. That was the majority of her problem. On a sigh, she dropped to the corner of the bed. "It's not you. I can't thank you enough for your help. And I'd be lying if I didn't tell you how nice it is to be taken care of. But I hate feeling so helpless."

"I know."

"It's like one moment I had a life, and now I'm someone's burden."

"I know."

The words that had escaped in hasty frustration lingered between them like a storm cloud ready to burst with rain. But it was the understanding beneath his quiet acknowledgment that finally penetrated her gloomy thoughts.

"You haven't been helpless in a long time."

"But I was." Ethan sat down next to her and took her hand, tucking it between his palms. "And it's not a feeling you forget."

"You were seven."

"Seven. Twenty-seven. Heck, eighty-seven. Does it matter? Fear is fear. And feeling helpless doesn't have an age limit."

"None of it changes the fact that you didn't go looking for this, Ethan. Or ask for this."

"And you did?" His hands tightened on hers, his easy strength going a long way to calm her nerves.

"No."

They sat like that for several long minutes, her hand tucked in his, their soft breaths the only sound in the room. She wanted to ask him about his father and why he needed to go visit Matthew Colton.

Was he afraid to see his father? Or maybe sad? Did it color how he really felt about becoming a father himself?

All questions freighted with the weight of a lifetime.

Despite her need to understand the man beside her, Lizzie was loath to mar their quiet kinship.

So she held her silence.

"Lizzie. Wake up."

The deep, husky voice sent a delicious chill down her spine, and Lizzie tried to burrow more deeply under the covers. She turned to snuggle in, only to come awake in a snap when she banged her head against the window of Ethan's truck.

"Ow."

"I'm sorry to wake you. We're home." When she didn't respond, Ethan added, "My place."

"When did I fall asleep?"

"About three minutes after we left your house. I didn't have the heart to wake you on the drive."

The events of the morning and the mental roller coaster that seemed to have her in its thrall came rushing back, and she fought to surface from the dreamless state where she'd hovered for the past hour.

In the crash of memories—an intruder in her home, another visit with cops and new locks on her doors—one other thought rocketed through her: she was moving in with Ethan Colton.

Had she lost her mind this morning?

While his help was welcome, the idea they'd be living together even temporarily seemed like some cruel torture for her heart. *And your hormones*, an impish voice whispered through her mind.

Locking down that train of thought, she took his

extended hand and allowed him to help her out of his truck. The ranch house looked different somehow, and she puzzled at how it could look like another place barely six hours after she last left it.

It was only when Ethan handed her a key that it hit her. When she'd left, she had been nothing more than a visitor.

And now she was home.

"This works on all the house locks as well as the office entrance to the stable."

"Thank you."

Late afternoon sunlight dappled his hair with gold highlights, and small crinkles edged the corners of his eyes as he squinted. "You're welcome to come and go as you please, but I would ask that you let me know if you're going to be gone."

"You're not my keeper."

He held up a hand. "And I promise to do the same. We're no good to each other if we don't know where one another is."

She tightened her grip on the key, unable to argue with his reasonable logic. "That's fair."

"And necessary. I don't want to scare you, but we have no proof the problems you experienced at home won't follow you here. I'd like to tell my ranch hands about what's been going on. Extra pairs of eyes can only help our cause, and my men are loyal to me."

"Of course."

Although the hands she'd met thus far all seemed well able to care for themselves, their safety was yet another facet she'd not even considered. What had only seemed dangerous to her had now grown to involve others.

"What's that look for?"

"You've been so kind to offer me help, and now I'm putting even more people in the line of fire."

"My team can handle themselves."

"Against a crazy person?"

"A few of them are pretty damn crazy all on their own."

The joke was meant to lighten the mood, but she couldn't summon up any laughs. "Please tell them to be careful."

He sobered at her request. "I will. And don't be surprised if you get a few shadows following you around the ranch. Once they know you've been threatened, they'll all close ranks to make sure you're safe."

Her gaze drifted to the stable in time to see two large men walk Dream and another horse she'd not yet met out of the barn. Their shoulders rivaled Ethan's for sheer breadth, and both carried themselves with a quick confidence that suggested there was little they couldn't handle. "That will be nice."

More than nice.

"Look, I know you've had a long day, but do you think you're up for a visit with my siblings? Chris mentioned a family gathering when I spoke with him earlier."

"Then you should go."

"I'd like you to go with me."

It had been years since she'd seen any of Ethan's family. The Coltons had visited regularly when she and Josie were younger, until her friend had requested the visits stop the year she turned twelve. It had been yet another scar on her heart, and it had taken Lizzie a long time to accept her myriad feelings about Josie.

Hurt. Anger. Sadness. And somewhere underneath it

all, a deep confusion that her friend had simply walked away. Like her own family had done so many years before.

She'd loved Josie's five brothers and sister, Annabel. The excitement when all six of them came to visit had always been anticipated for days, then recounted for months after they left again.

So why did the idea of seeing them again bring such a sense of trepidation?

"I can't intrude. It wouldn't be right."

"It would mean a lot to me if you'd go."

"But they don't know about the baby. I'm not sure springing a pregnant woman on them is quite the way you need to tell them."

Although the baby was a bit of a grasped straw, the sheepish look that came over Ethan's face gave her the strangest urge to laugh. He hunched his shoulders, and the hands shoved into his worn jean pockets only completed the hangdog look. "Chris already knows. I told him earlier when I asked him to look into those cops. And if I know my brother, it's already spread like wildfire to each of my brothers and my sister."

"Men don't gossip."

"Men gossip plenty." He looked up from his shoes then, a wry grin at his lips. "We're just usually quieter about it."

"Ethan… I don't know."

"Please. I'd like you to see them again, and I think the baby might take a bit of the focus off the endless discussion about my father and the Alphabet Killer."

"That's not the most comforting argument, you know."

He dragged his hand from his pocket and captured

hers. The warmth of his palm sent a shot of calm winging through her body, even as his touch generated a fresh round of jittery nerves.

"I don't mean to use the baby as an excuse. At all. But I do think we need something joyful to talk about. For the past few months all we've discussed is our father."

"It must be hard to talk about it."

He dropped her hand and looked out over his property. With a swift kick he sent a small rock arcing out over the front lawn. "Talk about it. Dissect it. Go over it ad nauseam."

Matthew Colton was far more than just a sensitive subject, and she wanted to be understanding of that fact. Even so, she also knew it wasn't fair to have half the story. She'd never been one to probe into others' private moments, but Ethan was inviting her in by virtue of the offer to meet with his family. She might as well step all the way through the door.

"Does this mean you're ready to talk to me about what you know?"

The afternoon air had warmed underneath a bright Texas sky, but the sun had begun its descent and a distinct chill whipped through the front yard. Ethan wanted to move Lizzie inside, into the warmth, but the stubborn light reflecting from the mossy green of her eyes suggested she wasn't going to budge an inch. "I've told you what I know."

"No, you've told me what I've managed to squeeze out of you. I'd like to understand in a broader sense what's going on. I asked you earlier if you think your father's engineering the Alphabet killings from prison, and you sidestepped the question."

"He's in maximum-security lockup. It'd be awfully hard to engineer something this extreme."

"That's not an answer—it's just another evasion." She turned her back to him and marched to the front door, her new key already in the lock before he could stop her.

"Come on. Wait."

"For what? For you to decide you can trust me? That you can talk to me about all the pain you carry and how it's all been churned up by what's going on?"

He might have been more open with Lizzie than any other person in his life, but her accusations boxed him into an inescapable corner. Ethan fought the rising sense of panic that lodged in his throat before it spilled over in a rush of words. "I don't want to go back to that time! Ever! I told you before I'm not helpless, and I sure as hell don't want to relive a time when I was."

"Talking about it and letting out what's bottled up inside isn't helpless. It's necessary if you ever want any sort of life."

She'd already tried to enter the house once and he'd stopped her, but this time, when she turned toward his front door, he let her go.

Why did they keep coming back to the same place? He knew damn well he'd opened the door on his emotions that night at the rodeo. He'd been shaken up about his father's cancer diagnosis and he'd shared far more than he'd ever intended.

None of that changed the fact he was entitled to his own thoughts. He'd spent two decades dealing with his memories of his father and his late mother, and he'd done just fine.

He was *fine*.

And she had no right to keep pushing.

He stalked to the truck to remove Lizzie's things, but once his gaze caught on Dream and Cappie, circling the ring, he changed gears.

Ethan gave a quick whistle for Cappie, and the horse responded in kind, his elegant neck rising at the call. His ranch hand glanced up, his ready smile dropping as he kept a hold on the chestnut gelding's lead. "You okay, boss?"

"Fine."

Ben's gaze was skeptical, but the man had worked for him long enough to know when to hold his tongue.

"Has Cappie been out for a ride yet today?"

"Nope. Cap loves when you take him out."

"Then he's about to get his wish. Please keep an eye on the house. Miss Lizzie went in to rest for a bit."

"Will do, boss."

In a matter of moments, he had Cap fully saddled and was out riding his property. The cool air that had swirled around them had grown raw, whipping and buffeting Ethan and his horse as they rode across the back pasture. Several herds grazed, paying them no attention, and he spurred Cap on even harder, giving the horse his head.

"Thatta boy."

He let his thoughts roam, the helpless infuriation that had filled him on the porch morphing into a self-righteous anger that echoed in his head louder than Cap's hooves.

"How dare she?"

The muttered words caught in his throat as he pulled hard on the reins, his gaze pausing on a flash in the trees. Even though he'd been running hard, Cap responded instantly to the change in direction, and Ethan moved them on toward the stretch of woods that rimmed a section of his property.

Had he seen something, or was it the play of his imagination?

He and Cap had ridden to the far side of the property, about a mile from the house. Although they moved the cattle around, this section was rarely used for grazing due to the thick copse of trees.

Did one of the cattle get separated?

He scanned the area once more and didn't see any indication one of his steers had got separated from the others.

Had he seen a person?

Cap sensed his anxiety and moved them more deeply into the trees at Ethan's subtle urging. The cool air whipped through the branches overhead in a piercing whistle, the sound subtly eerie.

Ethan stilled his horse, giving the area his full attention. He followed the various nooks and crannies of the tree line, scanning from the treetops to the brush that covered the ground. Whatever he'd thought he'd seen—if he'd actually seen anything at all—had vanished.

"Come on, Cap."

Ethan wheeled his horse around and headed back for the house. The air had grown even colder than when he'd started out, and he still needed to talk to Lizzie. He might resent her probing, but he couldn't fully fault the curiosity. Or her need to know what he and his siblings were dealing with, especially after what she'd been through that morning.

He hated discussing his father. But he also knew it wasn't fair to keep Lizzie in the dark.

As Ethan rode away, his focus on the house and the discussion that awaited him, he missed the woman who stepped out from behind the trees.

Chapter 8

Lizzie sipped on a club soda and watched the conversation swirl around the long table in Trevor Colton's dining room. The oldest of the Colton siblings, Trevor still had the same ability to take charge at thirty-four as he had at fourteen.

All these years later, she could still remember him giving orders as they all ran around the Carltons' farm, corralling his younger brothers and taking general responsibility every time the Colton siblings came to visit Josie.

Although she'd have thought him the most affected by Matthew's criminal history next to Ethan, the strong, sensitive man who led their meal had a quick smile and an easy way about him.

Everyone deals with grief differently. Just because you can't see it doesn't mean it isn't there.

Unlike Ethan.

He attempted to hide his childhood grief behind a stoic face, but she knew it was there. And she knew he needed a way to discuss the pain that never fully faded.

Her earlier frustration crested over her in a hard wave, and she took a quick sip of her drink to cool her tight throat. She didn't want to be mad at Ethan—and certainly didn't want to stay mad—but she hadn't quite got over their tense words on the porch.

He was the one who'd insisted she move in, especially with the heightened actions of her stalker. She hadn't even made a connection between the Alphabet Killer and what was happening to her until he brought it up. It was only natural she'd have questions, and she wasn't going to apologize for that.

Which made this evening that much more important.

If Ethan was going to stay silent, maybe his siblings wouldn't. She was nervous about coming tonight, but she couldn't say she was sorry she was here. Perhaps some time spent with the Coltons would shed more light on their father and the current rash of murders.

Annabel Colton laid a hand on Lizzie's arm and leaned over with a conspiratorial whisper. "Have we put you to sleep yet?"

"No!"

"I think you're just being polite." Mischief sparked behind Annabel's gaze, and Lizzie couldn't help noticing the resemblance between the woman and the image of Josie she still carried in her mind. Her friend had got that devil-may-care look in her eyes many times. As she thought back on it, most of the fun adventures that resulted from that look still lingered as some of her best memories.

"When Trevor and Sam get going with the law-enforcement talk, it can get sort of tedious."

Banishing thoughts of Josie, Lizzie couldn't resist asking, "Aren't you in law enforcement, too? I'd think you'd love this sort of conversation."

Annabel's subtle grimace was gone as fast as it appeared. "I love a good case. But an accounting of my father's sins hardly makes for an enjoyable evening."

"Ethan said something similar earlier."

Annabel's warm sky blue gaze flicked toward Ethan before drifting back. Even though he was sitting nearby, his sister spoke of him with simple honesty. "He's got the biggest scars, make no mistake about it. And talking about it doesn't make it any easier to live with the reality of who and what my father was."

"What about you? Has going into law enforcement helped? Learning about the criminal mind and what motivates some people toward such dark choices?"

"Most of my experience—my work at the academy and a few cases I've observed—has been theoretical." That grimace was back, but with the context of Annabel's words, a sense of what the woman was dealing with began to take shape in Lizzie's mind.

She knew Annabel was a rookie on the Granite Gulch police force—information that had been intimated earlier by Annabel's twin, Chris—but it was only with her description of her experience that the pieces fell into place.

"I'd imagine Granite Gulch is a quiet town. Or was a quiet town until the murders began again."

"We're fortunate that few of our officers have ever even needed to fire their service revolver," Annabel said. "But police work is also more than helping old women find their cats and running down missing pies."

"People call the police for that?"

"They do in Granite Gulch."

"This must be an awful strain on local resources."

Annabel hesitated, her shoulders stiffening before she gave a reluctant nod. "Yes, it is. We're a small police force for a small town. And while we have larger resources nearby in Dallas and Fort Worth if we need them, as well as the FBI, the recent murders have been a lot to deal with."

A hard slap of a hand on the tabletop startled her, and Lizzie snapped to attention as Trevor's voice rang out. She'd listened attentively through dinner to the ongoing conversation about Matthew but had allowed her attention to drift over dessert as she enjoyed the quiet reprieve talking with Annabel.

"We each need to get our clues. It's the only way we'll get to the bottom of this and find out where Mom was buried."

Trevor's mention of their mother put Lizzie on high alert.

Clues?

"And if one of us doesn't want to go?" Ethan's husky voice was the opposite of his brother's. Where Trevor's comments dominated the table, Ethan's subtle resistance went a long way toward quieting the din.

"It's the only way, Ethan." Ethan's older brother, Ridge, just above him in age, had been quiet for much of the evening, so his words stood out with similar gravitas. "The old man's stubborn, and he's not going to give us what we want if we don't play his game."

"It's not a game." Even without the broader context of what they were talking about, Lizzie would have been hard-pressed to miss Ethan's stiff shoulders and the rumbling anger that increasingly filled his replies.

She laid a hand on his thigh, not surprised to feel the steady, nervous tapping that had brushed against her leg repeatedly through dinner. He stilled, his hand covering hers under the table, and Lizzie had to admit to herself she was glad she came.

Glad she was here for Ethan.

She cared for him. And no matter how she looked at it, that fact remained unchanged. The past few days had only reinforced feelings she'd believed long dormant. A fanciful notion from childhood that had been abandoned years before, yet had sprung so easily back to life.

Which meant she'd need to tread carefully. Decisions were no longer simply what was right for her and her alone. She had a child to think about. And feelings for its father didn't mean she had a right to lose her head.

Focusing on the matter at hand, she keyed back in to the active conversation Ethan had been having with his brothers. "What's this about clues?" Lizzie kept her voice low—for Ethan's hearing only—and felt his hand tighten over hers.

"It's noth—" He stopped, then squeezed her fingers. "It's a ridiculous little fantasy my father's playing. If he sees us, presumably he believes he can atone for his sins."

It hardly sounded like a game, as Ridge called it, if it involved their late mother, but she pressed on. "I find it hard to believe he has that much freedom from prison. How can he orchestrate anything?"

"Think again." Ethan hesitated another moment, considering, before he turned toward Trevor. "Why don't you enlighten Lizzie on our father's latest request."

The grief she'd suspected earlier finally made an appearance. Trevor's engagement as their jovial host promptly vanished, replaced by the stoic FBI agent who had built a strong reputation for closing some of the state's toughest cases. "Our father's decided he wants time with each of his children. A dying man's request."

"It seems awfully late to get sentimental." She knew the words were harsh, but so help her, she couldn't summon up any apology for them. Matthew Colton had spent his free years sowing his own personal brand of evil across Blackthorn County. The lives he'd taken hadn't just ended individual existences—they'd ruined families.

And his family had been affected as much as—or more than—so many others.

No, she had no remorse, and she'd live with the judgment she carried inside.

"Our father has his reasons," Trevor said. "But he hasn't been very forthcoming with any answer save he wants to see each of his children before he dies."

"So you're just expected to fall in line?" Even as she asked the question, the somber faces that stared back at her around the long cherry table suggested that, yes, in fact they did need to acquiesce to the man who might biologically be their parent but who had never been a father to any of them.

"If we want information about our mother's resting place." The words were clipped and quiet, Ethan's voice such a low register she barely heard him.

But she understood the implications.

Although the window of time had been short, Matthew Colton had managed to move his wife's body between Ethan's discovery and the arrival of the police. The Colton property was extensive, and despite continued searching, her body had never been found nor had Matthew ever divulged where he'd placed it.

"Have any of you gone to see him?" Lizzie asked.

Sam nodded, his fiancée, Zoe, by his side. "Trevor

told us about the deal our father wanted to make, and I was as resistant as anyone. But after Z's sister was murdered—" He wrapped an arm around Zoe and pulled her close. "After we lost Celia, I knew I needed to try. Trev was already commandeering the old man's fan mail, so I went along and tried to get as much information as I could."

Lizzie knew it had been only a short time since Zoe lost her sister, Celia Robison—the Alphabet Killer's third victim, whose murder had officially meant the police were dealing with a serial killer. The poor woman's death had been all the news could talk about for a week, the coverage making national headlines.

Although grief still ghosted Zoe's petite features and pale blue eyes, beneath the pain, Lizzie saw something else.

Love.

It arced between Zoe and Sam like heat lightning, and for the briefest of moments, Lizzie felt a shot of jealousy wing through her chest before it skittered away to the corners of her mind.

She wasn't jealous. And she would never begrudge another their happiness. But it did seem extra special, somehow, that in the midst of her deepest pain, Zoe had found Sam.

"And you got zilch for your troubles," Ethan muttered.

Although Sam looked ready to argue, it was Trevor who interjected. "It was a clue, Ethan, and it was damn more than we had before."

"Texas." Ethan shook his head. "That was the old man's clue. Like it was a big surprise he'd bury my mother in the largest state in the contiguous forty-eight.

Where the hell else was he going to take her? On a cruise to Alaska or a trip up to Maine?"

Sam said nothing further, but Lizzie made a mental note to ask Annabel and Zoe if Sam had suffered any repercussions by opening up old wounds. She might not be Ethan's girlfriend, but she *was* his friend. And she was the closest thing he had right now to an impartial observer.

As she filed the clue away, another thought struck, along with a wistful shot of hope she'd believed long dead. "If Matthew wants to see each of his children, what's he going to do when Josie doesn't show up?"

"We'll cross that bridge." Trevor reached for the large pot of coffee that sat at his end of the table, its twin on the opposite end next to Chris. "She's the youngest, so if we tell Matthew she'll go last, maybe we'll get enough in the first six clues not to need her involvement."

It seemed like an awfully big gamble, but Lizzie knew she'd monopolized enough of the conversation. And despite her interest, she couldn't say she wasn't creeped out by what Ethan and his siblings were going through. Annabel's comment about how their father had begun to dominate every conversation was also making more sense.

What she couldn't quite reconcile, other than the fact that it gnawed at her with dull teeth, was the strange shot of hope that seemed to fill the room. It was almost as though they all felt if they could only outsmart their old man, they'd finally put the ghost of their mother to rest.

Lizzie allowed her gaze to drift to Ethan, his attention focused on the fresh cup of coffee he doctored, and amended her assessment.

Five of Matthew Colton's children had hope they'd discover their mother's final resting place.

And the one who carried the discovery of Matthew's sins had no choice but to follow along.

Ethan dropped an armful of recyclables into the blue bin in Trevor's garage, then swung a large bag of trash into the garbage can. He'd have preferred to walk the trash to the neighbors'—anything to get away from the cloying focus of his brothers and sister—but a few stolen moments in the garage would have to do.

This wasn't the first time the subject of visiting his father had come up, but Trevor's pleas for Ethan to take a ride up to the maximum-security facility that housed Matthew Colton had grown more urgent. They needed information, Trevor continued to argue, and Ethan was the big prize as far as Matthew Colton was concerned. The old man wanted to see him—wanted to look him in the eye—a pleasure Ethan had denied him for twenty years.

Damn the freaking bastard.

He slammed the lid on the garbage can, that same fear that had coated his throat a million hours ago rising up in a cloying rush. He stilled, breathing air into his lungs. And willed away that feeling of helplessness that had come on him at the age of seven and had never fully left.

He'd put that ghost to rest a hell of a long time ago, and he had no interest in rattling it back to life. Nor did he have any interest in dancing on the old man's puppet strings.

The garage door opened and his brother Ridge stepped out with another full bag and his own arms full of items for the recycle bin. "You okay?"

"Fine."

"Sure you are. Which is why you're hiding in the garage." Ridge dumped his wares in the same order as Ethan, the empty bottles and aluminum cans making a hard thunk as they hit the bottom of the bin.

"Drop it, Ridge."

"Why? So you can pull the old Ethan Colton switcheroo and check out on us? Go back to your ranch and not come out for a month or ignore all your phone messages and texts unless one of us comes out to get you?"

"I own a working ranch. My job's not nine-to-five."

"None of us work a simple day job. Doesn't mean a text or a phone call is that hard to place."

Ethan swore as he kicked at a small can that had slipped from his grasp. The metal rolled across the concrete floor before slamming into the plastic bin, ricocheting right back to his feet.

Just like his damn life.

He'd spent years putting his father and his miserable childhood as far behind him as he could, only to find it had all come back full circle.

"It was a fun surprise to see Lizzie again." Ridge hesitated, a broad smile breaking over his hard features. "Although there's a bit more of her to see than last time."

"You haven't seen her since she was a teenager. Of course she's grown."

"That wasn't the direction I was suggesting." Ridge moved closer, the smile falling. "Why didn't you tell us you were going to be a father?"

"Because I had no idea I was going to be one until yesterday morning, when I walked in on Lizzie in my kitchen."

"I didn't know you two were an item. I mean, we all knew you and little Lizzie Conner had a connection as kids, but this is a bit more significant. You're going to be parents."

"We ran into each other at the rodeo last year. Things just happened." Ethan left it at that, the tender moments he and Lizzie had shared something private.

Ridge hesitated a moment, and Ethan let him work up to what he wanted to say. His brother was nearly as quiet as he was and not one to poke into others' business. "Are you going to marry her?"

A hard pain slammed into his midsection, and Ethan could have sworn he'd lost his breath. *Marry Lizzie Conner?*

Why would he do that?

Yes, they were going to have a baby, but he'd be damned if he was going to saddle her with the Colton name. It was bad enough his child would grow up with Matthew's blood coursing through his veins. He had no interest in forcing a name that had been spit with outrage by half the county on an unsuspecting child.

On a hard cough, he shook his head. "I wouldn't do that to her. Or the baby."

"You won't do what?"

Ethan knew this was sensitive territory for Ridge, his own childhood sweetheart taken from him by parents who didn't approve of their daughter dating the child of Blackthorn County's most notorious serial killer.

"I won't marry her. I won't make my child carry the Colton name." He scrubbed at his face, his evening stubble rough against his fingers.

Ethan saw the flash of old memories cross his brother's face in craggy lines and knew he'd hit a nerve. But when Ridge spoke again, his past hurts were nowhere in evidence. "But the bigger question, little brother, is do you want to?"

"Lizzie and I haven't seen each other for six months. And before that it was years."

Ridge slapped him on the back. "Maybe you need a few more minutes out here to consider why you didn't answer my question."

The urge to argue was strong, but Ethan kept silent as Ridge headed back into the house. The sound of conversation drifted through the door, and he didn't miss the mix of feminine voices echoing above the lower baritones of his brothers.

It was no longer just Annabel, but Zoe, too.

And now Lizzie.

The door closed, effectively shutting out the noise once more, leaving Ethan with nothing but his thoughts.

How had he ended up here? He'd made a nice life for himself. He had his ranch, his own little piece of heaven on earth. His business was going well and he had managed to carve out a place of respect in Granite Gulch despite his parentage.

So how had the clear and certain path he was traveling on managed to change so abruptly?

Even as he asked himself the question, he knew he had no right. There were four victims of the Alphabet Killer. Four families and extended families who were now bereft of a loved one because someone wanted to mimic his father's crimes.

No matter how fast they worked, they had no leads on a killer who seemed determined to make as dark a mark on Granite Gulch as his father had. Unless he wanted to start believing the rumor Josie had taken up where Matthew had left off.

Ethan bent to retrieve the can he'd kicked away, anguish and sorrow churning in his veins that he'd even given another moment's thought to his sister's involvement.

Josie *wasn't* Matthew. It simply wasn't possible.

The garage door opened once more and he almost had a smart-ass retort winging back at Ridge when he caught sight of Lizzie. She'd clearly caught round three on the recycles, her hands full of aluminum cans and several empty plastic bottles.

"You don't have to do that." He rushed forward and pulled the detritus from her, only to get a dark look in return.

"You're as bad as your brothers. Annabel and Zoe, too, as a matter of fact. I'm having a baby, not lingering on the verge of death. I can carry a few empty items to the recycle bin."

"Do you make guests in your home carry trash?" He dropped the items into the blue bin, amused to see, based on the handful of empty cans, that Trevor still drank the same soda he'd loved as a kid. There was sugar and then there was *sugar*, and Trev seemed to thrive on the latter.

"No."

"So why should we be any different?"

"But it's like people see a pregnant lady and immediately assume I'm helpless."

"Trust me, Lizzie. Anyone who spends more than two minutes with you doesn't think that."

She seemed to blossom under the compliment, her pretty green eyes growing as wide as her smile. "I'm glad to hear it."

The reality was, his siblings hadn't thought her helpless at all. If he'd read their faces correctly—and he had a pretty good idea he had—they were all far more preoccupied with the fact Lizzie was pregnant at all than with whether or not she was going to help with the dinner dishes.

"Your father is certainly the topic of conversation.

Has it always been that way?" Her voice remained light as a summer rain, but he didn't miss just how sharp and pointed the question was.

"No. We did rather well avoiding any and all mention of his name except when necessary."

"That's a hard way to live."

"It went pretty smoothly from my perspective."

The lush lips that drew his attention like a moth to flame thinned, her frown replacing the easy smile she'd worn since entering the garage.

"Attempting to bury the elephant in the room really doesn't make it go away. It just throws a lot of dirt on top of it."

"I don't question what works."

"That's the problem, Ethan. It hasn't worked. You're all right back where you started, you most of all. Surely you can see that?"

"What I see is a problem to be dealt with. I'll deal with it." He knew it for a lie, the churning oil slick in his stomach an obvious reminder of just how large, but still he pressed on. "I appreciate that you know our history and like us anyway. It doesn't make this any less my problem to handle."

"Why can't you see I'm here to help?"

"Like you've been here the past six months? Tell me something." He moved up into her space, so close the edge of her belly pressed to his hip. "If you didn't have some ass skulking around your house, would you have even told me about the baby? Or were you going to spend your life hiding the fact you'd given birth to Matthew Colton's heir?"

The barb met its mark, and the gentle pressure of her stomach vanished as she took several steps back.

"We've been over this! I told you I was going to tell you after the baby had arrived."

He wanted to reach for her—wanted to take her hand and ask for forgiveness for his cruel words—but stayed rooted to the garage floor instead.

And only heaped on an additional insult.

"Easy words now. But awfully hypocritical to accuse me of an elephant in the room when you blithely ignored your own."

The vivid green gaze that had been so brightly amused only minutes before filled with a wary, battle-hardened grace. Her still shoulders only completed the image. "Take this out on me if you want—I won't break. But don't use me or my behavior to excuse your own. You've spent your life ignoring the events that shaped you. And you're out of places to run."

Chapter 9

Lizzie threw the covers off and got out of bed. She'd headed straight for her room after they'd arrived home and knew Ethan had done the same. Even with the self-righteous anger that had carried her through the first few hours of tossing and turning, somewhere in the midst of her anger, something had changed.

Transformed, really, as she'd relived each and every moment of their fight. And as each hateful word repeated over and over in her mind, she increasingly had to acknowledge Ethan's side of the story.

He'd acted the jerk, to the extreme. But she'd also backed him into a corner and he'd come out swinging. The emotional backlash was unwarranted, but the words had needed to come out.

The truth was, she hadn't told him about the baby. And while it was easy for her to believe she'd have gone to him after their child arrived, he didn't know that.

He hadn't known anything.

His impending parenthood. The results of their one amazing night together. Or her long-buried feelings for him.

While she'd keep the last thought to herself, she had to own her role in his feelings of betrayal.

She wrapped herself up in the robe at the foot of the bed, the oversize T-shirts she'd begun sleeping in too cold for walking around. The thick cotton enveloped her, and she pressed a hand to her belly after she tied the belt.

The baby was quiet after having kicked along with her roiling thoughts earlier in the evening. Their matched rhythms filled her with a strange sense of wonder that only punctuated a bigger point she'd conveniently—or deliberately?—overlooked.

She'd had almost six months to get used to the idea of becoming a parent, and Ethan hadn't even had two days.

The fears she'd carried to his front door—that his lifelong feelings about never having children would create an insurmountable rift between them—hadn't manifested. In fact, he'd seemed committed to the idea, maybe even excited. But it was still an upheaval during a time when his entire world had been turned upside down.

The well-oiled door didn't even creak when she opened it, and she headed down to the kitchen to get some water. The house was still, with nothing but an overhead light above the sink to help her navigate the quiet. She had to dig through three cabinets before she found a glass, but finally found what she needed. Glass full, she settled against the counter to drink her water and think about how she wanted to approach Ethan the next day.

Her normal go-to—an apology—flitted through her mind, but she discarded it. While she hated how the situation with his father had caused such emotional upheaval, she wasn't going to apologize for her curiosity or her heartfelt outreach of help and support. That said, she wasn't content to leave any question in his mind that she might not have told him about the baby. Her reticence wasn't based on a desire to keep him in the dark for his child's lifetime, but—

Something skittered across the back of her neck like a whisper, derailing her thoughts at the sudden intrusion. Goose bumps rose over her arms, and her first thought was that she wasn't alone. The image of a silent watcher quickly gave way to a darker threat, Ethan's words from earlier in the day pounding through her mind like jungle drums.

Your name begins with an E, Lizzie. Elizabeth is your given name.

Did someone know she was here? Someone who meant to do her harm?

The heavy rhythm of her pulse throbbed in her ear and she took a sip of her water, surprised to see her hand shake as she lifted the glass to her mouth.

What was wrong with her?

This reaction was awfully extreme, she admitted to herself, especially considering the fact that she had protection sleeping one floor away and had seen for herself how tightly locked Ethan kept his home. She'd even heard the dead bolt fall into place this evening as she walked away from Ethan in the entryway after they returned home.

Quit being silly.

Lizzie pushed herself away from the counter, determined to shake off the weird reaction. Maybe something else had spooked her. With a quick glance around the kitchen, Lizzie cataloged the room's contents to see what might have caught her attention. She was in a strange house—maybe a noise had caught her unawares during her late-night musings.

Or maybe Ethan had come downstairs and she'd been oblivious to his presence. A glance at the empty doorway eliminated that possibility, and she glanced toward the ceiling, taking some small comfort that the master bedroom was directly above her head.

Setting the glass down on the counter, she moved toward the mudroom. Ethan had no pets, but this *was* a working ranch. Had something sneaked inside, seeking warmth or shelter? She flipped on the overhead, oddly comforted when fluorescent light flooded the room. She scanned every inch of the small space, but once again, she came up empty.

When the baby gave a swift kick just beneath her ribs, Lizzie rubbed her belly. Whatever had her spooked was waking the baby, and she needed to settle down. It had been a long day, filled with more upheaval than she wanted to admit. Between the creepy stalker leaving her notes and the dark talk among the Colton siblings, it was more than natural her mind would be on high alert.

Lizzie snapped off the light and walked back to the kitchen. She needed to shake off the stress of the day, refill her water glass and go back to bed. The window over the sink looked out over the stable, and she let her gaze wander over Ethan's property.

She switched off the tap and turned to head back to her room. She took a few steps, then turned back to the window, that strange awareness slamming into her with brute force. The yard had been dark when she first came downstairs. Only now lights blazed from the overheads that rimmed the stable.

Just as though someone had walked through them.

Ethan had drifted in and out of a fitful sleep, but he sat straight up at the sound of running water. A glance at the clock told him it was shortly after three. Was Lizzie still awake? He rubbed his eyes, then ran a considering hand over his stubbled jaw.

Should he seek her out? Or was it a temptation he couldn't afford to risk?

He'd acted like a complete ass earlier, and he owed her an apology. He'd known it as the words were blasting out of his mouth like a broken foghorn, yet he'd let them come all the same.

Worse, he'd allowed his comments to linger between them like the proverbial elephant she'd mentioned, unwilling to engage in more than surface conversation on the drive home.

He had already resolved to apologize in the morning, but if she was awake, maybe there was a chance to apologize now.

The room was dark, but his eyes had already adjusted and he slipped into his discarded T-shirt and jeans. *Bit late for modesty, Colton.*

The wry thought kept him company as he padded his way toward Lizzie's room, but it was the wan color of her face—visibly pale in the dim light of the hallway as she reached the landing—that had him rushing forward.

"What's wrong?"

"Nothing."

He wrapped his arms around her and led her to the guest room where she slept. "You look like you saw a ghost."

"No. I—" She broke off, tension clogging her throat so her voice came out in a husky whisper. The glass in her hand tipped as her arms came around him, and he quickly steadied her before removing the water from her grip.

"Come on in and sit down." He flipped on the overhead light in her room and set the glass down on an old dresser that had been his mother's before walking Lizzie to the bed. "What's the matter?"

"It's nothing. I'm being silly." She hesitated before adding in a stronger voice, "But it didn't feel silly."

"What's going on? Did you have a bad dream?"

A husky laugh slipped through her lips. "A dream would imply I'd slept."

The oddest sense of satisfaction filled him. Not that she'd been unable to sleep, but he did take an odd sort of gratification that they'd spent the night equally miserable.

Which made absolutely no sense.

"I went down to get a glass of water. The pregnancy makes me extra thirsty and I usually take a glass of water to bed, but…but I headed up so fast when we got home, I forgot."

Remorse rose up to squelch the satisfaction, and he pulled her close as he settled them on the edge of her bed. "I'm sorry I upset you. My words were unkind and terribly insensitive."

She lifted her head from his chest, her green eyes clear and determined. "We will discuss that, as I was a willing participant. But that's not what has me upset. I felt something."

"The baby?"

"No, no." She shook her head. "The baby's fine. It was

something outside, I think. One minute I was standing there thinking about the things we said at Trevor's, and the next, I had the oddest sensation of being watched."

He tightened his arms around her as something dark and raw settled itself under his skin. There was nothing he wouldn't do to protect Lizzie and the baby. He'd brought them here to keep them safe, but if something had followed her, there was nothing he wouldn't do to protect them. "You were in the kitchen?"

"Yes. In front of the window over the sink."

"Did you see anything?"

"No. It was more of a feeling." Her expression turned dark, even as her hands tightened against the material of his T-shirt. "A silly feeling."

"Silly feelings happen for a reason. Take me through what you felt."

Whether it was his matter-of-fact acceptance of what she said or just her need to get it out, he wasn't sure. But she seemed to come to some internal conclusion before she nodded and continued, her voice growing stronger. "First I thought maybe you'd come downstairs and I had been so lost in thought I'd missed you come in. But when the kitchen was still empty, I checked the mudroom. And then I came back to the sink. The lights around the barn were all blazing."

"They're motion activated."

"They were dark when I came into the kitchen."

"Are you sure?"

"Yes. The window was dark, and I remember because I could see my reflection in the window as I filled my glass."

Ethan ticked off in his mind what could have triggered the lights—anything from a coyote to a restless ranch hand fit the bill. "I'll go out and check. While my men usually bunk down for the night, maybe someone couldn't sleep or needed to check on one of the horses."

Relief washed over her cheeks, and it broke his heart to see her so scared. "That makes a lot more sense than my hyperactive imagination."

He didn't want to burst her bubble—and it still could have been an animal—but his men wouldn't have scared her like that. If any of them had seen her standing there, they'd have announced their presence in some way with a wave or a smile from beneath the lights.

But he kept the thought to himself as he patted the hand splayed across his chest. "Let me go check and I'll be right back."

He was going to stand—he had every intention of doing so—when his gaze locked on hers. Emotion swirled in her eyes, everything from relief to fear to embarrassment and a host of things in between he couldn't quite name.

A renewed wash of anger stiffened his spine. He'd brought her here to keep her safe. But what if his home was the last place she needed to be?

He'd do everything in his power to protect her, but even he couldn't account for everything that went bump in the night. Especially if it was someone determined to do harm.

His father's life had taught him that much.

Matthew Colton's legacy wasn't simply tied to the people he'd murdered. His methods and the cruel way he'd stalked his victims were as much part of his legacy as the reputation he'd amassed during the years he committed his crimes.

Evil images flashed through the back of his mind and

it took him a moment to key back in to the woman next to him. The veneer of fear that had glazed her eyes had vanished, those green orbs growing dark with something far more enticing.

Desire.

Ethan wanted to shake his head. The rapid play of thoughts pummeling him from every angle—from anger to protection to the hate-filled deeds of his father—seemed wrong when faced with the innocent beauty that was Lizzie. Her eyes grew even darker and he might have excused it as a play of the light, but the bright overhead made the heat emanating from the depths of her gaze more than evident.

He needed to back away. She was scared and she didn't need him adding to her problems. But the lure of her—the lips he craved and the body that called to him and the heart that seemed to understand him even when he didn't deserve it—won out. Ethan bent his head, only to meet Lizzie halfway as she lifted her lips to his.

Fear for her transformed into a rush of need and a desire that simply couldn't be assuaged, no matter how much he tried to talk himself out of it. Their kiss was tentative at first, seeking, before a desperate craving overtook them both. Her mouth opened beneath his, her tongue rising up to meet his in a carnal feast they shared equally.

Oh, how he wanted her. This woman who confused him and made him want things he'd sworn he would never take part in. Love. Family. Fatherhood.

Yet here she was, offering all three.

Despite his fears—and the ready knowledge he wasn't prepared for anything she offered—he focused on what he could control. He could give her pleasure.

Could assure her there was no woman more beautiful or more desirable than her.

His hand drifted to the tie of her robe, slipping the knot before his hands slid over her rounded belly. Something deeply profound touched him at that moment—an odd juxtaposition of needs so deep they cratered his soul.

He would never, no matter how long he lived, sate the need to protect his child, to keep him or her safe and secure, until he took his last breath. Nor would he ever fully sate the desire for his child's mother. Her ability to give life—to carry his child within her—had made the need and desire he carried for her crest like the deepest wave.

She carried life. His child. And he'd never felt anything so deeply profound.

"Where did you go?" Lizzie's voice was husky, her eyes warm emerald pools as she shifted to look at him. Her fingers drifted through his hair, the light touch at his nape sending a renewed wave of desire racing down his spine.

Words failed him and he could do nothing but press his forehead to hers. "I'm sorry. So sorry for what I said before."

Her fingers were replaced by her hands and she drew him close, her lips pressed to his ear. "I'm sorry, too. I would never keep the baby from you. Please know that. I needed time, but I'd have made sure my child knew his father."

He nodded, the truth of her words embedding deep in his soul. She'd have done as she said. Events had collided to change that, but he wouldn't doubt her intentions again. "I know, Lizzie. I know."

Ethan knew he needed to go outside, even as he knew whatever spooked her was likely long gone.

But he held on for a few more moments.

And hoped with every part of his being that he could keep her safe.

Ethan walked the full perimeter of the stable, looking for anything that might give him a clue to what had spooked Lizzie the night before. He'd come outside to check for himself the previous night but couldn't see anything in the dark. Nor had he seen any of his hands when he'd investigated inside the stables.

By the time he'd returned inside at around four in the morning, Lizzie had fallen asleep on the couch. He'd covered her with a blanket, then taken a seat in the recliner opposite and watched her sleep. His mind was full of the moments they'd shared in the bedroom, and he had sat there, awake and watching her, even as the sun rose and flooded light through his living room windows.

He wanted her with him. There was no one he trusted to keep her safe save himself, and that was nonnegotiable. He'd believed himself able to resist her by focusing on her safety and the safety of the baby.

But the previous night, alone together in her bedroom, he'd realized just how deeply in trouble he was. And how delusional he'd been to think he could resist her.

Their night at the rodeo had been the most incredible night of his life. It was the first time in his life he wasn't Ethan Colton, son of a killer, but just Ethan. Although he hadn't lived his life looking for marriage and a family, he did date from time to time. He was as human as the next guy and sought companionship.

But nothing went very far. Inevitably, the women

he dated either came into the relationship knowing his background or they learned quickly once they mentioned the name of the man they were dating to a family member or a girlfriend.

Colton.

There was only one connotation for that name in these parts.

His siblings' entrance into various fields in law enforcement had gone a long way toward restoring the family name, but it couldn't solve everything. And it had made him a surprisingly easy target for thrill seekers or misguided women who felt they needed to save him from himself and his cruel past.

But not Lizzie.

She knew him—had always known him—and simply accepted him.

Ethan walked past Dream's stall, pleased to see her happily munching on oats. She whickered softly to him and lifted her head from her breakfast to give his hand a head butt.

"Hey, girl. How are you feeling?" Ethan stroked the long line of her neck, his gaze drifting to assess how his favorite mare was doing. Her stomach bore the distinct marks of her pregnancy, the distended flesh heavy with her foal, but her eyes were bright and clear, no sign of the pain she'd suffered the other night.

Had it really been only two days?

So much had happened, he still couldn't get a full grasp on how fast the trajectory of his life had changed.

"She's looking good, boss." Bill's voice pulled Ethan from his reverie, and he turned to see his foreman, a thick clipboard in hand and a toothpick hanging from the edge of his lips. "Doc came out late yesterday and gave her another once-over. Pronounced her fit and back on track."

"I didn't know Doc Peters was out this way."

"Said he wanted to look in on her himself, then was headed to see his daughter and son-in-law for a few days."

Ethan turned back and patted Dream's neck once more. "You make sure you don't give us another scare while the doc's out of town, sweetheart."

Bill leaned against the stall next to Dream's. "Saw your note on my desk. What were you doing out here in the middle of the night? Did Dream have another tough go of it?"

"No." Ethan glanced up and down the row of stalls. He hadn't seen anyone come in since he'd been up but wanted to double-check no one had got past him.

"Lizzie saw something last night."

"What sort of something?" Bill stood up straighter from where he leaned against the stall door. "Do we have a problem with someone not following ranch rules?"

"I don't know. I haven't got a sense from anyone lately. Most of the guys have been here at least a few seasons, and Jason, who we hired a few months back, has been nothing but focused on the work."

"What spooked her?"

"She felt like someone was watching her as she stood in the kitchen getting a glass of water. She went to look around in the mudroom, and when she came back, she realized the motion-activated lights around the stable had turned on."

As soon as the words were out, an image of riding Cap the day before hit him. He'd felt as though he was being watched, too, the flash in the trees deliberate enough he'd gone looking for who might be out there. He'd discarded it at the time as a trick of the wind, but maybe he'd been too hasty.

"Someone watched her? Who?"

Ethan trusted Bill to a fault and likely would have talked to him anyway, but Lizzie's agreement to share what was happening made the decision that much easier. "She's had some trouble at home."

Ethan brought the man up to date on what he knew, finishing up with the break-in at her house. "The police don't have any leads, and until they do, she's staying here."

"You think it was the guy after her, here last night?"

Ethan had wondered that very thing, especially through the long hours as he watched her on the couch, but he'd discarded the notion just as quickly.

The asshole stalking her had clearly worked out a plan of attack, but he'd likely be hard-pressed to find Lizzie that quickly. She and Ethan hadn't had contact up until two days ago, so it wasn't as if anyone following her during her pregnancy would know he was the baby's father. Add on he'd been careful on the drive home to make sure they weren't being followed and he found it difficult to believe her stalker had found her.

So who had? Was it possible she was in the Alphabet Killer's sights? The murders so far had taken place in and around Granite Gulch—not Lizzie's side of the county—but that didn't mean the killer wasn't looking to branch out.

"Damn it!" Ethan kicked at Dream's stall door. "Why would anyone target her?"

"I can make a few inquiries. See if anyone was up and about. Gotta say, I don't see any of our guys for late-night wandering unless someone was out enjoying a bit of company in town and came home late."

"You think one of the guys would have ignored her at the window if he'd seen her there?"

"Maybe." Bill shrugged, a distinctly uncomfortable glint shining in his eyes. "She's new here and all. And, well…"

"Come out with it."

"No one's going to look sideways at Miss Lizzie for fear of upsetting you."

"No. I suppose not."

Bill snapped the clipboard over his free hand. "I'll keep my eyes on them. Make sure no one seems out of sorts."

"I'll do the same."

Bill headed off and Ethan thought about the day before and his own sense of being watched. On a whim, he dragged down Cap's saddle and prepared himself for a ride.

No one's going to look sideways at Miss Lizzie for fear of upsetting you.

Although he hadn't hesitated to bring Lizzie to his home, he hadn't given much thought to the situation of her actually being there. He owned a working ranch, with men living and working on the property. He had no fear one of them would hurt her, but he did need to consider her presence from their point of view.

Her pregnant presence, his conscience rose up to taunt him.

The men who worked his ranch might be respectful to a fault, but they weren't blind.

Maybe it was time he put that fact to good use.

Chapter 10

Trevor Colton was used to conflict. Where others avoided it like a plague of locusts, he'd learned to embrace it and the chaos that churned in its wake. The skill had served him well in the FBI, born out of his position as the oldest of Matthew Colton's seven children.

But his ability to manage—and often persuade—in a conflicting situation was absolutely useless against his second-youngest brother, Ethan. Quiet and stoic, the man had the patience of Job and the ability to stubborn his way through any situation the world threw at him. Simply put, if Ethan Colton didn't want to do something, it didn't get done.

On a muttered curse, Trevor got up from his desk and headed for the small kitchenette down the hall from his office. He refilled his coffee cup from a single-serve unit and puzzled through the problem of Ethan.

Oddly enough—though he'd never say this to Ethan—

his brother's stubborn refusal to go along with their father's wishes was a carbon copy of Matthew's behavior. That stubbornness was one of the few traits Ethan had inherited from their father, but it was as infuriating in a man who wouldn't harm a barn mouse as it was from a man who'd made it his personal mission to ruin the lives of others.

Trevor returned to his desk and opened up the old, worn file he maintained on his father. The information dated back years, from even before he'd joined the FBI. In the time since, he'd added various pieces. Small clues or snippets of conversation overheard by prison guards and reported back to the authorities. Visitor logs. Prison psychology reports.

But no matter how much information he gathered, his father had never given any indication—to anyone— where he'd taken their mother's body after he'd killed her.

Instead, the old man had been content to rot, year after year, in prison. Although his crimes were heinous enough to qualify him for the death penalty in Texas, Matthew had narrowly escaped death row thanks to a few misguided politicians who'd pleaded on his behalf. Trevor had never directly asked, but he'd assumed life in lockup was better than the alternative.

As the brother of Big J Colton, Matthew was something of an anomaly in the criminal world. He was less than a nobody to his brother, but his death at the hands of the Texas state prison system would make for some damned uncomfortable press for Big J. So the man paid well to leave his brother hidden away in prison, avoiding a death sentence for his crimes.

Trevor sighed. He hated the realities, but he knew how the game was played. So he kept tabs on the politicians he knew were well paid to keep Matthew Colton off death row and continued to add snippets to his file.

Did it frustrate him? Hell, yes. But he had no choice. Until recently.

Matthew's cancer diagnosis had ensured death was coming for him anyway. It might not be at the hands of the state, but the outcome would be the same. So the old man had offered up a bargain. He wanted to speak to each of his children before he died and to each he'd give a clue as to where he'd buried their mother.

Although Matthew hadn't dictated the order of his children's visits, Trevor knew their father was anxious to see Ethan. And while Trevor would prefer to spare Ethan entirely, he desperately needed any information his brother might be able to secure.

Ethan's discovery of their mother—before Matthew had a chance to hide her body—had changed the course of Matthew's life. Up to that point, he'd escaped detection for his crimes, but it was the murder of his wife that had finally put Matthew Colton in jail. The evidence had been overwhelming, but it was the tearful testimony of a seven-year-old that had ensured their father would never breathe free air again.

Ethan was the one chink in Matthew's armor. Trevor's file was full of the old man's references to his son Ethan and his regret that the "boy found his mother that way." It was the only shred of remorse Matthew had shown for any of his acts, and it was the one thing Trevor hoped to use against him.

But he needed Ethan to do it.

Gathering up his suit jacket and downing half his coffee, Trevor grabbed the worn file from his desk. He needed to go see Ethan and find some way to jostle the immovable rock that was his brother.

* * *

Lizzie put two pans of her legendary pound cake into Ethan's oven and set the timer for forty-five minutes. She felt silly spending what used to be a workday baking a cake, but the act had kept her busy. She'd already cleaned her room, washed the sheets and done the crossword puzzle in the newspaper Joyce had brought over for a catch-up over morning coffee.

She was grateful for the woman's company and appreciated that Joyce had given up an hour out of her own day full of duties to visit, despite having met only a few days before. Lizzie had mentioned the cake recipe while they were talking and decided to put her money where her mouth was and make up a few for Joyce and Bill as well as the men in the bunkhouse.

Enjoy the time, she admonished herself as she took a seat at the table and flipped through the newspaper pages she'd already read. *Soon you'll be keeping up with an infant and you won't have a moment to yourself.*

Even though life as she knew it would change dramatically in three more months, she wasn't comfortable with idleness. She'd always found work kept her mind occupied and been satisfied with a full day's labor.

Yet here she was.

Her gaze caught on a small counter by the door and her small work tote. She'd added her laptop at the last minute before she and Ethan left her house and now remembered she had it with her. Playing on the computer was still idle time, but she'd go online and look up some more ideas for the baby's room as well as check into the online pregnancy center she used to track her weekly progress.

As the computer booted up, she peeked into the oven to check on the progress of her cakes. The golden batter had small bubbles in it and she was satisfied she'd have something delicious to share in another hour. It would be nice, she mused, to do something for the rest of the ranch. Joyce had been very welcoming, outlining how the ranch worked, how many men bunked on the property and how much livestock Ethan worked over his land.

It was impressive, she had to admit, to see what he'd built in such a short period of time. He was only twenty-seven, and while he'd lived a lifetime in those years, he was still young to be sole owner of a working ranch.

With that thought came another. She had no idea what he'd named the ranch. He had to call it something, as he took his livestock to market and showed his horses in statewide events. She made a mental note to ask him and then took her seat, a fresh glass of water in hand as the log-in screen popped up on her computer.

She typed in her credentials, then used the Wi-Fi password she'd seen pinned to a small message board on the counter to get internet access. Once she had Wi-Fi, she quickly logged into email and began separating the junk from the things she truly wanted.

Her gaze caught on a subject line—DUE DATE— and she clicked the message, an image of holding the baby in her arms come May filling her mind's eye.

The beautiful image vanished as the email message registered.

YOU THINK YOU CAN RUN AWAY FROM ME? THERE'S NOWHERE YOU CAN RUN. YOU AND THE BABY WILL BE MINE.

Lizzie dropped her water, the glass shattering as it hit the hardwood kitchen floor.

* * *

Ethan drew Cap up to the stables, their morning ride good on exercise but empty on any possible clues to who might have been on the property the night before. He'd spoken to each of his hands and got universal confirmation that no one had been out late the night before or anywhere near the stables.

His ride out to the section of trees that rimmed his property had proved fruitless as well. He'd left Cap to graze and taken the wooded area on foot and still was no closer to finding information.

Was it possible it really had been a coyote or some other critter tripping the lights last night?

It was equally possible he hadn't seen a thing the day before other than a play of the light, especially when he saw no tracks or markings in the trees. Thoroughly frustrated, in the same way you tried to remember the lingering vestiges of a dream that simply wouldn't piece together, Ethan dismounted from Cap's saddle. He'd wash him down and settle him with some oats and then head in for his own lunch.

Joyce waved him down from the porch, her voice carrying across the open expanse from the house to the stable. "Bobby! Help Mr. Colton with Cap."

One of his younger hands working the corral nodded and came to take Cap. "I've got him, Mr. Colton. Looks like Miz Joyce needs you."

Something hit low in Ethan's gut, his stomach turning at the sheer concern in Joyce's face. Was Lizzie hurt? Or had the baby decided to come early?

A thousand scenarios swirled through his mind as he ran for the porch. "What is it?"

"Lizzie's upset. She got—" Joyce broke off. "Come see for yourself."

Ethan rushed into the house and stopped short at the image that greeted him at the kitchen table. Lizzie sat there, her face wet with tears, her arms wrapped around her midsection.

"Lizzie?"

She didn't acknowledge him; instead she sat there in the same position, her arms wrapped tight around her.

"What's wrong? Is it the baby?"

The bright-eyed woman he knew was nowhere in evidence, and he knelt down beside her and tentatively reached for her shoulder. "Please talk to me. What is it?"

"There," she whispered. "Look at the screen."

The tension in his chest that something had happened to the baby faded at the mention of the computer, and he turned as she'd directed. And saw the message someone had deliberately sent to frighten her.

Ethan scanned the words—the acknowledgment she'd fled her home and the continued focus on the baby—and also the fact that the creep had somehow managed to use an anonymous account. He was far from computer savvy, but didn't doubt there were those who understood how to send such messages.

He turned the screen away, willing her focus off the hateful words. Prying her hands away from her body, he linked his fingers with hers, desperate to make some connection. "Don't look at it anymore. We'll get to the bottom of this, but don't look at it."

Her hand tightened in his before a hard sob burst from her. "Oh, Ethan! What does he want with me? And with my baby?"

"Shh. We'll get to the bottom of this. We will." He stayed next to the chair on his knees and held her as close as he could. He pressed her head against his shoulder and continued to repeat words of reassurance.

"You're safe here. I promise." He saw Joyce give a firm nod before she slipped from the kitchen but knew she stayed close, hovering in the living room to help out wherever she could.

Lizzie's head was heavy against his shoulder, her hands cold where they wrapped in his. "Who could this be? Do you think this is the person watching me from outside last night?"

"We haven't been able to find anyone."

"He was there, I know it." She lifted her head, fire sparking deep in her eyes. "It had to be him."

"And I believe you felt someone watching you. But that doesn't mean it was this creep. How could he have found you?"

"He found my email."

"Yes. A computer program. Distant and cold, no matter how personal and intimate it feels. But that doesn't mean he'd have any way of knowing you were here."

He dropped her hands and pulled the computer closer. "What is it?"

"Give me a minute." He took a quick screenshot of the image, then turned off her internet access.

"What are you doing?"

"Disconnecting you from this jerk." Satisfied when the Wi-Fi notification blinked off, Ethan flipped over to another program and saved the image of the message.

Lizzie's innate curiosity seemingly won out and she leaned forward to look at what he was doing. "How'd you know that?"

"With four brothers and a sister in law enforcement, you learn a thing or two. We'll give Sam or Annabel the screen grab later."

The doorbell rang, interrupting their discussion, and Joyce's voice echoed back toward the kitchen that she'd answer it. Fascination turned to horror as Lizzie pushed herself back in her chair. "She needs to be careful. She can't just answer the door."

"She's fine. And believe me, no one's going to make trouble during the day. I've got over twenty able-bodied ranch hands in addition to myself. Joyce knows what she's doing."

A familiar voice sounded from the foyer. "It's Trevor."

Lizzie got to her feet, brushing away the last few tears when Ethan's oldest brother walked into the kitchen, Joyce at his heels.

"Mr. Colton's timing seems perfect, don't you think?" Joyce ushered Trevor in before going to the counter. She nodded to Ethan before giving a small smile to Lizzie. "I want to get this broken glass out to the trash. I'll leave you three alone."

For the first time Ethan noticed the broom and dustpan leaning against the counter. Before he could ask for more details, Lizzie smiled at Joyce. "Thanks for your help. I'm sorry I broke that glass and spilled so much water."

Joyce pressed a quick kiss to her forehead before bustling out. "It's easy enough to clean up. Don't you worry about it."

At Trevor's puzzled look, Ethan and Lizzie brought him up to speed on what had taken place since they'd left his home the previous evening.

"Why didn't you call me?"

"Until a few minutes ago, there was nothing to call about."

Trevor tapped on the edge of the computer. "I'd like to see the message."

When Lizzie only nodded her agreement, Ethan

pushed the computer toward his brother. "I screen-grabbed the email."

Trevor busied himself with the computer, and Ethan settled back to watch his brother. Although he'd had his challenging moments with Trevor—with all his siblings—he couldn't deny how much closer they'd become in the past few years.

He also couldn't deny just how proud he was of all of them. Trevor's ascension at the FBI was a particular point of pride. He'd faced odds as Matthew Colton's son, yet he'd proved himself an incredible asset to the Bureau.

Trevor let out a subtle "hmm" and continued tapping on keys.

"What is it?" Ethan asked.

"I'm not entirely sure, but it looks like the IP address wasn't yet tapped into. Best I can tell, the message was sent yesterday. The sender must not be online right now."

"Wouldn't he have a way of tracking where I was? Finding my location since he sent the message?" Although fear still tinged the edges of her words, Ethan saw the steel had returned to Lizzie's spine. She obviously wanted answers.

"That works both ways." Trevor closed the laptop. "If he leaves the connection open while he's not there, there's a chance you can trace it back. For now I think you're good, but I'd like to ask a colleague who specializes in cybercrime."

"Of course." Lizzie shuddered and pushed at the edge of the laptop as if it were a dead snake. "Take it if you need to."

"I'll do that."

Ethan poured two mugs of coffee from the counter,

handing one to Trev. "Funny timing showing up when you did."

"I'm glad I did and I'm happy to help." Trevor took the offered mug. "But you're right—it's not why I came. I wanted to talk to you about visiting Dad."

"I thought we covered this last night."

"You avoided the subject last night. But I need to discuss this with you."

Ethan didn't miss Trevor's pointed glance toward Lizzie, but he quickly stepped in to set his brother straight. "I'd like Lizzie here. There's nothing you can say that she shouldn't hear."

"Fair enough."

Ethan left it at that. He loved his brother and respected him beyond measure, but he sure as hell wasn't going to make this easy on him. So he sat quietly and waited for Trevor to state his case.

"Here's what I need you to do."

Lizzie watched the byplay between brothers and marveled at the silent battle of wills. Although she'd had foster siblings growing up, she'd never had a biological brother or sister. In hindsight, she had to admit she'd likely painted those relationships to be more rosy and perfect in her mind than the reality.

Love didn't mean agreement. And it certainly didn't mean the relationship was frictionless or battle free. She knew Ethan and Trevor cared for each other, but the two pillars of stubborn male pride that sat before her only reinforced the idea that just because you were family didn't mean you saw everything through the same lens.

"Sam made his visit last month and got some additional information from Dad."

"Yeah, yeah. He got the clue—Texas. Mom's some-where in Texas. Like we didn't know."

"He also got his hands on the letters Dad receives. We've been going through them and some have stood out, but nothing concrete. And nothing that's got us close enough to understand who's murdered four women in rapid succession."

Although she had no interest in being a lascivious bystander, Lizzie had to admit the mind of a killer fascinated her. In a keep-her-distance way, yes, but it fascinated all the same.

"I've asked Ethan this, but I'd be curious to get your take. Do you think your father's controlling the killer from jail?"

Trevor tapped one of his folders. "My father's activ-ity is closely managed and monitored. While I wouldn't rule anything out, we've kept a very close eye and don't think he's involved beyond being the inspiration for what's happened."

"Why would someone be inspired by a killer?"

"You'd be shocked what people are inspired by. His notoriety helps with the overall attention, but there are people who believe my father is a hero."

"But he killed so many people!" Everything in her rebelled at the idea Matthew Colton's actions could be perceived as anything other than the heinous crimes they were. "How could anyone want to emulate that?"

"You'd be surprised. There are a lot of unstable peo-ple, and to them my father's willingness to take action is heroic."

"Action." Ethan practically spit the word. "He had a lifelong problem with his brother, so he took that out on innocent people. That's not action—that's sick and twisted revenge."

Trevor didn't argue, but neither did he agree. Lizzie wondered at the things Ethan's oldest brother had seen in the course of his job and how he could choose a living that put him so close to others like his father.

"I don't know how you can do this, day after day. It must be horrifying to live and breathe people's most horrendous actions."

Trevor's smile never reached his eyes. "Let's just say my childhood prepared me well for the worst that human beings can do to each other."

"So what do you want me to do, Trev? Go see the old man and give the bastard what he wants? Explain to me why I should do that. Aw, hell, it's not just that." Ethan stood to pace. "Explain to me why he deserves it."

"He doesn't deserve it."

Ethan stilled, his hazel eyes as bleak as a winter sky. "So then why do you want me to go?"

"The people of Blackthorn County deserve it. The women who've been murdered so far deserve it." Trevor stood and faced his brother. "And you deserve it. You deserve to look the old man in the eye and tell him he's a bastard. To tell him that you've made a life for yourself. A damn fine one, at that."

"It's just giving him what he wants."

"No, it's using him to get what we want. You think this is the first time he's asked to see his kids?"

The question seemed to knock Ethan back, and Lizzie was surprised at the sudden, urgent need to offer comfort. She sensed the outreach wouldn't be welcome as he processed his brother's words, but she couldn't deny how heartbreaking it was to watch.

The little boy she always imagined in her mind—the one with serious eyes and painful thoughts that shone out of them—was back. It was as if the years faded away and that small, vulnerable boy once again stood in the kitchen.

"You never told me this."

"It wasn't the time. Nor was it anything I'd have encouraged. He didn't deserve to see any of his children."

"But I deserved to know."

"We did what we thought was best."

Ethan caught the slip as soon as Lizzie did. "We?"

"Me." Trevor stopped. Shook his head. "We. Chris and I discussed it and felt telling you of the old man's request would do you no good."

"I had a right to know."

"And we had a right to protect you."

"When?" Trevor's answer obviously wasn't quick enough, and Ethan shouted the request again. "When!"

"About a year after Josie stopped the visits."

Lizzie did some quick math in her head and figured Trevor for about twenty-three or twenty-four back then. Old enough to know better but still green enough to want to protect his underage brother.

"I deserved to know."

"You were still a kid. And you were our responsibility. There wasn't any reason to tell you."

"I had every right to know and you had no right to keep it from me." Ethan slammed a hand on his chair, the movement enough to knock the sturdy piece to the floor.

Chapter 11

Ethan struggled with the demons that raged through his blood. Anger. Frustration. Grief.

And now disillusionment.

How dare Trevor keep something like that from him? And to use the excuse that it was for his own good was a massive pile of BS if he'd ever heard one.

His gaze landed on Lizzie, her eyes wide in her face. He instantly regretted the violence of his outburst and bent to right the chair.

"Ethan, you have to understand. You were still young. We would never have let you go there to see him."

His knuckles grew white against the frame of the chair but he refused to raise his voice. Refused to let the never-ending anger that seemed to burn to the very depths of his toes rage out of control. "I never wanted to see the bastard. But I should have been told. I was a teenager by then and old enough to understand. I had a right to know."

He'd trusted his brothers. Had believed them when they'd promised to stick by him no matter what. Hell, he'd followed their lead, even when the pain was too thick and too heavy to breathe through, to trust they knew what was best.

"Years ago, we made a pact to stick together, no matter what. To be honest about where we came from, always, to each other. And I believed in you. It's why I got up on that witness stand and told the jury about Mom. About what I'd seen."

Images of that day in the courthouse flooded back. CPS had the responsibility to escort him in and out of the courthouse, but it had been his brother who'd sat with him while his caseworker explained what was going to happen and what sort of questions would be asked.

"Just tell them what you saw, Ethan. It's okay to tell them." Trevor's voice was firm, but he didn't miss that small waver underneath. The one Trev had so often, even when he tried to look brave.

"But Dad will be there. I mean, here." Ethan glanced around the courthouse, wondering where they were hiding his father. His dad would be so mad at him, especially when he described the bull's-eye on Mom's forehead. And the holes in her chest.

And the blood.

His tummy turned over like the day he found his mom, when he was still sick from the flu. He felt like that a lot. As though something had punched at his belly and he was going to throw up everything he'd eaten.

Because he'd seen the news stories and he knew what that bull's-eye meant. Saralee Colton was dead *and not because she'd had a heart attack or been bit-ten by a rattler. Someone had shot her. Murdered her. Just feet away from their house.*

He'd come to understand that person was his father.

"No one will hurt you, Ethan." The caseworker had patted his shoulder, the same way she'd done the day she picked him up at the police station after he'd found his mom and called for help. The same way she'd done when she dropped him off at the Rosses' house—they'd be his foster family, she'd explained. She'd even done it that morning, when they'd gone over his testament—no, testimony—again.

"She's right, Ethan." Trevor nodded with all the worldly wisdom of his fourteen years. "You can't get in trouble for telling the truth."

Trevor had looked so earnest that day, trying so hard to be the man of the family. His other siblings hadn't been allowed to come, but Trevor had pleaded as the oldest Colton child that he needed to support Ethan. His brother had made a promise that day that he'd always be there. Always.

Lizzie's hand wrapped around his. "Come sit down, Ethan. Trevor came here for a reason."

He looked down at her hand, so small and slender against his, and fought the rush of emotion that swelled in his chest. He didn't want a commitment and he didn't do forever, but at that moment, the support she offered meant everything.

"Your brother needs your help."

"I do." Trevor passed over a thick folder. "This is the file I've kept for years on Dad."

"Trevor Colton's infamous file." A harsh laugh echoed in his ears as he took in the worn edges and yellowed paper that stuck out from the bottom. "Something else you've never shared with me."

Trevor's voice stayed steady, but a determined fire lit his dark eyes. "When I started it you were too young to see the various pieces. And by the time I went into the Bureau and began adding additional information, it wasn't something I could share."

"So why now?"

"I need your help. And maybe if you understand what we're up against, you might have a better sense of why I need you to go see Matthew."

The oven timer rang, almost like a bell signaling the end of a round in a prizefight. Lizzie leaped up. "The pound cake! I forgot."

At the mention of cake, Ethan registered the warm sugary smell that pervaded the kitchen. He'd been so focused on getting to Lizzie when he entered the house he'd completely missed the yummy smell that permeated the room. The warm scents of vanilla and sugar comforted in the same way her touch did.

In a matter of hours, she'd made his house more of a home than he'd managed in any number of years.

He let go of her hand, pleased she would be turned away from the table while he flipped through the pages of Trevor's file. He didn't miss his brother's sharp, knowing gaze but ignored it in favor of focusing on the matter at hand.

And opened the file that told the sordid tale of his childhood.

Erica Morgan stocked the bar at the Granite Gulch Saloon, checking off her inventory list item by item. The lunch crowd had been light, and after she made sure her last orders were laid out from the service bar, she'd switched gears to manage inventory.

"You've been busy lately, girlfriend." Erica glanced up at her friend Sandy, who was her partner in crime on the lunch shift. With a wink, Sandy added, "You're making the rest of us look bad."

"I've seen you humping your way through those tables like your ass is on fire. You're no slouch yourself."

Sandy patted the pocket of her apron, a small bulge indicating the tips there. "Ever since you put the idea of taking a cruise in my head, I've been saving like crazy. Four days in the Bahamas is worth every extra minute in this hellhole."

The image of pristine beaches and bright sunshine— the opposite of what they'd had around here for the past few months—filled Erica's thoughts. "Don't forget the hot guys we'll meet and the daiquiris we'll drink."

"Yes to that!"

"Can I get some help over here!" A harsh bark from the end of the bar pulled Erica from her vacation fantasy, and she stood to help the rude patron who'd hollered for her attention. She gave Sandy an eye roll—not visible to their new patron—before turning around with a large smile.

The plain woman who'd hollered at her sat at the edge of the bar, her face set into hard lines. Despite the unremarkable features and drab clothes, Erica could have sworn she recognized the woman. She didn't want to stare—the bitch was already in a snit—but something about the woman nagged at her.

"What can I get you?"

"It's about time. I'd like a gin and tonic."

"Of course."

"And make it quick."

The afternoon was quiet, and while she had no desire to be spoken to that way, images of the Bahamas still swam through her head. Determined not to ruin her good mood with someone else's bad one, Erica fixed the drink and kept a discreet watch on the woman.

She was slender, with medium-length, mousy brown hair. Erica figured her for early to midforties, but still couldn't place why she knew the woman. Sandy was already off to see if one of her tables wanted dessert, so she'd have to wait until her friend got back to see if she knew the woman.

Erica set the drink down and tried to reset the conversation. "Can I get you anything else?"

"No."

"You sure? Dessert, maybe? The kitchen cooked up some fresh apple pies this morning. They're good."

"I don't eat things that will make me fat. I'll never meet a man that way."

When she smiled and still got that stone-cold visage, Erica tried one more tack. "Oh, I don't know. Plenty of cowboys like a woman with curves on her. Surely a piece of pie won't hurt."

"I said no!"

Erica backed off, her friendly smile dying on the vine. "I'll leave you to it, then."

She went back to her inventory and tried to shake off the rude woman, even as something continued to nag her. Why did she feel as though she knew her? As she restocked a case of vodka, a strange sensation settled over the back of her neck.

Was the woman watching her?

Erica turned slowly, but her customer was looking down, focused on her G&T, muttering something she couldn't hear over the subtle din of the bar. Chalking it up to the strange things that made up a bartender's repertoire of stories, she went back to scanning in the tags that the liquor commission required for proper inventory control.

She got through a few more bottles and, once again, that sensation curled up her spine with cold fingers.

Damn woman. If she asked for another drink, Erica would refuse service. It was her right as a bartender, and vacation or no, she wasn't going to sit by and get treated like this. The woman probably didn't even tip well anyway.

With the last bottle checked in, Erica stretched her back and used the move as an excuse to glance down once more at her surly customer. The woman was gone, but a few crumpled bills lay at her place. Erica walked down to collect the payment, content to see the woman had vanished when something caught her attention near the door. The woman stood there, her gaze on Erica, a dark, evil look spitting like fire from her dull, washed-out face.

A harsh shiver gripped her and, unbidden, an image of the dead bird on her patio swamped her thoughts.

Was this woman somehow responsible?

Before Erica could shake off the weird connection, the woman stepped through the door and was gone.

Ethan closed Trevor's folder and fought the wash of images that painted his mind. Blood. Death. And a red bull's-eye drawn on the center of his mother's forehead.

He'd made the mistake of reading the file from newest detail to oldest, and the last images were of the individuals his father had murdered. Each image stared back at him in vivid color, and every one included the distinctive red bull's-eye on the forehead Matthew had used to mark his victims.

All save one.

There were no photographs of his mother, but he carried her image in his mind, as clear as if he'd looked at her yesterday. She lay on the small back patio of their farmhouse, her body at a strange angle, blood pooling around her shoulders and that telltale red mark on her forehead.

He'd stayed home that afternoon, a stomachache forcing him to miss out on the endless games of tag and flag football he and his siblings had played on the wide expanse of their farmland. He'd been sick upstairs in his bed, and after calling for her, he'd finally come downstairs to get some ginger ale to settle his stomach.

Tamping down the miserable memory that still haunted him when he closed his eyes, Ethan slid the folder across the table. "I'm not sure what you hoped I'd get out of this, but I've got nothing for you, Trev."

"There's something we're missing when we look at the evidence, and no matter how hard we look, nothing makes sense."

His brother slid one more folder over. "These are images from the new crime scenes. Four women, murdered in alphabetical order by first name."

Lizzie still stood at the stove, and Ethan gave her a quick glance to make sure she stayed there before opening the fresh file. Although he hadn't seen any of the crime-scene photos, he'd read the news stories and had a damn good idea of what the women likely looked like. Two neat gunshots to the chest and a red bull's-eye on the forehead, matching Matthew Colton's calling card.

He flipped quickly past the images, grimacing at the

photo of Zoe's sister, Celia, before he closed the file. "Still nothing."

"How can this possibly be productive?" Lizzie took a seat at the table, and Ethan realized how naive he'd been. She'd been paying attention all along—she'd simply chosen to give him some space as he reviewed the information.

"The cops have always believed Ethan's discovery of our mother interrupted Matthew's process. As a serial killer, he had a ritual pattern to his behavior, and Ethan's arrival interfered with that."

"But it was also your mother. Why assume Matthew would follow a pattern at all?"

Ethan was surprised at Lizzie's question and her knowledge of the matter. Although he'd done everything in his power to ignore the situation that had made him, he'd done occasional research through the years on the mind-set of a serial killer. The ritualistic nature of the killer's crime was significant and formed a pattern that often helped the police find necessary clues.

"Ethan's arrival on the scene did break the pattern. Our father was hiding when Ethan found our mother's body. It was when he ran for help that Matthew had to improvise, and it made him sloppy. There were clues and evidence he hadn't left behind before. It's how they caught him."

While he knew Trevor wasn't detached from the situation, the cold retelling of their father's crimes swirled up emotions best left alone, and Ethan had had enough. He pushed himself back from the table and headed for the coffeepot. "Sorry I can't help you, Trev, but I don't have any answers."

"Think about it. That's all I ask."

Ethan didn't turn around and figured his stiff back and lack of agreement told Trevor all he needed to know.

But it was Lizzie's soft voice that broke the silence. "What's that last folder, Trevor?"

"Letters my father gets in prison. Sam's been going through them with me as a fresh pair of eyes."

"You think they have clues?" Lizzie asked, and Ethan saw her reaching for the stack as he turned back from the coffeepot.

"Don't look at those, Lizzie." The thought of her reading the twisted thoughts of sick individuals—of exposing herself and the baby to such depravity—had him moving close.

She stilled but didn't pull her hand from the thick stack of papers. "But they might have clues."

"They're letters from psychos. Sick people who have given my father some sort of status and importance in their minds."

"But what if there are clues to the creep who's been after me?"

Trevor's focus shifted immediately. "The email from earlier?"

"Yes. I thought it was an isolated problem targeted at me, but Ethan has made me question if it's possible it's the Alphabet Killer. If we look at the letters, we might get some sense if they're the same person. I also have the other notes the creep has sent."

"What made you think this, Ethan? We've not got any sense the killer has expanded their target area. Lizzie lives clear across the county, nearly an hour's drive away."

"That's not very far."

"No, but it would be a break in pattern."

Ethan had run through the same questions in his own

mind and was no closer to answers. Yes, the timing of Lizzie's stalker and the Alphabet Killer's murders was oddly coincidental. But was he putting them together for the right reasons?

Or had he somehow convinced himself that the Alphabet Killer's connection to his family had spilled over to the woman carrying his child because it was easier to combine them than to assume his life was under attack from two separate quarters?

"I don't like the coincidence, that's all."

Frustrated at the seeming impasse, Ethan opened the folder and flipped through a few of the letters on top. Several had red bull's-eyes on them, like a psychotic calling card. "These are ridiculous. Scented paper. *Pink* scented paper. Hell, half of these are love notes."

Disgusted, he snagged one and held it up, scanning the contents that spoke of a depraved mix of hero worship and dreams of love. "Ida Wanto?"

Trevor leaned forward at that. "Can I see it?"

Ethan handed it over but wasn't fast enough to stop Lizzie from snagging the envelope that had come with it. "The postmark is Rosewood."

"That's awfully close." Trevor glanced over the top of the letter. "And nowhere near Lizzie's side of Blackthorn County."

"It's also clearly a fake name." Ethan didn't bother to hide his disdain but did temper his tone when Trevor appeared to catch himself, refocusing on Lizzie.

"You've shared the notes you received with the police?" When Lizzie nodded, Trevor pressed on. "I'll contact them and see if we can't at least run the handwriting through the FBI database. See if anything pops up."

"You can do that?" Lizzie asked.

"A Bureau badge can bypass a lot of red tape." Trevor's smile fell. "But it's not an omniscient resource. Please promise me you'll be careful. It's good that you're here, where we can all watch out for you."

"There's nowhere else she should be." Ethan closed the file and placed a hand over the thick stack of letters. "And I'll do anything to keep Lizzie and my child safe."

"So you will look through the letters?"

Ethan fought back a grim smile at his brother's tenacity. "Yes, leave them with me. I'll take a look and see if anything stands out. I can't afford to ignore anything, no matter how much of a long shot it might be."

Ethan sat hunched over a stack of paperwork in the kitchen, a laptop open to the side. He scratched a few numbers on a notepad and muttered under his breath. Vet bills had been higher than expected this month, as had fuel costs. Although they usually skated by on a fairly mild winter in North Texas, the New Year had been unseasonably cold so far.

The folder full of letters sat on the counter where Trevor had left it earlier, and he glanced at the stack, debating whether or not he should give up on the billing tonight. He hated doing the bills—he'd rather vaccinate a herd of bulls seven times over—but he had no choice. They came like clockwork, month in and month out.

The TV hummed gently from the living room. He'd suggested Lizzie stretch out after dinner, wrap herself in a blanket and relax after the few days they'd had. She'd been quick to protest that she was fine, but he hadn't missed the circles beneath her eyes. Joyce had noticed, too, and had rushed over late that afternoon with one of her famous casseroles so they wouldn't have to worry about dinner.

He'd suggested she and Bill join them, but she'd waved him off, happy to take the pound cake Lizzie pressed on her before she ran out as fast as she'd run in.

Dinner had decidedly domestic overtones, and they'd both made an effort to talk about something other than his father, the Alphabet Killer or her stalker. Instead, she'd amused him with stories of her coworkers and her time in college.

He'd been surprised to learn she'd spent a semester studying in France and had half-decent French skills to boot. He had, however, drawn the line when she'd suggested Etienne as a name for their child should it be a boy. She'd laughed at his reaction and he realized she'd been teasing him.

It was funny, he thought as he entered a new item into his accounting program, how easy she was with him. He knew his surly nature typically had people keeping their distance. Even his siblings kept their distance, only pushing so far.

But Lizzie pushed right on through any barriers he put up with effortless grace.

Etienne.

He smiled in spite of himself. He'd enjoyed the quiet time with Lizzie. In fact, as he snapped his laptop closed, he had to admit to himself she was more than he'd ever imagined. He cared for her—he always had—and he remembered their time together as kids fondly. She'd been one of the gang, his little sister's friend and another pal to play dodgeball with or go swimming in the Carltons' pond.

It had been that last summer, though, before Josie had requested the visits stop, that Ethan had looked at Lizzie as something more than a buddy to pal around with. She was thirteen and he was almost sixteen. She'd blossomed since their last visit, and even now he remembered being surprised at that fact and embarrassed by his awareness of her.

So he'd kept his distance, content to watch her from afar as she and Josie had bugged Annabel relentlessly about hair and makeup and boys.

"Are you at a stopping point?"

As if he'd conjured her up, Lizzie stood in the kitchen. Her eyes were a soft mossy green, still hazy with sleep, and a lethargic smile completed the picture.

"I'm at the point where I appreciate the intrusion." He tossed his pencil down and rubbed at his eyes. "Monthly billing comes around way too fast."

"Why haven't you hired someone to do it?"

"For a long time the business wasn't big enough. And now. Well." He shrugged. "It's a monthly chance to keep tabs on what's mine." On impulse, he asked her, "Do you remember that last summer? Before Josie stopped the visits?"

"Of course." The sleepy haze fell from her eyes and she took a seat at the table. "I always looked forward to the visits you and your brothers and Annabel made to the Carltons'. It's only now that I realize what a logistical nightmare that must have been. Seven kids all in various foster homes, coordinated and corralled for three visits a year."

"Trevor was out by that time, and Annabel and Chris were close." He ran a finger over a wet ring his iced tea had left on the table. "But yeah. A logistical nightmare."

He traced the water ring, dispersing the liquid, unsure of his next move. It unnerved him, this need to share his thoughts. He didn't do that—he wasn't wired that way—yet Lizzie brought something out in him.

"I, um, noticed you that summer."

He might as well have told her the president was at the door for the shock that reflected back from her face. Any vestiges of sleep were well and truly gone, her eyes bright, shiny emeralds above the high arch of her cheekbones.

"Why didn't you tell me?"

"You were too young. I was sixteen and it wasn't right. I knew it wasn't right."

Although he wouldn't change any of his choices, a small, lingering part of him wondered what it would have been like to let her know he'd noticed her that day. To have flirted a bit and acted like a carefree teenage boy with a crush on a pretty girl.

She dropped her chin into her hand. "I wanted you to notice me. I must have spent weeks agonizing over that bathing suit every time Josie and I went to the mall with Rhonda. She'd find me in the juniors section at the department store, walking around and around the swimsuit section."

"Did Josie know how you felt?"

"I never told her, but she was probably smart enough to have guessed." Lizzie stilled. "She never mentioned it, though. It was like she somehow knew I wanted to keep that small thing to myself."

Ethan waited for the raw shock that always stabbed him in the chest at his sister's name, only to draw an easy breath instead. Discussions of Josie were usually fraught with pain and sadness, but here, with Lizzie, it was nice to share the memories.

"She was always sensitive that way, my baby sister. Gentle. Even as a small child, she understood boundaries and space. Being the youngest of seven, that's not all that easy, but she always shared toys and she never got into the bigger kids' stuff."

"You miss her."

"I do. We all do."

She laid a hand over his, the touch as easy as a breeze on a warm spring day. "I do, too."

"Thank you." Ethan laid his hand over hers where it still rested on his forearm. "Memories of her are usually painful. It's nice to remember I have more than a few that are wonderful."

"I'm glad." Two spots of color lit her cheeks. "And I'm also glad to know the bathing-suit shopping wasn't totally a bust."

He couldn't hold back the grin, especially now that all the teenage angst and longing was behind him. "What did you want me to do? You were off-limits."

"Why?" She cocked her head, a strange light shining from her eyes. "It's not like kids don't experiment. Test the waters. You could have flirted with me. It didn't have to go past that."

"I never wanted to—" *Why* had he avoided her that day? She had a point—a bit of innocent flirting wouldn't have been out of line. Even as he asked himself the question, he knew the reason.

"There's a stigma being Matthew Colton's kid. I never wanted to add to it in any way."

He'd got used to her easy responses and running litany of questions, so it was a bit of a surprise when she hesitated, as if summoning up courage.

"Was it hard? Being Matthew Colton's kid?"

"Yes."

"Because he betrayed you?"

"Some of it."

She waved a hand. "I'm sorry I asked."

He reached for her, taking her hand, midair, in a

tight squeeze. "It's okay you asked. It's just not easy to explain."

How could he explain living his life bereft of the person who was supposed to love him beyond measure? Who was supposed to love his mother and respect her above all other women? Who was supposed to raise him and his siblings with a firm hand and pride shining from his eyes?

Because his father was none of those things.

Lizzie knew the memories were painful for Ethan—it was stamped all over his face every time the subject of his father came up—yet she couldn't apologize for her questions. He needed to get these feelings out.

She'd done enough time on a therapist's couch to know the memories that were left buried always found a way to rise from their graves. And while she wasn't a licensed psychologist, she could provide a listening ear and the promise his comments would go no further.

Perhaps it was the upheaval of the past few days or just the quiet moments as the day ended, but she was pleased when he eased into the conversation and answered her questions.

"My life has been shaped by my father's actions. I was only seven when he killed my mother and was caught by the cops. I don't remember a whole lot before that time. Kid things, but not a lot of specifics."

"Was he around?"

"Much of the time, as I remember. Despite the atrocities he committed, they weren't something that engaged him every single day. He had a job or something he went and did every day. Obviously a family, too."

The simplicity of that wasn't anything she'd ever considered. Matthew Colton's reputation was defined by his evil acts toward others, but Ethan was right. Those incidents made up a small number of hours in the man's life.

His family had made up far more.

So how had he managed to marry and have seven children and still see the world in that way? Wasn't there some joy—some hope—that came from staring into the eyes of a child?

And Matthew and Saralee had created seven.

She laid a hand over her stomach, the idea of betraying her child—one not even born yet—beyond unfathomable.

"What do you remember?"

"Not much. Trevor remembers the most, followed by Chris and Annabel. They said there would be time periods when he'd just disappear."

"Is that—" She squeezed his hand. "Is that when he committed his crimes?"

"Many of them. Unfortunately, murder wasn't his only crime. Trev's convinced he had quite a bit of other bad stuff going on the side." He let out a harsh laugh. "When it comes to my father, that's all too easy to believe."

"What sort of things?"

"We're not sure, but Trevor said he's recently become obsessed with this watch he left buried on a piece of property out in West Texas. Says he wants to be buried with it 'when the cancer comes to take him.'"

"Does it have some significance?"

"My father has never been one to act without a reason. But Trev's hitting a big fat goose egg on every angle he tries. Even the location is a mystery. Texas is a big state, and there was no evidence my father's crimes ever extended that far west."

"And this request he's made. To speak to each of his

children. What is he going to do when you all aren't able to produce Josie?"

"I have no idea. Ridge is convinced the old man's going to blow his stack when he finds out Josie vanished."

"He doesn't know?"

"Best we can tell, he doesn't know."

Lizzie wasn't sure why, but that news struck her as the saddest part of the entire situation. Matthew had made his choices and now lived out the consequences, but Josie had been an innocent child when her family shattered.

What had suddenly spooked her so many years after their father went to jail?

So many questions that simply had no answers.

Sensing Ethan had said far more than he'd ever planned, she patted his hand before getting up to get some water at the sink.

He was out of his seat like a flash. "I can get that for you. Relax a bit."

He must have sensed the argument already springing to her lips, because he smiled and pulled her close in a side-armed hug. "And I know. You're pregnant, not helpless."

What was an innocent tease flipped quickly, the arm against her body like a brand against her skin. She stared up into his eyes, those gorgeous hazel depths going dark with attraction.

How was it so easy?

They'd been sharing a simple conversation—warm, friendly—and yet it was there, always simmering. That attraction that could consume at the smallest spark.

"You don't have to pamper me." Her voice came out

on a breathless rush, and she would likely have laughed at herself if she didn't want him so desperately.

He dropped his arm and moved to the sink, his movements stiff and awkward. She saw his reflection in the window, the same as she'd seen her own last night, and moved a few steps closer, curious to see if she could re-create those strange moments. It felt safer with Ethan here and might confirm whether it had been only inside her head.

Although it wasn't nearly as late as the previous night when she'd been up, the hands had all retired for the evening and the stable was quiet, with no light visible around the perimeter of the barn. Just a dark emptiness as the world quieted down to sleep.

He turned, a glass in hand, concern etching his features in the soft light from the small kitchen overhead. "What is it, Lizzie?"

"Nothing." She wanted to shake it off, but stopped herself. She wanted honesty from him and should do the same in return. "I was thinking of last night. Trying to re-crea—"

Like a flash, one of the perimeter lights flipped on, as if she'd thought her imaginings to life.

But it was the lone figure beneath the light that gripped Lizzie's entire body in a hard squeeze.

"Ethan." She hissed his name, like someone who was afraid to startle a frightened animal.

The wash of exterior light must have tipped the scale, because the tall, slender figure silhouetted against the barn glanced up, fear painting her features in harsh relief.

And then the woman ran.

Ethan pulled Lizzie close, his back still to the window. "What is it? Are you okay?"

"It's—" She struggled against the tightness of his embrace and the words that caught in her throat like dry, day-old bread. "It's her!"

"Who her? The baby?"

"Josie! She's outside, next to the barn. She's the one who was watching me!"

Chapter 12

Ethan didn't wait for clarification; he simply moved into action. He'd shed his boots earlier but had slipped on sneakers for his last visit to the barn and still wore them. Grateful for the thick soles, he ran from the house and raced toward the stables, cold ground crunching under his feet.

"Josie!"

Her name ripped from his lips, his breath pooling in the cold February air. When he heard no reply, he shouted again, adding a plea to come back. Was it possible his baby sister was here? That she'd been here all along?

"Josie!"

Her name continued to echo over the cold air, but no one responded. No one came forward.

The lights from the barn lit up the training circle, and he moved closer, anxious to see if there were any footprints or incriminating marks in the dirt around the paddock. Although he didn't have Ridge's tracking skills, he couldn't see anything that stood out between the booted feet that made imprints all day long.

"Ethan." Lizzie's voice was breathless as she came toward him, his coat in her hands.

"Get back inside."

"You need a coat. Come here and bundle up. It's freezing."

The adrenaline that had carried him outside began to fade, a deep cold settling in his bones. He took the coat she offered, slipping into it, considering her as he did. She'd taken the time to slip into her own coat, and while she didn't have on a scarf, she was pulling on her gloves even now.

"Was she here?"

"No." He kicked at the ground. "Or if she was, she's gone."

"I'm sorry." Lizzie stilled, her breath gathering around her in small puffs. "Do you think it's possible?"

"What did you see? Are you sure you weren't imagining something?"

"The lights were off, Ethan. You saw it for yourself. Then they flipped on at someone's movement."

"Yes, but the house is still some distance from the barn. Are you sure it was my sister?"

"I know what I saw." Although her coat stretched against her belly, Lizzie had no problem folding her arms, settling them above the roundness. "And I saw Josie."

"If it was her, why would she run away?" While the question was firmly of the moment, it was steeped in the same questions they'd all asked themselves for years. Why had she stopped their family visits?

And why had she run away in the first place?

"I don't know, Ethan. But I do know what I saw. Josie was like a sister to me. I know what she looks like."

"What *did* she look like?"

Lizzie's eyes narrowed, as if she pulled those few brief moments from memory. "She has the same petite frame she used to curse because she quit growing before everyone else."

"Squirt was the name Chris gave her, and it stuck."

"She hated that name. Or pretended to." The small smile that tilted her lips faded. Growing serious, Lizzie added, "She was always tiny, but she looks thinner than ever. And she had an old barn coat over thickly padded clothes. Like she knew she'd be outside."

"So why did she run?"

"She's frightened. That has to be it."

"Of me?"

"Maybe she's frightened for you."

Although it was nothing more than nuance, Lizzie's words filled his mind with any number of images, none of them good. "Why would she be scared for me?"

"That's what we need to find out."

Erica flipped through the various playlists she'd created for the bar until she found the one she was looking for. The crowd was quiet tonight and a bit thin, the mix of cold weather and weeknight routine keeping folks away.

While she wanted the bar full—butts on bar stools meant job security as surely as a Cowboys win on Sunday—she couldn't deny the lighter crowd would mean she could get home at a decent hour tonight. The past few days had dragged at her, and she was ready for a bit of downtime. She was about to get two days off and had already decided to head into Dallas for a bit of window shopping. She might even dip into her vacation savings and spring for a new pair of shoes. Something—anything—to break the funk that seemed to have descended.

"Another draft, Lou?" She smiled at the grizzled man at the corner bar stool. He came in like clockwork, two beers and one shot his limit each night.

At his nod, she snagged a fresh pilsner glass and worked the stick of his favorite brand, her gaze drifting to confirm who else needed refills.

The corner opposite Lou was empty tonight, but a small wave of anxiety seized her stomach as she remembered the strange woman who'd sat there earlier. Her plain features had flashed through Erica's mind more than once since lunch, the weird fury that filled the woman's eyes still haunting her, all these hours later.

Drop it, she ordered herself. *Think of the shoes. Something high and sexy that would garner some appreciative stares on the cruise.*

She handed Lou his beer and worked her way through three more refills before turning her attention to the work behind the bar. She had already washed the used glassware but needed a fresh bottle of margarita mix and more maraschino cherries from the storeroom. Taking quick stock of anything else that needed refilling, she grabbed a full bag of garbage to save herself a trip and slipped out toward the back.

Images of a pair of shoes she'd seen the prior month in her favorite celebrity magazine filled her thoughts as she exited the back of the bar. The thin gold straps were sexy yet elegant, and she could add a matching polish to finish off the whole look.

The lid of the garbage can made a loud thunk, effectively banishing images of sexy shoes and hot guys on the dance floor of her cruise ship. But it was the bright flash of a gun—pointed directly at her heart—that had Erica going still.

"Scream and I'll pull the trigger before anyone can get here."

Heart rabbiting in her chest, Erica felt herself lift out of her body, the moment was so surreal.

The gun.

The cold night air that turned her breath to frost.

And the woman who stared at her, tall, plain and unforgettable.

It was her patron from earlier that day. The unfinished gin and tonic who'd left her with a serious case of the creeps.

Erica eyed the gun but kept her voice low as she'd been told. "What do you want with me?"

"I want an apology."

The response was so at odds with what she'd expected, her mouth actually fell open. "But I don't know you. Whatever you think I did, I'm sorry."

The woman's gaze narrowed, her brown eyes full of a crazed sort of fury that scared even as it fascinated. "You really don't remember?"

Unbidden, her mind filled with thoughts of the past few days. The weird noises and flash of light on Sunday morning when she'd gone to her car. And the dead bird on her back porch.

"It's you. You've been following me."

"I like to know my enemies."

"But I didn't do anything to you."

Erica's gaze skittered to the back door of the saloon— she'd need her key for that since it locked from the inside—lessening her chances of clearing the garbage area to make her way to the parking lot. The Granite

Gulch Saloon was quiet tonight, but someone was bound to be walking in or out.

"Don't try it." The woman's eyes were bleaker than an ice storm and equally volatile. But her arm was steady and sure, the gun never wavering.

"Please tell me what I did. Whatever it was, I'm sure we can fix it. I would never intentionally hurt anyone and I am sorry if I did."

"You kicked me out a few months ago and now you can't even remember who I am?"

The same fuzzy sense that had assailed her earlier—that she *did* know this woman—struck once more, only now Erica was able to place her. They'd exchanged words a few months back, after the woman had come in and harassed other patrons, muttering dark, ugly things under her breath, hissing them at anyone who would listen.

"You seemed to be having a difficult night. I felt it wasn't right to serve you any more liquor."

"I was fine."

Erica knew it was fruitless to argue, yet something small and hot ticked inside her.

How dare this woman scare her like this?

"Who are you?" Erica moved closer. "I'd like to know your name."

"You don't need to know. All that matters is that I know yours. Erica. *E. R. I*—" The rest of the letters fell away in singsongy tones, brittle leaves on the cold wings of winter.

With brutal clarity Erica knew why the woman had come.

Her name began with an *E*.

She rushed the woman, more than willing to take her chances, but the pressure that hit her chest was like a wall, catching her at an odd angle and pushing her backward with inhuman strength.

And by the time the second shot sounded, Erica knew she'd never see the bright blue waters of the Caribbean.

Lizzie rewrapped the towel tightly around her head and sat on the edge of her bed, shea butter in hand. Her nightly ritual had become routine, and she used the thick creamy lotion in the hope of keeping the skin of her belly from getting too many stretch marks.

Not that she'd mind a few.

They were proof of the life she carried inside. Visual memories of the nine months she'd waited before bringing an infant into the world.

To her mind, the real question was, what sort of world was she bringing her child into?

Although she'd been convinced earlier, had she really seen Josie? Even though it had seemed real at the time, was it possible it was just a fanciful notion, conjured up out of the thick wash of memories that had assailed her for the past week?

The Coltons had been the closest thing to extended family she'd ever had. She knew what a significant part they'd played in her life and her memories. Perhaps being around all of them again was just playing havoc with the present?

She smoothed the lotion over her stomach, then rubbed her hands together with what was left, smoothing the oil over the length of her fingers. Whether it was the repetitive motion or memories that hovered too close to the surface, Lizzie had no idea, but unbidden, a conversation from long ago filled her mind.

"His name's Michael. He's been flirting all year in

math class and he finally got up the nerve to ask me out."

Lizzie knew Michael Evans. She'd always thought he was cute, in a sweet, quiet way. And while she'd admit to a spot of jealousy that Josie had a boyfriend, she was so happy to have her friend back she would be nothing but the most supportive soul.

Josie had become so distant lately. She'd tried to understand—had even got her courage up to ask if Josie was mad at her, but the noncommittal answer had left Lizzie more confused than before.

So the news about Michael and the willingness to once again tell secrets was welcome.

Josie had initiated the conversation, hopping on her toes as if she carried a wonderful secret she was dying to share. So Lizzie had suggested they beautify with manicures and pedicures. When Josie had been receptive, Lizzie couldn't pull out her shoe box of polish fast enough.

"Where's he taking you?"

"To the movies."

"Will you—" Lizzie broke off, not sure if she was being too intimate or if it was okay to ask.

"Will I what?"

"Well. Kiss him."

Lizzie wanted to kiss Ethan Colton so badly she could barely stand it. Ever since the summer two years before, he'd played center stage in all her best dreams.

But that was all he was. A dream.

"I hope so." Josie giggled again, and Lizzie fought the shot of sadness. They'd been such good friends—like sisters—until Josie had got so strange. She'd just closed up, unwilling to answer questions or explain

*why she'd become so distant. She didn't even want to
see her brothers and sister.*

*Maybe Michael was just what she needed. And de-
spite his shyness, he had more nerve than most boys
she knew, asking Josie out on an honest-to-goodness
real date.*

"What do you like about him?"

"Everything. He's cute. And he's smart. And he likes
me for me."

*Lizzie looked up then, pulling her focus from the
small daisy she was dotting so carefully onto her big
toe.* "We all like you for you."

"Not like this. He doesn't care I'm a Colton."

"I don't care, either."

"Yes, but I don't want to kiss you."

*Lizzie tossed a pillow at her friend, laughing in spite
of herself.* "I don't want to kiss you, either. But what
does that have to do with us liking you? I care about
you. Rhonda and Roy do, too. Even Charlie and Wade
like you plenty."

"Charlie and Wade are gross and fart all day."

"I bet Michael farts on his sisters, too."

*Josie giggled, tossing the pillow right back at her,
and Lizzie breathed an inward sigh of relief. She knew
she needed to tread carefully, the subject of their foster brothers a sensitive one. Josie had wanted Sam or
Ethan to come live with them at the Carltons', but Charlie and Wade had already been there and there wasn't
any room.*

*It didn't change the fact that Charlie and Wade were
decent enough. Gross with all their farting and burp-
ing, but they were good brothers.*

"What I mean is Michael doesn't look at me weird

because I'm a Colton. He says he likes me for me. Just the way I am."

Lizzie stood and walked to her bedroom window, the memory still lingering in her mind.

Just the way I am.

Ethan had said something similar earlier.

There's a stigma being Matthew Colton's kid. I never wanted to add to it in any way.

While she'd known the family through the lens of one lonely kid to another, it did stand to reason their father's actions would color what others thought of them. It was hardly fair, blaming children for the sins of their father, but fair didn't make it any less true.

Was that why Josie's name had been bandied about along with the Alphabet crimes? Was she an easy target? A possible suspect with a family history and too many people willing to believe she carried her father's blood *and* his bad intentions.

The knock at her door pulled her from her thoughts and the darkened view out her window, replacing both with a ribbon of anticipation that curled in her belly like smoke. "Come in!"

She was covered neck to toe in an oversize bathrobe—her concession to a belly that wasn't nearly done growing—and suddenly felt fat and ungainly as Ethan entered the room.

He was so beautiful. That long, rangy form, capped by shoulders that made a woman's fingers itch to roam over their breadth. Even with the layer of terry cloth she wore, she was helpless to stop the desire that swirled in her core or the purely feminine need that gripped her at the sight of him.

"I wanted to check on you. And apologize for doubt-

ing you before. It's just so hard to believe Josie would
be outside my home and would run from me."

Desire took a backseat to compassion and comfort
and Lizzie gestured him into the room. "It's so hard to
understand her decisions."

"She's not the Alphabet Killer. That I know without question."

"I know. And I agree with you."

And she did know. The police and the FBI could
speculate all they wanted, but nothing would make her
believe the sweet girl she'd known and loved like a sister had become a mindless killer.

But no amount of certainty could explain why Josie
Colton had chosen to run from her family, either.

He glanced around the room, as if surfacing from
his thoughts. "I'm sorry to bother you. I just wanted to
check in and make sure you were okay."

"I'm fine."

"Um. What are you doing?"

"My nightly ritual."

His eyebrows rose at that, but he didn't say anything.
Suddenly awkward with the silence, she pointed toward
the small end table that stood next to her bed. "My ob-
stetrician is a big supporter of pampering as much as
possible during pregnancy. So I take a long shower and
use lots of lotion to make sure my skin stays hydrated."

"Can I help?"

What had been a factual, functional exercise mere
moments before had suddenly become fraught with sensual overtones.

"I—"

Ethan moved closer, his gaze growing heavy. "It's
the least I can do, after all."

While the bigger part of her screamed to dive head-first into the moment without another thought, her curiosity still won out. Intrigued by his word choice, she couldn't resist pushing. "After all?"

He tugged at the edge of her hair towel, pulling at the tight twist. The towel hit the hardwood floor with a thump as his gaze followed the curly mass of damp hair that spilled over her back. "I am half the reason you're in this condition."

"Technically you're entirely the reason."

Ethan pressed closer, his body flush against her stomach. "Yes, but I had help."

His lips hovered at her ear, and Lizzie wanted nothing more than to reach out and take what he offered.

But sex—or the ripe promise of it—couldn't change what they were dealing with. It wouldn't make her stalker suddenly vanish. Nor would it bring any sense to the mystery surrounding Josie.

"I thought—" It seemed wrong to toss cold water on the moment, yet she couldn't hold her tongue. "I thought you didn't want a child?"

"Before." He stilled and she saw the genuine battle he waged inside. "That was before you came here. Before I knew."

The hope she'd tried to keep in check flared, a bright vivid spark in the darkness. "Knew what?"

"It's us, Lizzie." He cupped the round fullness of her stomach, his hand instinctively cradling the baby. "New life. A new start. This baby is us."

His whisper sent a mass of shivers coursing down her spine and she shifted, suddenly anxious to shut out the world. As if sensing her willingness, he closed the distance with a sensual drag of his lips against her cheek before taking her mouth fully.

The hands she'd held still at her sides lifted, cupping

his shoulders before wrapping fully around his neck as she opened her mouth to his. The imagined kisses she'd longed for at fifteen gave way to the reality of the desire shared by two adults.

The night of the rodeo he'd made her feel things she'd never experienced before. She had dated—even seriously at times—and had believed she knew what it was to share physical intimacy with a man.

But none of them had been Ethan.

He'd taken full possession of her body, drawing out sensation after sensation with every touch. He'd masterfully painted her body with his mouth until—finally— they'd physically joined when neither could wait any longer.

How amazing, then, to realize she now bore the anticipation of discovering him once again.

Only now she knew how potent was the need that pulsed between them.

Only now did she understand the way he made her feel.

Only now did she truly grasp the power of loving Ethan Colton.

Ethan breathed in the warm woman in his arms, the subtle mix of scents from her pampering no match for the more earthy tones of woman beneath. He wanted her with the sort of need that drove sailors to the rocks. And as he wrapped the long length of her hair in his hand, still damp from her shower, he finally understood those sailors went to the rocks willingly.

His other hand still played across her stomach, the outline of their child heating his palm.

Once again, he was assailed by the heady mix of protection and desire that swirled through him. He wanted this woman with his very last breath. Wanted to possess her and brand her with his body as surely as his heart beat in his chest.

Yet he'd give that very last breath and every one in between to keep her and their child safe and secure.

Trailing his fingers over the roundness of her stomach, he reached for the tie of her robe, slipping open the knot.

"Ethan." She dragged her mouth from his, her voice soft. "I'm so—"

He refused to let her finish, letting the tie fall from his fingers before opening the robe. "You're so beautiful."

"I'm huge."

"You're perfect."

Entranced by the sight of her creamy skin, still soft and pliant from her shower, he allowed his hands to roam along with his gaze. Although the baby created a barrier between their bodies, he was enthralled to realize the curves he'd loved already were only more generous, more beautiful.

And he could still create a series of fires every place he touched.

He traced the full outline of her breasts, his hands filled with their heavy weight, fascinated at the lushness of her body. Her breath quickened and he narrowed his focus to the tight points of her nipples. She moaned on a hard breath, and he moved closer, pleased at the flush of color that suffused her chest as he teased the distended flesh.

"Ethan…" His name floated from her lips and he caught it with his own, their tongues mating in a carnal feast. He refused to break contact with her mouth, all the while keeping a steady focus on her sensitive skin, delighting in her responsiveness.

Another soft moan matched the restlessness of her body against his, and he braced his hands on her hips, turning her so her back was flush against his groin. A hard wave of pleasure swamped his system as she pressed against his erection, the tightness beneath his jeans nearly painful in its intensity.

Still, he pressed on, determined to make up for every lonely moment he'd spent since their night at the rodeo. Intent on washing away those endless hours with nothing but pleasure and joy.

Focused only on Lizzie, he ignored the demands of his own body and continued the exploration of her breasts with one hand while the other moved along the bones of her hips, the weight of her belly pressed to his forearm as his fingers sought her tight warmth.

A hard moan fell from her lips as he pressed his fingers against her flesh, seeking the small bundle of nerves at the very heart of her pleasure. Another wave of need punched through him as she burrowed more tightly against his groin, but he again ignored the discomfort as she rode his fingers.

"Lizzie." He whispered her name against her neck, his tongue trailing along her flesh. He was as lost as she, drunk on the pleasure he could draw from the very depths of her body, and Ethan knew it was the most erotic moment of his life.

The most *necessary* moment of his life.

Her breathing shattered on a moan and he felt her responsiveness down to his very marrow. Holding tight to her, he let her ride the wave, nearly as carried away by her beautiful answer to the pleasure he gave as she was.

A hard, jarring ring broke through the quiet moment.

His hands were still intimately pressed to her body and Ethan disengaged himself before reaching to his back pocket to flip off the call, sending it to voice mail.

"You can get that." Her voice was still husky with need, her body languid in his arms.

"Not on your life." Had he planned ahead before coming to her room, he'd have left his mobile downstairs altogether. Keeping a strong arm around her for support, he pulled them toward the bed. "Come over here."

Although he'd ignored the call, the digital interruption had effectively broken the sensual cocoon around them both, and he wanted to regain some equilibrium. He wanted her, but he also knew the last few moments had his knees shaky and the ground not quite firm beneath his feet.

Their night together after the rodeo had been a sensual feast. One he'd never thought he'd be lucky enough to repeat.

But after the past few days—their close proximity, his discovery of her pregnancy and the external danger that was far too close for comfort—he'd begun to question if there could be something more for them.

The robe still hung loose around her slim shoulders, but even with the slight covering, he knew the secrets beneath the thin material. Knew intimately the beauty of her body's response. He knew her.

Why didn't that fact scare him as much as he'd expected it would?

Another hard ring lit up the air, and he reached for his phone, determined to silence whoever called. When Trevor's name painted the face of his phone, he nearly sent it to voice mail before Lizzie's soft voice broke his concentration. "Answer it."

"It's not important."

"Maybe it is."

Her voice was quiet, but her steady hand over his had him reconsidering answering the call. On a resigned sigh, he accepted the call. "What's going on, Trev?"

"There's been another murder."

Chapter 13

Ethan huddled in the parking lot of the Granite Gulch Saloon with his brother Ridge, matched cups of coffee in hand. The cold night air whipped around them, but it was no match for the brutal cold that had settled beneath his skin.

The *E* murder had been committed.

He was torn—appalled yet overwhelmingly relieved—at his relief it wasn't Lizzie, yet he couldn't shake the sheer horror at the evil that had once again marred their lives.

An evil that had its roots in his father's depravity and warped sense of the world.

"How are we back to this same damn spot?" Ridge nearly spit the words, his breath punching out in hard bursts.

"I'll give you a better question. Why can no one get a handle on this? The woman was shot in a public place."

Ethan and Ridge stood separated from the action,

the parking lot now filled to the brim with professional crime-scene investigators. Even with the harsh flood-lights and silently flashing blues and reds, a fair number of civilian cars and trucks peppered the lot. Certainly enough to deter a crazed killer from targeting their next victim.

Yet someone had. The techs were all busy doing their work, but Ethan and Ridge had already got three key bits of news.

The woman was shot on the premises, not dumped there.

She had the distinctive red bull's-eye marked on her forehead.

And her name was Erica Morgan.

Ridge buried his hands in his jacket pockets. Ethan knew his brother was anxious to begin tracking the area in his role as one of Blackthorn County's search-and-rescue team, but Trevor and his FBI buddies were still working through the crime-scene specifics. Another murder—with the clear mark of the serial killer haunt-ing Blackthorn County—had brought out the top brass, and everyone wanted to be crystal clear about how the scene was handled.

"Trev's convinced the answer is to go see dear old Dad."

Ethan eyed Ridge over the edge of his cup. He never considered himself small, but standing next to his brother always reminded him that Ridge had landed the biggest shoe size of all the Colton boys. His brother was hard and angled, and no one with a working brain cell would mess with the man.

So it was a shock to see his brother's normally rigid jaw and determined brown gaze rife with indecision.

"You don't agree?" Ethan was intrigued by Ridge's reticence. "I thought I was the only holdout."

Ridge frowned. "None of us are exactly looking forward to it."

"And?" Ethan couldn't resist asking.

"It's giving Dad what he wants." Ridge crumpled the cup in his hand. "I don't like it, and I really don't like how it's coincided with the murders."

"Trevor thinks Dad's innocent of what's going on."

"Not buying it. He might not be behind it, but he's got a sense of who's doing it. Hell, he's the one who told Sam to focus on the letters written by women."

"For clues?"

"That and because he thinks they should be looking at a woman for the crime."

Based on the information his family had already shared, Ethan knew this was a new direction for the case—and one that had made the consideration of Josie's involvement seem slightly more plausible—but it still seemed like a strange outcome. While it was well documented women could be serial killers, it was a set of crimes more associated with male behavior.

"Is he just being a crafty bastard and trying to throw everyone off?"

"Sam doesn't think so. But the angle of the chest shots indicates someone tall enough to be either male or female."

Ethan thought about the stack of letters sitting on his kitchen counter and the woman he'd left at home with them. He'd not planned on taking things so far tonight with Lizzie. Things had just…happened.

Wonderful, beautiful, amazing things. Incredible moments with the mother of his child. Heartbeats in time with a woman who meant far more to him than he was comfortable admitting.

And then a dark, depraved call had interrupted their quiet moments together, stamping what was pure and lovely with something ugly and sinister.

His brother's call had only reinforced what Ethan had known all along. He'd never be free of the sins of his father. Instead, they would continue to leave dirty, oily marks on his life that would ruin anyone who came into contact with him.

He and Lizzie were bringing a child into the world. How could he ever hope to spare his child from the dirty name of Colton?

Movement at the crime scene caught his eye and he watched—horrified—as a long black bag was hoisted onto a stretcher. "That's her?"

"Yes." Ridge pointed toward the coroner's van. "They'll look for additional forensic evidence when they get her to the morgue."

"Do you think they'll find anything?"

"No." Ridge kicked at the ground, a rattle of stones grinding beneath his booted foot. "Not if the killer follows pattern. The bull's-eye is precise, but leaves nothing human on the marking. And the body won't be touched."

"It's so cold." Although he'd never had the urge to take a life, Ethan was shocked at how impersonal it all felt. "You'd think the act of killing someone else re-quired something—anything—human from the killer."

He'd been surprised his family wanted him at the crime scene, but in retrospect he was glad they'd called. The time with Ridge was time well spent. Ethan also knew the call was another step in Trevor's "convince Ethan to go see dear old Dad in prison" plan.

And damn it all if his brother's efforts weren't beginning to chip away at his resistance.

"Trev brought the file of letters over earlier. Asked if I'd take a look. Especially with what Lizzie's been dealing with."

"What's Lizzie dealing with?"

At Ridge's immediate shift in attention, Ethan muttered a thick string of expletives. "Trev hasn't spread the word?"

"No."

Ethan gave his brother the benefit of a catch-up, surprised to realize how much it helped to talk each incident through with someone new.

"It's someone she knows. The sense of intimacy the jerk's trying to create is too close. Too familiar."

"But who? She's confirmed there's no ex-boyfriend making a nuisance of himself. No weird neighbors or strange guys at the coffee shop."

"Someone at work, maybe?"

Ethan vowed to ask her again with Ridge's prompts before he realized his brother was owed the rest of the story. "There's one more thing. Lizzie thinks she saw Josie tonight."

"What!"

Ridge's voice was loud enough to draw the attention of a few of the techs on the periphery of the crime scene. He lowered his voice, but the softer tones were no less urgent. "Where? How?"

For the second time in as many minutes, he caught his brother up on the latest in his life, and it was only when he finished that he caught something specific in Ridge's dark gaze. "What?"

"I think—" Ridge stopped and ran his hands over

the day's worth of scruff on his cheeks and neck. "It's stupid."

"Out with it."

"I think I've seen her, too."

Ethan respected his brother's need to keep his own counsel—hell, he did it on a regular basis himself—but this was big news. *Huge* news. "And you've been sitting on it?"

"Not sitting on it, exactly." Ridge narrowed his gaze as he looked out over the crime scene. "I wanted to be sure. There're too few facts floating around and far too many rumors for my taste."

"What makes you think you've seen Josie? None of us have seen her for a long time."

"I don't—that's the rub. But I've seen a woman twice now, while out working two different jobs. Something about her is familiar." Ridge balled the coffee cup even harder in his hands. "Familiar like my sister."

Ethan knew he needed to tread carefully. They all missed Josie—as a family and each in their own way—but their sister's disappearance had hit Ridge harder than the rest of them. He'd wanted to become her warden when she first separated from the family, and she'd denied him.

Ridge still looked for her in every case he worked.

Sam and Annabel worked their way over from the crime scene, their matched looks confirming for anyone who even gave them a glance that they were siblings. "How's it going?"

"Slow." Sam blew out a hard breath. "And Trev's pushing the Bureau's involvement hard on this one."

"They are involved," Annabel reminded Sam, her tone gentle. "And they need to be. We don't have nearly the same resources here in Granite Gulch."

"I know. Damn it, I do." Sam's hunched shoulders straightened and he firmly turned his back on the scene. "But it still chafes, you know? This is our town. Our people. Heck, I went to school with Erica. She was a sweet girl. Content, you know. She wasn't overly ambitious, but she gave every project she worked on her all."

"No witnesses?" Ethan asked, already knowing they had no visuals on the killer.

"Nothing, and the back of the saloon wasn't a high priority for security cameras." Annabel's gentle, soothing tones vanished. "The owner couldn't even spring for a cheap monitoring system."

"Did you get anything out of the people inside the bar?" Ethan knew his brother and sister had spent the past hour culling through the saloon's patrons, taking personal information and statements.

"One of the waitresses is especially upset. She's good friends with Erica. Was even planning an upcoming cruise with her," Sam said.

"She's smart," Annabel added, "and pays attention to her surroundings. She mentioned a strange, nondescript woman who was in earlier today, acting belligerent."

"Which only gives further credence to looking for a woman." Ethan caught Ridge's dark gaze before his brother gave a subtle nod. "Lizzie thought she saw Josie tonight."

He got the same shocked reaction from his siblings as from Ridge before something sharp and tangible took shape in his mind. "But if Josie's been hanging out somewhere on the ranch, there's no way she's the killer."

"Look. Aside from the fact I don't believe my sister's a killer, you're only about ten miles out of town, Ethan," Annabel argued. "That's not an impossible distance."

"When did Lizzie think she saw her?" Sam's eyes were as dark as Ridge's, but they were all cop.

"Around eight."

His brother shook his head. "Time of death's estimated around eleven. Annabel's right. Ten miles isn't an impossibility."

"Oh, come the hell on." Ethan fought the need to grind his back teeth. "Aside from the fact that we all know Josie and don't think her capable of this, can you honestly tell me you think she hiked ten miles into town to kill someone?"

"She could have a car." Sam continued to poke holes. "Or a partner."

"I haven't seen anything foreign on my property, and my ranch staff would tell me if they did."

"I think I've seen her, too." Ridge finally spoke up, his timing impeccable after Chris and Annabel had already voiced a series of questions.

"Maybe it's time we shifted the investigation," Sam said.

"Where?" Even as he asked the question, Ethan already knew the answer.

"I'd like to ask Lizzie Conner a few questions."

The creepy, ugly letters stared up at her from where she'd placed them around the table. Lizzie had maintained a protective hand over her belly—as if she could shield her child from the depravity and ugliness in the letters—even as she continued to read them one by one.

Sympathizers. Hero-worshipers. And the ones she'd dubbed the worst: imitators.

Matthew Colton's letters held all of these and more.

"What sort of person idolizes a serial killer?" She

muttered the words to herself as she stood to get herself a fresh glass of water.

She did a quick walk past the entrance to the living room. Bill dozed in the ancient recliner that sat in direct view of the TV, and Joyce was fast asleep on the couch. Their insistence on keeping Lizzie company had given way to end-of-the-day exhaustion.

For her part, Lizzie had left the couple to their illusions of playing watchdog, feigning the need for sleep and heading up to her room shortly after Ethan had left for the crime scene. She'd only sneaked back down after she couldn't stand another second alone in her room.

A hard shudder gripped her as she imagined what Ethan had spent the past two hours dealing with.

The *E* murder.

She hadn't been the target. But some poor young woman had. A life was now snuffed out at the hands of another, and the clues were possibly in the stack of letters on the table.

Lizzie filled her glass at the tap and stared out the window. The lights were blazing on the barn, and she could see the movement of two ranch hands near the paddock. Men Ethan had deliberately put on duty to keep watch.

And to keep her safe while he was gone.

Headlights added to the view, and soon she saw Ethan's truck followed by another as well as a police car. The sight of his brothers Ridge and Sam, as well as his sister Annabel, added a layer of nerves to ones she hadn't realized were so close to the surface.

In moments, the kitchen was full of Coltons, their faces long with sadness, worry and grief.

"How was everything?" Lizzie briefly thanked her

foresight to slip into yoga pants and a sweatshirt as she took in the people who now crowded Ethan's kitchen.

Sam spoke first. "What you'd expect. Managed chaos."

"Do they have any more clues than before?"

"Nothing yet, but it's early." Annabel smiled and Lizzie didn't miss the attempts at kindness beneath the comment.

The reality likely was they didn't have any clues, only another dead woman.

"I'll put some coffee on." A sleepy Joyce bustled into the kitchen, her focus on helping a sweet balm to the tense air. Bill had already pulled Ethan to the side for a conversation. In moments, the older couple was on their way, leaving her with Ethan, Ridge, Sam and Annabel.

"You were looking at the letters?" Ridge pointed to the even sheets of paper spread over the table.

She took a seat next to him and attempted to explain her sorting system. Although the letters in the file were all uniform in size—copied on standard-size printer paper—it had only taken her flipping through a few to realize how many had been handwritten on stationery before being photocopied.

Various shapes of handwriting filled the folder, from large loopy swirls to small, neat, slanted script to block printing. The lack of uniformity reminded her of her own job. Mortgage applicants were as varied as their handwriting, and she'd often played a game with herself, imagining the person who filled out the form.

The game wasn't nearly as intriguing or lighthearted with the letters sent to Matthew Colton.

"They seem to fall into three major categories. First, the ones who worship your father and his crimes. They either idolize him for his choices or claim to love him for what he's done."

"Sick and twisted minds," Ethan muttered from the counter where he poured coffee into a line of mugs.

"Yet focused. Determined, even," Lizzie added as an afterthought. "They might seem sick and twisted to us, but there's a strange sense of purpose in the notes. Like they've finally found someone who understands them."

When Ethan only shook his head, his back to them, she pressed on. "Then there are sympathizers who seem to feel he was wronged by the justice system."

"And what's the third?" Sam probed.

"They're the worst." She again laid a hand over her stomach, fierce in her need to protect her child. "They are the ones who want to imitate his crimes as their own."

Annabel reached for her free hand, squeezing it in her own. "That's quite insightful. You've taken them down to their essence."

"Why do people think like this?"

Ethan distributed the mugs, then took his own and sat down next to her. "Because they're sick. They have some ridiculous need to focus on another to give their lives meaning or value or to validate the twisted thoughts in their head."

"It's not that simple." Lizzie thought about the letters she'd read—the words and their patterns—and realized it wasn't accurate to simply sum up Matthew's letter writers as those suffering from mental delusions. "Some of these people connect with your father. Their arguments are cogent and rational and they are in support of his crimes. They feel disillusioned with the world around them and they see him as someone who felt the same and who took action."

"Motive isn't always just about greed or opportunity. This one, for example." Sam tapped one of the letters Lizzie had left on top and picked it up. "'You grew up in a broken home and you understand the pain of family rejection. How could you have made any other choice but what you did?'"

Lizzie felt Ethan stiffen next to her, his gaze focused on his steaming coffee. She knew this had to be difficult for him, but she also knew they'd never get to the bottom of the situation they were dealing with if they didn't try to look beneath the surface.

The letters had disgusted her and upset her, but they'd also confirmed something she already knew. So many people lived with pain and suffering. If they didn't look at the problem through that lens, they risked possibly missing the person who was systematically killing women in Blackthorn County.

"Lizzie. Ethan told us about Josie. Do you really believe it was her?"

Annabel's change in subject pulled her from her musings, and Lizzie was shocked at the stab of pain at the mention of her old friend. She'd managed to put Josie out of her mind for a few hours, but now images of the woman silhouetted in the barn lights re-formed in her mind.

"I think it was her, yes."

"You think?" Sam pushed, even as he kept his tone gentle.

"It was through the window and I haven't seen her in several years, but yes, I believe I saw Josie tonight."

No one said a word, but four matched faces surrounded her at the table. Each was full of their own private misery, their thoughts full of memories of their baby sister.

She'd seen Ethan close up at the mention of Josie, and it was humbling to see Ridge, Annabel and Sam all do the same. While she didn't want to add to that, she refused to let the subject continue to lie quietly in the corner, like a snake waiting to strike.

"Do you ever wonder why she stopped the visits?"

Silence greeted her until Ridge finally spoke. "All the time. We all do."

"Maybe there was a reason."

"Be careful there, Lizzie. The police and the FBI are all over reasons." The gentleness in Sam's voice had vanished. "They're looking for any reason our sister could be the Alphabet Killer."

"You don't really think that?"

"No," Ethan said. "None of us do."

"Yet those in charge of the investigation continue to look at her. Why?"

Sam spoke first. "When we were investigating the murder of Zoe's sister, Celia, the profilers put together a noticeable trend in the victims. They all have long dark hair."

"So do lots of women. And I still don't see what that has to do with Josie."

"Serial killers have a known pattern. There's a reason they go after a type, usually because it reminds them of the thing they're trying to eradicate in their life."

Although she didn't doubt Sam's wisdom, it seemed silly that something as simple as hair color could put a literal and figurative target on someone's head.

"What Sam's trying to tell you," Ethan added, "is that since the FBI's been investigating women for the crime, we've had to look a bit closer to home. Josie's fiancé was seen kissing a woman with long dark hair the day before she disappeared. The day their engagement ended."

Her earlier memories again filled her mind's eye, an odd punctuation to the discussion. She hadn't thought about Michael Evans in years, yet here he was, popping up twice in one night.

His name's Michael. He's been flirting all year in math class and he finally got up the nerve to ask me out.

"Wait. Whoa. You think Josie's the Alphabet Killer because she had a fiancé who kissed another woman?" She knew Michael, and the idea he'd cheat on anyone wasn't a match for her memories of the quiet student in her biology class. That didn't mean he couldn't, but it still seemed so incongruous.

What seemed even more ridiculous, though, was the idea that a single kiss could somehow unleash something more. "Engagements end all the time, and they don't result in either party becoming serial killers."

"We don't think she's the killer," Annabel insisted. "But the feds are willing to look at every path, no matter how silly. It's one more line to tug."

"Or a dead end to make people feel like they're doing something when they have nothing to go on." Lizzie knew she was being unfair—she knew nothing about law enforcement and even less about tracking a killer—but this was insanity.

"How can any rational person possibly see this as a lead? Yes, she dated Michael Evans in high school. And after she ran away, their relationship obviously ended. That does not make her suddenly pop up six years later, killing women in alphabetical order like some beast unleashed."

"She *is* the daughter of Matthew Colton." Ethan's

words were like a gunshot in the room, the exposure of the elephant they all did their damnedest to ignore.

She reached for his hand, willing him to somehow understand what she knew in her heart. "And you're his other children, along with Trevor and Chris. None of you are killers inside, lying dormant, waiting for some small slight to tip you off. And neither is the girl I grew up with and considered a sister."

His hand lay still beneath hers. "Until we figure out who's doing these things, the gun's going to continue to point in the direction of our family."

"Then let's focus on finding the one truly responsible. Because any other outcome is unacceptable."

Yes, it was more challenge than statement, but Lizzie meant every word.

Lizzie had expected to fall right to sleep after the night's events, but after nearly an hour of tossing and turning in bed, she decided to come back downstairs and finish what she'd begun.

The letters she'd read through earlier had been neatly stacked on Ethan's kitchen counter, and she picked them up again, reordering them into her previous bundles.

Although she wouldn't call her conversation with the Colton siblings a revelation, they had helped her focus her thoughts. And at the heart of that was the continuing question of who the Alphabet Killer was. The feds and the cops didn't know; that was patently obvious.

Especially if they were investigating the woebegone love story of a seventeen-year-old runaway as their lead clue.

"Lizzie?" She glanced up to see Ethan's unfocused gaze quickly sharpening. "Why are you looking at those?"

"I'd like to help."

"Don't put that crap in your mind. It's not healthy."

He'd dragged on a pair of jeans but not a shirt, and she fought hard to keep her attention focused on the moment rather than the golden hue of his skin or the delicious play of thick muscle across his chest and stomach.

Despite her best efforts, she gave herself a few extra moments to drink her fill, eyeing the light dusting of hair on his chest and the way it tapered to the snap of his jeans.

Even as her gaze traveled that glorious path, she couldn't stop the response of her body or the memories of how he'd made her feel earlier. Her body tingled from the mind-blowing orgasm he'd given her, and she could still feel every place he'd touched, like a brand that had transferred from his hands to her skin.

He reached for the letters on the table, effectively snapping her from the hot memories.

"I'm going to put these away, and I'd like to ask you not to look at them again."

"Excuse me?"

She'd never considered herself a shy, wilting violet, and no matter how attractive the man opposite her was, she didn't tolerate caveman behavior. "You'd like me to do what?"

"They're disgusting and soiled. I'm thinking of you and the baby. Those letters are stressful."

Although his comments hardly placated, Lizzie wasn't blind or stubborn enough not to recognize he had a point about the baby. She also knew her limits and didn't need constant reminding. "But it's okay for you to read them and process their contents?"

"I'm dealing with it, along with my family. You're being dragged along for the ride."

She'd had every intention of staying calm, soothing, even. But something about the unyielding set of his jaw and the dismissive tone had her hackles up before she could even think to back down. "The baby's fine. I'm fine. You're the one who's not fine, Ethan."

"What's that supposed to mean?"

"You tell me. You're in the middle of a nearly inhuman upheaval in your life, and you keep acting like it will go away if you just don't pay it any attention."

A wave of muscles flexed in his shoulders as he straightened off the doorjamb. "I'm well aware of my current responsibilities."

"Then why won't you discuss them with me?"

"I can handle what's going on."

She wasn't a confrontational person by nature, more eager to handle a crisis with a smile and a small joke. But there was nothing funny about the current situation, and she was done trying to approach it with anything but brutal honesty. "You keep thinking that if it makes you feel better."

"Like you know so much."

"I know so much because I care about you! I can see you're in pain and I can see you're hurting. You don't have to be alone. I'm here to help you!"

"This isn't your battle, Lizzie. And you're not here to help me."

The urge to throw something—anything—had her clenching her hands into tight fists. But what hurt the most was the evidence in his absolute and complete shutdown that Ethan hadn't really changed.

He'd told her in many ways over the past days that he was prepared to care for their child. Somewhere along the way, she'd translated that to mean he cared for her, too. And that maybe, given enough time, he'd want something that went beyond caring.

Something that went to making a life together.

But building a life meant caring for each other. Crafting a relationship meant unloading what was inside before you imploded with it. Creating a future meant sharing burdens and helping each other.

The stoic, unyielding soul before her was unable to do any of those things.

Sadly, in the quiet space that separated them across his kitchen, Lizzie was forced to acknowledge the truth. Ethan Colton was a man determined to face his life alone.

Chapter 14

Lizzie woke to a quiet house and a note from Joyce on the kitchen counter. The woman had made a breakfast casserole and left a fruit bowl in the fridge and instructed Lizzie in no uncertain terms to eat both. She smiled to herself at the motherly tone and set out to do as she'd been told.

It was only a few minutes later, after she'd filled a cereal bowl with fruit and pulled a serving of egg casserole out of the microwave, that she realized what was missing.

The file folder of letters had disappeared from the counter.

"Damn fool man."

The baby punctuated the comment with a kick, and she smiled at the small show of solidarity.

And while she'd have liked nothing more than to go hunt Ethan down, Lizzie couldn't deny the delicious smell of breakfast or her ravenous—empty—stomach.

So she sat down to eat her eggs and sausage and fruit and decide how she was going to handle Ethan.

Their fight—and she absolutely classified their discussion the night before in the fight camp—had left her with a sense of hopelessness when she got into bed. But the fresh light of morning had her rethinking that late-night decision the moment she climbed back out from beneath the covers.

Ethan Colton was an immovable rock on the subject of his father, and she wasn't immune or insensitive enough to question why. But it didn't give him leave to either ignore the obvious or not work to keep his sister's name from being dragged through the mud.

Yes, the authorities were looking for a woman for the crimes. But focusing on Josie was not only a dead end, it gave the real killer more time to roam free and potentially harm others. They needed to divert attention back to the proper channels, and she had as much at stake as Ethan.

It was her baby's aunt whose name was in question, after all.

Lizzie had nearly finished her breakfast when her pocket rang, and she dug into the folds of her robe for her cell phone. She couldn't hold back the smile when she saw her boss's name on the readout.

"Cheryl! How are you?"

"I'm good, sweetie. How's the baby doing?"

She caught Cheryl up on how she was feeling and traded pleasantries. Although she'd avoided giving the specifics around her decision to leave the bank, Cheryl had always had a keen eye and Lizzie knew the woman wasn't completely fooled.

"I know you said your decision to leave was based on wanting to work things out with the baby's father, but I have every confidence I can figure something out here. We'd love to find some way to keep you, and I've already had discussions with Zane about finding a way to do that. He values your contribution and he's willing to consider some sort of revised schedule to let you work at home."

Although she had minimal contact with Zane Hardwick, as he was Cheryl's boss, he'd always been friendly to her. But she'd had no idea she was on his radar to the degree that he valued her enough to find such an accommodating solution.

"That's awfully generous of Zane."

"He's adamant we find a way to keep you. He told me himself."

An opportunity to work a flex schedule—even a few days a week—would allow her to stay closer to the baby and possibly even determine shared parenting time with Ethan. It was only an hour's drive to his home from her office, and she could manage that a few days a week if she moved herself and the baby to Granite Gulch.

It didn't fully solve her problems, but it did give her something new to consider. And being physically closer to Ethan might deter the stalker or draw him out. A stranger in Granite Gulch wouldn't go unnoticed by the locals, which would make identifying who was after her a heck of a lot easier.

"Please give Zane my thanks. Really. But I still need some time to think."

"I understand. But promise me two things."

"What's that?"

"Promise me you'll think about it enough to say yes. And promise me you'll come to the annual awards dinner. You've earned your award as best loan officer of the year, and I'd like to see that you get your honor in person."

She'd completely forgotten the banquet in the rush of all that had happened. "It's this week?"

"Tomorrow night. I know you didn't want to go, feeling it would be awkward, but you earned it, Lizzie."

"I—"

"I'll only call you later and nag you some more, so go ahead and say yes and save me the time."

Lizzie couldn't hold out against the force of nature that was Cheryl Banner. "Okay. Okay. You've convinced me."

A small voice whispered she should talk it over with Ethan first, but...well. Damn it, she was going. Cheryl was right. It was an honor.

And she was sick of playing the sitting duck.

She'd earned her award and she wanted to collect it. And if it happened to incite her stalker to reveal himself? Well. She'd deal with that, too. The banquet was going to be an evening with a room full of people. How dangerous could it be?

"I'll see you tomorrow night."

Foolish, foolish woman.

The words repeated themselves over and over in Ethan's mind as he stared at Lizzie. She'd come into the stables with a fresh thermos of coffee, and he'd initially felt remorse for his harsh comments the night before.

But her latest scheme was beyond the pale.

"You are not going to draw your stalker out. No way. End of story."

"I'm going to receive an award I earned with a heck of a lot of hard work. It's not drawing anyone out."

"Which basically waves a red flag in front of a bull."

"I'm not—"

He cut her off before she could come up with any further arguments. "You left the company less than a week ago because you were convinced your stalker was tied to the workplace. Have you forgotten so soon?"

"I've forgotten nothing. But I have a right to my life. This is something I've worked incredibly hard for and it will be a good way to keep my name in front of those who matter. They're considering giving me a flex schedule so I can keep working after the baby comes."

In the back of his mind Ethan knew he had no right to keep her from doing as she pleased, but somewhere on the path from his brain to his mouth that fact was forgotten.

"Absolutely, under no uncertain terms, are you going back to that job."

"Excuse me?" Her green eyes widened, shooting fire as they did. "I don't recall needing your permission."

"You do now."

"I'm not sure where you've come up with the idea you've got a say in my life, but you can shove it right back where you found it. We're not married. We're not even in a relationship. So you'd better rethink how you're speaking to me."

"You're having my child. That gives me a huge say."

"About our child. Not about me."

She whirled around and stomped off. Ethan didn't miss Bill's averted gaze or the uncomfortable look on the face of one of his hands as he stalked past both of them, chasing after Lizzie.

"Lizzie."

The baby might have slowed her down a bit, but her ire had those long, long legs moving fast over the grounds. He hollered her name once more before she turned around.

On a hard sigh, she stopped, her voice hoarse with her frustration. "Look, Ethan. It's clear neither one of us can have a calm, rational conversation right now. Let's discuss this later."

"I—"

Her hair whipped around her face in the cool breeze, her cheeks glowing pink, and he felt his anger vanish, morphing into desire in the speed of a heartbeat.

He'd held all that glorious hair in his fist last night. Those soft strands had wrapped around him, still damp from her shower, while her lush body had pressed against his front. The heavy weight of her breasts had filled his hands.

And the last—that glorious moment when he'd pressed his fingers against the most intimate part of her and she'd fallen apart in his arms.

The images slammed into him, layered over each other in such painful clarity he could swear he still felt the imprint of her in his arms. Could still hear her soft moans and the husky timbre of her voice as she called his name.

"Ethan?"

He knew he had no right to her. Hadn't the later events of last night proved that? The Colton family was right back in the center of Blackthorn County's biggest problem since his father.

And yet…

Even with all the chaos that surrounded them, he wanted her.

"Ethan?"

"What?"

"Let's discuss this later."

"Okay."

She moved closer and laid a hand on his arm. "I didn't mean to upset you. I'm not changing my mind, but I didn't come into the stables to pick a fight, either."

"I know."

"Do you?" She stared up at him, the anger already faded from her eyes.

"Do you understand I'm not trying to stifle you? Or hold you back? I want to keep you safe."

"Keeping me safe doesn't mean putting me on a shelf. I'm not a museum piece. I've got a life ahead of me and I am going to live it."

She stopped, but he heard what she didn't say loud and clear.

With or without you.

The moment hung there before he nodded. "I know."

"Okay, then. I've got a few things to do. I'll see you at lunch."

He let her go but stood at the paddock rails, unable to turn his back on her. She still moved with steady grace, her pregnancy not yet fully slowing her down, and it was lovely to simply stand and watch her.

It was only when she reached the front porch and bent toward the front door that something hit him as off.

But it was the scream that echoed from the house that had him running, bone-deep fear stabbing his heart with every step he took.

Lizzie put one foot behind the other, moving slowly away from the front door. The mangled doll lay where she'd found it, its sightless eyes staring to the sky, a long knife embedded in its chest with a note beneath.

The image was silly—stupid, even—yet the intent behind it was deadly serious.

"Lizzie!"

Strong arms came around her from behind and Ethan's soothing words filled her ear. "You're okay."

She turned in his arms, pressing her head against his chest, unable to understand why anyone would possibly want to target her like this.

What had she done to attract such awful attention?

Ethan's hands roamed over her back, a soothing counterpoint to the fear that still pumped adrenaline through her system like a fire hose. He painted her back in large, arcing circles with his palm while she did her best to slow her racing pulse and find some equilibrium.

To think they'd been fighting only minutes before.

Now she couldn't think of anything but hanging on to him, her ally in the storm.

"I'm sorry, Ethan. So sorry."

"For what?" He brought a hand to her chin, lifting her face to look at him. "What could you possibly feel the need to apologize for?"

"I brought this…this depravity here. Literally to your front door."

"I can handle it. And I'd far prefer it at my front door than yours."

"Why's it at anyone's door?"

"I don't know." His arms tightened once more. "Damned if I know."

They stood like that for several long moments, the morning sun warming them on the porch as they diligently ignored the threat that lay a few feet away. It was only after she couldn't withhold her curiosity any longer that she stepped from Ethan's arms. "There's a note."

"I can see."

"Let's read it."

"I'd prefer to have Sam or Annabel come out and take a look. Dust for prints."

"Of course."

While she agreed with his assessment, she knew the police would find nothing. Just as they'd found nothing the other day when the stalker had actually come into her home.

They'd find nothing this time, either.

Ethan pocketed his phone after disconnecting the call. "Sam'll be right out."

"Good."

She moved to the edge of the porch railing and stared out over the grounds. While this part of Texas wasn't exactly known for being covered in forest, the property was old and there were plenty of large trees that dotted the yard on down to the main road. The house was set back pretty far but it wouldn't be impossible to move through it unnoticed.

"How long do you think this thing's been lying here?"

"Can't be more than a few hours. While we all use the mudroom door in and out, Joyce and Bill went out through the front last night."

"So sometime in the past eight hours." He and his brothers and sister hadn't got back from the crime scene until after two, and it was barely ten now.

The urge to hover was strong, but Ethan finally suggested she go inside. "I'll call you when Sam gets here."

Lizzie hated the fact that some whack job had managed to send her running inside with her tail between her legs, but she couldn't stand being near the doll for another second. The slender knife sticking out of the small body sent a very clear message, and she wasn't quite sure what to do about it.

Someone was after her and her child.

And no matter how safe she thought she was, the man who stalked her continued to come ever closer.

The tissue-thin walls of the boardinghouse in Rosewood seemed to telegraph every bit of noise in the dump. She'd already heard the high-pitched whine of the brat down the hall who decided he didn't like his toy truck or his sister touching it. The old woman across the hall had her morning game shows on so loud it was a wonder they weren't audible clear to Granite Gulch.

But it was the whore next door who took the cake.

Every day she had a different man with her. Trash who wanted nothing more than to get in her pants, and she let them. Each and every one of them.

She'd heard them when she got in last night and it had been going on ever since. Cries of "oh, baby" and "almost there" had filtered through the walls while the cheap headboard kept time like some sort of dirty metronome.

She fought the rage and jealousy at the way the woman flaunted her sexuality and the men she brought home, all salivating over her large breasts and narrow waist. She'd even thought to give advice one day when they passed in the hall. *Toss your hair back over your shoulder and put on a bright summer dress and the men will line up.*

But the men never lined up.

Her gaze drifted to the opposite wall, traveling over the beautiful lines of the wedding dress that hung on the frame of the small closet. The yards of silk and lace drooped on the hanger, and she knew she should bring it for cleaning, yet she couldn't bear to part with it.

Besides, he might come back, and then where would she be? They were on the verge of marrying, after all. It would do no good to have her fiancé come back home and her dress be with the cleaners. Wedding dresses took time to clean, and she needed to be ready.

So she pushed that idea back out of her mind and focused on other things.

She needed to get her latest letter to Matthew out and posted. Blocking out the latest round of *oh, baby*s, she focused on the letter. If he only knew what he'd inspired, he'd be so proud of her work.

The latest—that tramp Erica—had been rather satisfying. She'd thought she could say whatever she wanted, kicking her out of the bar. A public place, at that!

Erica wouldn't be kicking anyone out. Not anymore.

For the briefest moment, she allowed that sense of euphoria to fill her chest. It was as though each time she fired a bullet into the chest of another, a part of her became free.

Once upon a time she'd been so angry. She'd stared out over all her guests and had to thank them for coming but tell them there wouldn't be a wedding that day. Ever since, such a huge, heavy weight had lain on her chest.

But she'd finally found a way to take the weight away. Matthew Colton had shown her how. In his deeds she'd discovered the way to free herself.

It was only right that she told him.

With one last glance at her wedding dress, she focused on the sheet of paper before her.

Dear Matthew...

Lizzie changed into one of her favorite maternity tops and put on a pair of slacks. While she appreciated the more casual air of the ranch, the pretty green blouse and dark slacks felt like putting on armor.

It was silly, she mused as she came downstairs, but

the act of dressing formally actually made her feel better. More in control.

And she needed every bit of strength she could muster.

Sam was already at the table, a field kit spread out before him. That gross doll lay in the middle like a sacrificial victim, and she watched, eerily fascinated, as he took photos, then began to separate the knife and the note beneath it from the doll.

Ethan leaned against the kitchen sink, his lean hips pressed to the counter, his long legs crossed at the ankle. He was quiet while Sam worked, but his focus never left his brother.

"I'm sorry you're dealing with this, Lizzie." Sam made the apology as he ran a small dusting of fingerprint powder over the knife. "And I'm sorry you're stuck with me as your CSI man, but I promise, I can do it in a pinch."

"Thank you for coming. I'm sure you have better things to be doing."

Sam looked up at that, a small, supportive smile matching the warmth in his eyes. "You are the better thing."

Something hard lodged in the hollow of her throat and her thoughts from the night they were at Trevor's struck her once again. She loved this family. Josie had truly been a sister to her, and her family had adopted Lizzie as their own.

Coming to Ethan's after the threat to her and the baby hadn't just brought him back into her life. It had brought all the Coltons back as well.

While the threat was far from over, the realization that something very good had come of all this pain gave her the strength she needed to take a seat at the table.

"I'm good, Sam. I'd like to watch what you're doing."

She didn't miss the pointed glance he shot Ethan, but he did acquiesce. "Let me walk you through it, then."

Sam spent the next ten minutes describing what he was looking for. Anyone who'd ever watched an episode of a crime drama could understand the treatment of the evidence and the dusting for prints, but the other things fascinated even more.

He took copious notes on the doll itself. Shape, characteristics, the fibers of its small head of hair. He even made specific notes that the doll was undressed instead of dressed, indicating gender hadn't been identified by the stalker.

"You think that's important?"

"I think it's well worth noting." Sam stopped and set his pen down. "Do you know the baby's sex yet?"

"I haven't wanted to know." She turned toward Ethan. "We talked about it at first, but then haven't said much else. If Ethan wants to know, I am fine with asking my OB at my next appointment."

"Personally, I'm hoping for healthy and happy." Ethan pushed off the counter and took a seat next to her. "Beyond that, I can wait for the baby's arrival."

That lump she'd managed to swallow around grew larger, tightening her throat with tears. "If you're sure."

He put a casual arm around the back of her chair, his fingers playing along her upper back. "I'm quite sure."

As if sensing the weight of the moment, Sam returned to his work, his gaze focused on a new set of notes about the knife. Lizzie watched him work, willing away the tears.

She was grateful for his tact. And while her hormones regularly had her crying buckets, in the same way she'd put on the outfit for inner strength, she didn't want to become a great big blubberer at the table, either. So she settled into the warm fingers on her back and once again swallowed back the lump of tears.

"Have you been kicking around names?"

"Lizzie thinks Etienne is a winner."

Ethan's joke was so unexpected she couldn't hold back the giggle. A laugh that only grew louder at Sam's wide-eyed speculation.

"Oh. That's nice."

"We're not naming the baby Etienne. Aside from the fact we don't live in France, it was a small suggestion in a line of many."

"Have you landed on any others?" Sam glanced back up from his notes.

"We haven't really discussed it—" She was interrupted by the ringing of Sam's phone. He glanced down where it lay next to him at the table and, after an apology, got up to answer it.

Sam left the room, his voice muted as it drifted back from the other side of the door.

Ethan turned to her, the warm hazel of his eyes edging toward gold. "Let's discuss it now. Do you have any names you like?"

"A few."

She knew the ploy was an effort to keep her attention off the doll, but Lizzie couldn't help but feel the gravitas of the moment. They were discussing names for their child. An act practiced the world over by couples.

Two people eagerly awaiting the arrival of their child.

And now she and Ethan had come to that point.

"I've had an easier time with boy names. I like James and Eric. I also like Scott and Lawrence."

He nodded. "All good solid names."

"Ethan is a good one, too, if we want to go the junior route."

Ethan shook his head at that. "While I'm grateful for the suggestion, my son, if it's a boy, should have his own name. Any others?"

"George has become popular of late."

"No."

"You don't want to name him after a future king?"

"Nice though it may be, the king can keep his own name. Besides, I think you're thinking of a roguish leading man with that choice."

She had to laugh at that, her deep-seated love of a certain movie star *exactly* the impetus for the suggestion.

"So we've covered quite a few boy names. What about girls?"

She knew it was a risk—one she wasn't entirely sure she should take—yet she couldn't have stayed quiet if she'd tried. Taking a small breath for courage, Lizzie pressed on.

"If she's a girl, I'd like to name her Saralee."

Chapter 15

Whatever he'd expected Lizzie to say, the selection of his mother's name for their child caught him totally unaware. Emotion long buried flooded his system, and if he'd still been standing at the counter he had no doubt his knees would buckle.

Saralee.

The name of a woman who'd never see her own grandchild. Who hadn't lived long enough to see her children grow to adulthood.

A deep, raw well of anger opened up somewhere in the vicinity of his heart. Pain down to his very marrow filled him, and he wanted to cry out like a wounded animal.

His father was the reason.

He well knew there was no guarantee he'd still have his mother had circumstances been different, but he'd have liked to see her have the same shot at life as everyone else. Instead, she'd hitched her star to Matthew Colton and had paid for the decision with her life.

"Ethan?"

He was prevented from saying anything by Sam's return to the room, and he took that as a good sign. The anger and rage that drummed through his system needed an outlet, and it sure as hell wasn't going to be Lizzie.

"Everything okay?" His brother's question was fraught with curiosity, and Ethan only gave him a dark stare.

"Fine."

"That was Chief Murray. He promised an update when they had a chance to process all the witness statements."

"And?"

"Seems more than one person corroborated the waitress's statement of a strange woman lobbing insults and obscenities at Erica. Their descriptions all match. A plain woman in her early forties."

Lizzie leaped on the details, leaning over the table toward Sam. "So it can't be Josie."

"Chief said it removes practically all suspicion that she's been behind the Alphabet crimes."

Sam finished filling them in on his chief's update, relief palpable in his words.

"While I'm glad resources will be put toward finding the real killer, it still doesn't explain why Josie's back here," Lizzie said. "Why won't she come talk to anyone?"

"We might know that if we knew why she left in the first place." The frustration and anger Ethan carried over his mother's murder was nearly as potent as his emotions toward his sister. Josie's leaving had affected them all, her actions as senseless as his father's.

She might be innocent of murdering anyone—and he'd never doubted that—but she wasn't innocent of keeping secrets.

What was she hiding?

Ethan's gaze caught on the doll still lying faceup on the table, and the mystery of his family gave way to the reason they'd called his brother out to the ranch.

"Can we read that note?"

Sam nodded and pulled on a fresh pair of evidence gloves. "Yes. Let's get this over with. I've got all my notes in order, so the only thing left is to read the message."

Lizzie's breath stilled and Ethan placed his arm back on her chair. He wasn't mad at her—he could never be—yet he struggled to understand how to share all the rage and grief that filled him.

He cared for her. He knew he did, and he was finally beginning to come around to the idea that his life was better with Lizzie Conner in it.

Yet how could he make a life with someone—or even attempt to—when the life he was living was awash in murder, deceit and lies?

Worse, how could he raise a child in the middle of such depravity?

Questions without answers.

Unfortunately, there was one question with a very definite answer. "What does the note say, Sam?"

Remorse stamped itself in the set of his brother's shoulders and the apologetic tone of his voice as he turned the letter around to show them both.

THERE'S NOWHERE YOU CAN RUN. YOU AND THE BABY ARE MINE.

* * *

No matter how hard she tried, Lizzie couldn't put the image of that awful letter from her mind. The big block printing, written as if to be untraceable. The knife that held it in place. Even the discovery of the item on Ethan's porch.

All were signs her stalker had followed her to Ethan's front door.

Sam had taken the items with him, promising to open the case here in Granite Gulch as well as share the notes on the file with the cops working her case at home. Although it wasn't much, the use of the knife added another layer of menace that the cops took seriously, Sam promised.

Even as she appreciated his sincerity, Lizzie knew it wasn't that simple. The Granite Gulch PD was focused on catching the Alphabet Killer. Every hour and resource was put toward stopping the madness that had infiltrated their small town. No one except maybe Sam or Annabel was even going to be looking for some stranger in town.

It only added to the reason she and Ethan needed to go to the banquet tomorrow night. She had no interest in setting herself up as bait, yet she couldn't shake the idea that the problem rested with someone at her job.

Who, she had no idea.

Ethan came back into the kitchen after walking Sam out. She studied him, pushing away the attraction and need that normally colored her view of Ethan to focus on the man underneath.

And sadly, she realized he was hanging by as fragile a thread as she was.

Lines marred his forehead and the edges of his eyes, while his shoulders practically trembled from the emotional weight he was holding up. Still, he bore it all with the same stoic grace with which he lived his life.

Unbidden, an image came to mind of their night at the rodeo. She'd planned on going with a friend who'd had to back out at the last minute, but she'd refused to miss out on a fun evening, even if it meant going by herself. She hadn't been inside the arena more than ten minutes when she'd seen Ethan across the concourse.

Several large groups of people separated them, yet she'd have known him anywhere. She could practically *feel* him, it had seemed at the time, her gaze landing unerringly on the large man in the cowboy hat. He'd looked similar that day, his large shoulders stiff with responsibility and a dark weight that most people likely never noticed.

But she did.

And she knew what it meant. Knew the burden he'd carried since he was a small boy. It was that knowledge—far more than his attractive frame or impressive physique—that had propelled her forward, unwilling to let the moment pass her by.

She hadn't given a thought to the fact that she hadn't taken quite as much care with her outfit that night, tossing on jeans and an old comfortable button-down. Nor had she worried that her hair wasn't perfect and her makeup camera ready.

She'd simply leaped with joy at the chance to see him again. And maybe—just maybe—to make that burden a bit lighter for a few hours.

Well aware she was staring, she pressed him for details. "Did Sam say anything else?"

"No. Just another promise to keep the file open and their focus on the asshole who's stalking you."

"It won't help."

"You don't know—"

She cut him off, the idea she'd already worked out in her mind growing stronger by the moment. "The Granite Gulch PD is overworked already. You know that as well as I do."

"They're professionals."

"Yes, professionals with a horrible weight over them as these crimes kept happening on their watch. It's why we need to go to the banquet tomorrow, Ethan. We'll be surrounded by people, so the risk is minimal. You'll be there to watch out for me and you can look for things I've been blind to."

"I'm not dangling you in front of a madman." Ethan moved farther into the kitchen, those shoulders stiffening another few degrees. "Am I the only one who spent the last hour staring at that damn doll with a knife in its chest?"

"I stared at it, too. And that's why we're doing this."

"You're talking crazy, Lizzie."

"It's rational and it's our only option."

"No, our only option is to ignore this and let the damn police do their jobs."

He turned on his heel, obviously ending the conversation. Whether it was his immovable attitude or something else, she had no idea. But something inside her—something small and dark and rooted in the anger of her childhood—rose up and took hold of her throat.

"And you're not a man who sits idly by and lets life act on him!" The words shot from her lips like a gun, as lethal in their own way as a bullet.

He turned back to her as fast as he'd turned away, fire lighting the depths of his eyes. "You know nothing about me."

"I know everything, Ethan! I've known it for years."

The words continued to tumble out, one over the other, faster than she could try to censor herself. "I know the way you stare at animals as if they hold the secrets of the universe. And I know how you can look at the sky and know if it's going to rain, even if it's a bright, vivid blue."

He didn't respond, so she kept on. "I know you value your family, even if you don't know how to show it. And I know you like ice cream. Rocky road and pistachio are your favorites, but you'll happily do with vanilla if there's nothing else.

"I know you love the Boston Red Sox for reasons that make sense only to you and I know you hate spiders."

She held her ground, even though her arms ached to wrap around him.

"I *know* you, Ethan."

His head fell, his gaze on the floor, and for the longest time she thought he'd say nothing.

Endless moments later, when he finally lifted his gaze from the floor, she saw something warm in his eyes and an emotion she'd never seen in all the years she'd known him.

For the first time, she saw acceptance.

"Animals do hold the secrets to the universe. They're eternally pragmatic, with a million years of learning visible in the depths of their eyes." He moved closer, his gaze never leaving hers. "The rain's easy. I cut my palm on a rusty nail when I was a kid and it still hurts like the devil when a storm's heading in. I love my family with ice cream a close second. In fact, there are days all that sweet creamy goodness takes a definite lead over Trev's nagging or Chris's know-it-all puss."

He closed the last few feet and pulled her into his

arms. "Spiders are the only one of God's creatures I'd prefer vanish from the planet, never to be seen again."

She stared up at him, entranced by that warm golden gaze. "They're not wise?"

"Who knows? They're so damn ugly I don't want to be within ten feet of them."

He bent down and pressed his lips against hers. She almost kissed him back when another question popped to mind. "And the Red Sox?"

He pulled her close and smiled against her lips, murmuring, "A man's got to have a few secrets."

And then he was kissing her, all that strength and masculine perfection pressed against her, drawing out a response as surely as she breathed.

As their tongues met and mated, full of the eternal push-pull of need and desire, Lizzie had to acknowledge one more thing she knew.

She loved him.

Great, huge swells of love that had been there from the very first day she'd met a lonely eight-year-old boy sent to visit his sister. She'd lost her heart that day, even if she hadn't fully understood it at the time.

And if her instincts were correct, she was never going to get it back.

Sam's fiancée, Zoe, carried an oversize tray of meat into their dining room, her smile bright as she offered up a small wink to the group assembled around the table. "Sam's been channeling his inner Fred Flintstone for the last hour on the grill. Please, eat up. We have enough meat here to last us until the next millennium."

Ridge spoke first, answering Zoe's wink with one of his own. "Nothing wrong with a plate of meat."

"Amen to that." Ethan stood and helped Zoe with

the heavy plate, settling it on the center of the table. He didn't miss his brothers' matched looks of hunger or Annabel's sharp elbow into Chris's side as she ordered her twin to put his napkin in his lap.

He smiled to himself. Some things never changed, no matter how old they got.

As deliverer of the platter, he snagged a quick slice of steak and narrowly avoided a swat from Annabel. He wiggled his fingers in a teasing wave and shot her a triumphant grin before passing the sides as Zoe ordered.

Lizzie sat next to him, and in moments she'd filled her plate with an assortment of sides and several slices of meat. When she caught him eyeing her plate, she blushed and ducked her head. "I'm sorry. I'm hungry tonight."

He leaned in, unable to resist a quick nip at her ear as he teased her. "My look was one of impressed awe, not censure. You're eating for two, and Sam and Zoe cooked a feast. Enjoy."

While he had no doubt the baby added to her hunger, she didn't owe him an explanation for her meal. One of the things he'd always liked about her was that she acted like a real person. There was good food on the table—she had nothing to be embarrassed about by eating it.

Filing away the odd thought, he focused on his family gathered around the table. Conversation ebbed and flowed, a mix of the silly and stupid as well as the deadly serious. As he'd anticipated, they'd no sooner cleared the dinner plates than the subject of the Alphabet crimes came up.

"Hey, Ethan. That love letter you picked out sure gave Annabel and me something to do today." Sam patted his stomach before shooting his sister a look of sheer commiseration. "We spent half our day combing through an old boardinghouse in Rosewood."

"You found something?" Lizzie spoke first, her gaze eager.

"Depends on your definition of *found*." Annabel didn't bother to hide her disgust. "Bunches of love letters to Dad that were never mailed, all rambling on and on about strength and courage and sporting that crazy red bull's-eye."

"Was the center dot off?" Lizzie asked.

Annabel and Sam both snapped to attention but Annabel spoke first. "How'd you know that?"

"Is it like the note Ethan pulled out? The bull's-eye was off center in the letter from Ida Wanto."

Ethan shook his head, unable to quite hide the bone-deep pride at her words. "You sure you don't want a job at the precinct?"

Lizzie blushed at the compliment, and it was only after his siblings offered comparable accolades that she finally spoke. "I look at a lot of loan applications. While more and more they're electronic, I still see a lot of handwritten paperwork. I notice things."

"Well done." Sam nodded before he echoed Annabel's comments. "Unfortunately, we didn't get a lot out of the visit beyond those other discarded notes, but we have a few uniforms watching out for things after we left. No one's showed up yet and I think whoever Ida is, she's in the wind."

"Like Josie." Ridge spoke first, before rushing on to make his point. "I don't think they're the same person, but Josie's as elusive as that boardinghouse resident."

As the conversation turned to Josie, Ethan glanced once more at Lizzie. Although she'd contributed through-out the meal—and obviously had quite a lot to contrib-

ute on the mysterious Ida Wanto—she'd grown pensive
at the mention of their younger sister.

"Trevor, that can't be right." Annabel interrupted
their brother's latest set of updates on the case. "I never
knew Josie was engaged until the subject came up yesterday. Did any of you know?"

Annabel's surprise was palpable, and Ethan appreciated Lizzie's quick—and reassuring—response. "She
and Michael kept it very quiet, even from the Carltons."

"But she told you?" Ethan pressed Lizzie gently, well
aware the subject was fraught with emotion.

"It was more that I knew because I was in the house.
By that time we were seniors and Josie told me very
little. Even so, we shared a room. I got the feeling there
was a lot of on-again, off-again between the two of
them, but she couldn't hide the small diamond she'd
begun wearing."

"Is that why you went looking for him, Trev?" Ethan
asked. "Does he have some information about Josie
we're missing?"

"He might have, but now we'll never know." Trevor
pushed his plate away. "The FBI's been on it, and we
tracked down the widow of a Michael Evans. Her
name's Lorna and she had a good recollection of what
went on then."

"Michael's dead? *And* he married Lorna?" Lizzie
jumped on Trevor's remark, and it reminded Ethan yet
again that she had lived in the same house as his sister.
Josie had broken off contact with her siblings, but she
was near others, no matter how distant her behavior.

"Hang on—I've got the report." Trevor dug into his
back pocket for his phone, then searched for an email.
"Here it is. 'Michael Evans suffered from a childhood
illness that put him into congestive heart failure for

several years. He finally passed away about two years ago.'"

"Poor Michael."

"How sad."

Lizzie and Zoe spoke at the same time, and again, Ethan was reminded of the sufferings of life. His earlier thoughts of his mother wrapped around these fresh ones and he considered his mother's death through a new lens. Grief and sadness did come to all families, bringing its own sort of hellish pain, no matter the circumstance.

By all accounts, Michael Evans couldn't have been more than about twenty-one or -two when he died, leaving behind a wife and a future.

Trevor continued reading from his notes. "'Michael and Josie fought, with Josie breaking things off. By Michael's own admission, he'd kissed Lorna to make Josie jealous and consider coming back to him, but she vanished.'"

"That's new information." Chris furiously scribbled on the small notepad he always carried. He'd been investigating leads on Josie for years, and this was one line he'd obviously never tugged. "Why would she do that?"

Trevor glanced up from his phone, placing it back in his pocket. "Report said Josie never gave her reasons. The last thing my colleague got out of the interview was that Lorna and Michael were friends at the time of the kiss and that friendship had slowly turned into something more. They married about a year after Josie left town."

"More people she left behind." Lizzie spoke first. "I remember how much she liked Michael. She and I didn't talk about more than surface things after she grew distant, but I always got the sense she was so excited about having him in her life. When she talked about

Michael, it was like she'd forget how hard she was try-ing to be distant."

"Do you know why she grew distant?" Annabel asked.

Lizzie shook her head. "I don't. But it happened around the same time she asked you all to stop com-ing for visits."

"So she made the break with you and her family at the same time?" Zoe said. "One clean sweep across all her loved ones."

"Looks like." Sam nodded and wrapped an arm around his fiancée.

Although Ethan had never considered it from that angle, the idea that Josie shut out Lizzie *and* her fam-ily all at once gave light to a new idea. They'd always assumed they'd done something to hurt her. The fragile baby of Matthew and Saralee Colton.

But cutting ties with everyone, including her foster sister and then, years later, with the man she was sup-posed to love, suggested otherwise.

"We've been looking at this all wrong." Ethan stared down the table at each of his siblings before his gaze came to rest on Lizzie.

"How do you mean?" Other questions quickly fol-lowed Lizzie's, his provocation reframing their discus-sion.

"We've all assumed Josie didn't want to see us any-more. What if she was trying to protect all of us in-stead?"

Chapter 16

As she slipped into her gown the next day, Lizzie considered the earlier drive to her house. The hour had passed in companionable silence, as if she and Ethan had returned to their respective corners to regroup and reassess. It wasn't an entirely fair analogy, as it suggested they were in the midst of an emotional brawl where someone would be declared the winner and someone else the loser. Yet she couldn't shake the feeling they'd hit a strange sort of lull.

Yesterday had been a revelation, in more ways than one.

Her fight with Ethan had taken a surprising turn, his anger at her suggestion of attending the work banquet morphing into the oddly comforting moments of connection and understanding. And then they'd gone to the impromptu dinner at Sam and Zoe's, where they'd spent more time cementing their relationships as a family, as well as questioning the real reasons for Josie's disappearance.

But it was the personal changes that had her mentally regrouping most of all. She'd finally admitted to herself that she loved Ethan.

No, she amended to herself, she didn't simply love him. She was *in love* with him.

And she had no idea what she was going to do about it.

Yes, they'd grown closer over the past week. She had every confidence he cared for her and would do everything in his power to make a wonderful life for their child.

But loving him put an entirely new spin on things.

Someday he would find someone. And where would that leave her? The single mother of his child, helpless to watch as he brought a new woman into their child's life.

It wasn't fair of her to begrudge him happiness, but it chafed to think some day their circumstances would change. And when that day came, she'd be marginalized, pushed to the fringes, a woman he'd spent a bit of time with once.

A lone tear welled at the corner of her eye and she wiped it away, unwilling to dwell on such dour territory. She needed her wits and her focus tonight. She could break down later, alone in her own bed.

On a resigned sigh and a hard flutter of nerves, she grabbed the small clutch on the edge of her bed and prepared to face the evening. There might be emotional monsters in her future, but right now, there was a real-life monster raging out of control in her present.

Ethan tugged at the knot of his tie as he continued to pace Lizzie's living room. The evening had *bad idea* stamped all over it and he wondered, for about the millionth time, why he'd let her talk him into this.

When had he become such a freaking pushover?

As an image of large green eyes filled his thoughts, he knew exactly when he'd become such a damn pushover. The day Lizzie Conner waltzed straight back into his life.

He tugged extra hard at his cuff, pulling the material to the edge of his suit jacket. He hated dressing up, nearly as much as he hated spiders. And at the realization he'd compared a childhood fear to an evening of going out with a beautiful woman, he stopped his pacing and took stock of his life.

He was a grown man, for the love of all that was good. He could go out for an evening in something other than jeans and a flannel shirt. Heck, he was a businessman, even if he chose to overlook that aspect of his job most of the time. He might prefer the more cowboyesque aspects of his life, but the future of his ranch depended on his ability to add to his business and do more than simply maintain the contracts he had.

He'd do well to remember that.

The light click of heels on hardwood caught his attention, and in moments, Lizzie came around the corner. She was draped head to toe in formfitting black, the material cradling her body's swells with a flattering touch. She wore her hair down in long waves, curls spilling over her back.

"Wow."

The tense look that framed her face in hard angles vanished as she looked up at him. "Thank you. And might I add, wow yourself."

"Consider yourself unique, Miss Conner."

"Oh?"

"There hasn't been a woman since my old aunt Beatrice who could get me into a suit and tie."

"She made you dress up for an event?"

"Her funeral."

Her shock telegraphed across the room before a heavy laugh shook her shoulders. "That's terrible."

"But true."

She strolled over and Ethan struggled to keep his hands at his sides. He needed to be on his game tonight, and gazing on her like an overheated schoolboy wasn't the wisest move. But how she looked…

Her pregnancy had only added an extra, sexy dimension to her curves. The formfitting dress telegraphed that she was all woman, all while managing to showcase her spectacular legs.

Her fingers floated over the knot of his tie. "You did a good job on this for a man who only puts on a suit once a decade."

"My mama raised her boys right. She had me tying my ties for church by the time I was five."

Lizzie cocked her head at that, a soft smile replacing the high joviality of moments before. "That's a lovely tribute to her. And a beautiful memory."

It *was* a beautiful memory. Even now he could see it, himself and his brothers all lined up in a row for inspection in their pristine living room. Sam had been too small, so Saralee had helped him with his knot. Then she'd stood back to look at them all.

"My handsome men. All five of you."

Then she'd gone down the line, pressing a kiss to each of their heads before herding the lot of them into the car to head down to Granite Gulch's largest church, smack in the center of town.

"So it's not all bad memories?"

He stood there, trapped in a moment between present and past, before he leaned forward and pressed the lightest kiss to her lips.

"No. Not all bad. I think maybe I've forgotten that."

Her eyes twinkled even as she kept a hand on his shoulder. "I'm glad I could help you rediscover one of the good memories."

The gentle memories that had accompanied Ethan from Lizzie's house to the banquet faded as he came around the truck to help her out. While he was sorry she had to climb in and out of the same truck he used for hauling any number of items around the ranch, he'd made a special effort to get it washed.

And he wasn't in the mood to fold himself into her little sedan.

They'd have to think about getting her something else. An SUV, maybe. Still manageable in size but high enough for her to see over other cars when she drove and equally easy to get the baby in and out of.

They followed their place cards to their seats, images of their baby in a carrier still flooding his thoughts before he snapped himself out of his reverie.

When had he begun to think of, much less care, what Lizzie drove?

Because you do care.

The thought whispered through his mind like smoke, and he almost shook his head to rid himself of the erratic thoughts.

It was none of his business what she drove. And after they dealt with this bastard stalker, it wasn't any of his business where she chose to live, either.

Yes, they had a shared responsibility to their child, but beyond that, he had no claims on Lizzie.

"You want to drop the angry linebacker routine?"

Her soft poke to his ribs had him zoning back in to their table. "What?"

"You're a million miles away. Is something wrong?" She kept her voice low and her smile broad, and he knew the couple already seated across the table thought they were just sharing pleasantries.

"Yes. I'm fine."

"Add a smile, too. My boss is heading over."

He couldn't resist the slightest jab back. "You mean ex-boss, right?"

She was prevented from saying anything else as a petite woman descended on both of them like a tornado. After she'd managed to wrap both of them up in tight hugs, Cheryl regaled him with stories about Lizzie and what a good worker she was and how much they missed her, even though she'd been gone only a little more than a week.

Something odd skittered over the back of his neck, and he was about to turn around to see what it was when four more people came up to their table. All were anxious to say hi to Lizzie and congratulate her on her award.

And then the social landscape morphed again when an announcer discreetly asked them to all please take their seats.

He was shocked when he had to fight an overwhelming urge to press a kiss to her nape. The moment vanished as she turned toward him, but the need lingered, tightening his body and stealing his breath.

"Ethan. Let me introduce you to our division head." Lizzie had her hand on his arm and pulled him toward a tall man seated opposite Cheryl. "Ethan Colton, this is Zane Hardwick."

Ethan exchanged pleasantries, each man sizing the other up. Lizzie had mentioned Zane on the drive over and his support of her working a flex schedule, so Ethan went out of his way to be kind. Even so, something about the man's bright blue eyes and power suit rubbed Ethan raw.

Shake it off, Colton.

This man was important to Lizzie's career and he'd do well to hide his distaste.

"So you're the man who's swept our Lizzie away from us."

Ethan dropped the handshake, then reached for Lizzie, settling the same hand at her waist. He kept a congenial smile firmly in place. "Lizzie's more than capable of deciding for herself where her life takes her. No sweeping necessary."

Dark eyebrows narrowed over the clear blue eyes and Ethan had the vaguest sense of menace before Zane's face cracked into a wide smile. "Truer words."

If Lizzie was bothered by the exchange, she didn't show it, instead thanking Zane for all his support and for the job offer he'd extended through Cheryl.

"You're an asset to us, Lizzie. I want to make sure you know that."

She thanked him again before they took their seats, and Ethan tried to filter through what had bothered him. The man held a large job in a large corporation. Heck, Lizzie's bank was responsible for half the business loans in the state. Work like that made for some big britches. As he surreptitiously glanced around the hotel ballroom the company had rented for the evening, he had to admit there were more than a few Zane Hardwicks peppered among the crowd.

Settling in for dinner, he used the quieter time to

observe the table and the broader ballroom beyond. The servers moved through the dinner courses quickly, and he declined every offer of wine, choosing instead to keep his wits about him. As they got closer to the awards portion of the evening, the crowd began to move once more.

Conversation circles sprang up as people began making laps during coffee and dessert, and several of Lizzie's colleagues made their way over to say hello. She introduced him to each and every one, and Ethan didn't miss their curious stares. He suspected he and Lizzie would be the subject of quite a bit of discussion on drives home that evening and over the watercooler the next day.

He'd kept a close eye on everyone who'd made a point to come up—male or female—and was more than a little surprised when nothing stood out as dangerous or even remotely suspicious. Had he only imagined the problem was in her workplace?

Every person he'd met had been cordial and congenial.

But if it wasn't here, where had the problem originated?

Maybe they were looking in the wrong place. She'd said she didn't have any ex-lovers who exhibited inappropriate behavior, but maybe one of them had been pushed over to darker thoughts upon the discovery of her pregnancy. Or perhaps someone in the neighborhood had taken a shine to her without her knowing. The worst of the crimes had taken place in her home—it wasn't a huge leap to think they needed to look closer at her neighbors.

"I'm next." She squeezed his knee, effectively pulling him back from his mental list of suspects.

Excitement hummed off her and Ethan saw something in that moment that he hadn't understood earlier. On some level, he supposed, he'd known it was there, but until that moment he'd never articulated it to himself.

She took deep pride in the accomplishment of the evening. He'd seen it when she'd brought him to her home. And he'd seen flashes of it again when she mentioned her job. But here—watching her—he finally understood.

She'd been raised with nothing. Less than nothing, if you considered she had never even been given the love of her parents. Yet she'd still carved out a place for herself. With hard work and determination and a major gusto for living, Lizzie Conner had become someone.

Someone warm and wonderful. And very, very special.

Zane stood with her when her name was announced. Ethan had already seen in the program that he would present her with the award. It was only when they both stood, the man's hand pressed firmly against Lizzie's back, that Ethan had a flash of foreboding.

But it was the dark look of triumph the man flashed him over his shoulder as they walked toward the stage that had Ethan coming up out of his seat.

Lizzie walked to the long dais set up at the front of the ballroom. They'd been kind enough to seat her at one of the tables near the stage so she didn't have to waddle far, and Zane had been kind enough to help her. Although she didn't love the feel of his hand on her back, she accepted the man was probably afraid she'd fall on his watch.

He held the small glass statue that outlined her accomplishment, his smile overbright in the stage lights, an odd glow in his blue eyes. Predatory, almost. The urge to take a step back gripped her, but she was afraid of losing her footing. So she stood there, something strange settling in the pit of her stomach as he praised her work.

He smiled as the ballroom full of people clapped. This should be a moment of pride and enjoyment, yet no matter how she looked at it, all she could muster was an insane need to flee.

"I'm not letting you go, Lizzie."

His fingers brushed hers as he handed over the statue and she took it, her own fingers suddenly trembling with nerves.

I'm not letting you go.

The words echoed in her mind as she pushed forward, flashing a smile for the room even as wildly ringing alarm bells skittered up and down her spine with icy fingers.

She was suddenly grateful she'd written out her brief comments on note cards, speaking the words she'd rehearsed before her bedroom mirror earlier. Only after she'd worked her way through them, down to the very last thank-you, did she step away from the podium to a room full of clapping and encouraging whistles.

Zane once again placed a proprietary hand on her back, and she shivered at the contact but focused on putting one foot in front of the other. As she moved across the stage, the lights grew dimmer and she saw Ethan waiting at the base of the steps. Relief flooded her in hard waves, and the breath she didn't even realize she'd been holding escaped in a rush of air.

"Ethan." She kept her voice to a proper whisper but moved into his arms as soon as she got close.

"I think we're good, Hardwick." Ethan's sharp voice had decidedly dark edges, his hazel gaze full of menace and a clear threat. She'd noticed the two of them sizing each other up earlier and had chalked it up to silly male behavior, but in that moment she'd never been more grateful for silly male behavior.

Ethan had seen what had taken her far longer to realize.

Was it possible Zane was her stalker?

Zane Hardwick, vice president and well-respected senior officer of her bank?

Her mind cycled through her limited interactions with the man. She'd been with the bank a little over two years, and in all that time she might have been in three meetings with him as well as attended two Christmas parties. Had he been watching her that whole time? Lying in wait?

Cheryl seemed concerned as they collected their things and made their goodbyes, but Ethan was insistent they leave. Lizzie had enough time for a weak goodbye and a promise to call her in the morning before they rushed from the hotel.

In moments, Ethan had her bundled back up in his truck, heading for her house.

"I just don't believe it." The words seemed so inane— so useless—yet she couldn't seem to stop saying them.

Ethan had barely pulled out of the parking lot before he had Sam on the phone, his brother's voice filtering through the truck's speakers. "I need you to run someone for me."

He gave Sam the particulars before adding one more thing. "I need you to alert Lizzie's detective on the case here in town, too. The more people looking for this bastard, the better."

A hard string of expletives filled the truck as Ethan

took a tight turn into her neighborhood. "Ethan. Calm down. We're almost home."

"Calm down? You're lucky I didn't kill him right there in the ballroom."

"But we don't know for sure it's him."

He turned toward her as he slowed for a stop sign. "You can honestly sit there and tell me you think it's someone else?"

"No." She shivered at the cold, ghostlike handprint she could still feel on her back. "No. But we don't know for certain, and we can't just go around accusing people. He's a well-respected man of the community."

"Is he married?"

"No."

"Dating anyone?"

"No." She stopped, searching her mind for the latest office gossip. "Seems he might have stopped seeing someone about eight or nine months ago now."

"Did he become friendly after that?"

"No." Again, her mind whirled for any memory, no matter how small, of their interactions with each other. "Honestly, Ethan. He's my boss's boss. I am always cordial to him, and that's it."

She knew the words didn't mean a heck of a lot, but neither did it make the most sense to go around accusing well-respected members of the community without proof. An appreciative stare and grabby hands didn't make him a stalker, no matter how badly they wanted to get to the bottom of things.

And yet…it didn't mean they shouldn't look closer. She'd spent a lifetime trusting her gut, and something had both hers and Ethan's going off tonight.

She opened the garage door with her remote as he pulled into the driveway then on into the garage. Of all the intimacies they'd shared over the past week, this seemed like one of the most personal. This was her home.

And Ethan was here with her.

Zane knocked back the vodka, disgusted at the cheap swill someone had chosen to serve at the banquet. They should at least have the decency to save some of the good stuff for him and his fellow VPs. *Budget cuts*, they'd claimed when the president's assistant had walked them all through the final details for the party. *Gotta set a good example*, one of the other VPs had mentioned as he kissed their bank president's ass.

Good example.

As if that mattered. The room was full of semi-drunk losers who would never amount to anything beyond the desk jobs they currently toiled away at.

Even Lizzie had been a disappointment.

He'd had his eye on her since she started. Cheryl was one of his better team leads, and she'd been excited when she hired the recent graduate into their loan program. The young woman had shown such promise. Such drive. And such a fantastic body.

He'd kept watch on her, biding his time. He knew she was still new—and still in that stage where she wanted to prove herself—so he'd left her be, more than willing to wait. He'd been dating a model at the time anyway and didn't need to rush things too fast with Lizzie.

But oh, how he kept watch.

And the more he watched her, the more he realized she'd be the perfect answer to his problems. The rumors had begun that their president wasn't long for his position. Zane had been groomed at his right hand, set up in the bank's succession plan.

Until another set of rumors began. The ones that said he didn't know how to behave. How to be discreet. How to manage his personal business. Could a man who wasn't able to commit really make a strong bank president?

It was then that he'd realized he needed to amp up his game plan with Lizzie. Everyone loved her and she'd be the perfect bank president's wife.

Until she'd gone and got herself knocked up by that low-life cowboy.

Zane had thought he could find time to court her and build a power relationship in the office, but the damn whore had ruined everything.

Until he'd hatched his alternative plan. All he needed to do was scare her into his arms. She was a vulnerable, pregnant woman. It should have been a matter of weeks before he'd be able to swoop in and offer his kindness and attention. A warm sense of protection that suggested he was there to take care of her.

Instead the dumb bitch had run for the hills, right back to her baby daddy.

Zane ordered up another vodka, cursing his dumb luck. Realistically, he should cut bait and run. But he knew the decision was coming down soon on Jack's replacement, and he didn't have time to find someone new.

So he'd better figure out how to make things work with Lizzie.

The bartender had just handed him a fresh glass when a small tap on his shoulder had Zane turning around. Although the man standing opposite him was dressed in plain clothes, he stank of cop from head to toe.

"Mr. Hardwick? I'd like a word with you."

Lizzie drank the mug of tea Ethan had pressed on her the moment they'd walked into the house. She'd questioned why he wasn't drinking his own mug and had got a dark look in return before he crossed to her small liquor cabinet and poured himself three fingers of bourbon.

"I can't say I've had any craving for alcohol during my pregnancy, but consider me slightly jealous right now."

As jokes went, it was a dumb one, but it did at least push a smile through his morose expression. "Chamomile doesn't have an appropriate kick?"

Lizzie wrinkled her nose. "No, and it tastes like something I pulled out of my garden to boot. I thought I had regular black tea in there."

"It's got caffeine."

"Let me live a little."

She'd been diligent throughout her pregnancy to eat right and avoid things that were bad for the baby. While caffeine sat on the list of things to avoid, she figured a mug of tea was hardly going to stunt her baby's growth. Especially if the aerobics going on beneath her ribs right now were any indication.

The baby chose that moment to execute a particularly harsh kick, and Lizzie winced as she rubbed her belly.

"You okay?"

"I'm fine. The baby's active right now."

"Even more reason the caffeine's a bad idea."

She glanced down at her stomach and offered up a small whisper. "Traitor!"

Although he was obviously not moving on the subject of her evening tea, he did take the seat next to her on the couch. "You've had a scare tonight. Let me help you come down from it."

He had already kicked off his dress shoes and thrown his suit jacket on the chair when they walked in. In moments, he had his sleeves rolled up and his hands on her lower back. "Tell me where it hurts."

"It doesn't hurt."

"Then why have you been rubbing your back for the past half hour?"

Foiled again.

"It's the end of the day. It's just tired muscles."

"So let me help."

She was about to protest when the most delicious sensation ran down her spine. Ethan had one hand pressed to her lower back while the other exerted pressure on various points. The combination of both his large hands immediately created a sense of relaxation as he kneaded her flesh.

"That's—" Her head dropped as he hit a particularly sensitive spot, and she nearly cried out at the glorious release of pressure. "That's perfect."

He continued on like that for several minutes. Whether the baby's evening aerobic session had run its course or it was simply reacting to her own relaxation, Lizzie didn't know, but the activity in her womb began to slow. She could still feel movements, but they were more languid and relaxed.

"You should patent those hands, ace."

"Hmm?"

"Seriously. You're like the baby whisperer. The high kicks have faded to a few scattered taps."

"I'm sure your adrenaline had her wound up." Ethan stilled, then smoothed a path over the back of her gown before pulling her against him. "Are you doing okay?"

"I'm still in shock, but yes, the shock has faded."

Although the magic of his hands was gone, the tension release had helped clear her head. With that foremost in her thoughts, she turned the subject of Zane Hardwick over in her mind.

"What would he gain by doing this? The man's well respected. He's got a good job. He's a pillar of the community. Why?"

"He's a massive jerk. Didn't you see the way he was glad-handing the crowd?"

"He's the divisional VP. He's supposed to do that. Make everyone feel welcome. Even more important, make them feel that their contributions matter."

"And you don't think that's a load of BS?"

Lizzie was so shocked by his statement she sat up and turned toward him. "Why? He has management oversight for nearly a hundred people. I'd hope he knew how to make them feel like their contributions mattered."

"Even if he looked down on each and every one of them?"

"Were we even at the same event?"

"You don't see it because you're in it. It's like my brothers and sister. They're all in law enforcement, so they think that's the only way to be. They spend their days on the hunt for criminals, so it informs the way they see the world."

Was that true? Had she been the proverbial frog in hot water, boiling without even realizing it?

"I like what I do. It's good work and I'm good at it. What's wrong with that?"

"Nothing. So long as it doesn't become the definition of you."

"And you're not defined by the ranch? By the work you do with animals?"

"It is a part of me. Like breathing." He said it so simply—so easily—she knew it to be true.

"Well, why can't banking be a part of me?"

"Do you want it to be?"

Although she'd believed herself happy before things had got bad at work, Ethan's question forced her to look at her situation.

Was she happy? She was proud of the hard work, naturally. And hadn't she worked her way through college specifically to come out and get a good job, support herself and build a life?

"I like what I'm doing. I have a home. A retirement fund. I've nearly paid off my car. Those are good, honest ways to live."

"I never said it wasn't an honest way to live. But I asked if you were happy."

For the first time since she discovered she was pregnant, Lizzie stopped and took stock of her life. Had she been going through the motions? One foot in front of the other, living the life she thought she should—the good girl who did no wrong, who grew up to get a good job with a 401(k)?

"What's your point?"

"It seems to me you were someone living their life and going through the motions. What would you have done if you hadn't seen me at the rodeo? Would you be here six months later, still alone? Still working your job and making your car payments?"

The question was so pointed—and the picture he painted bleaker than she'd have wanted to ever admit.

"What would you have been doing?"

"The same thing."

"I thought you were the chilled-out cowboy, whistling a happy tune with your animals." Lizzie heard the petulant tone and ratcheted it back. She could hardly fault the man for pointing out the truth. "Weren't you?"

"I thought I was. And then you showed up, pregnant

and burning bacon on my kitchen stove, and I've had to rethink a few things."

She watched, mesmerized, as he reached out and wrapped a curl of her hair around his finger. "I realize I'm not great with words. I don't see the world in flowery terms and I probably never will. But I do know I've been sleeping. And since you've come back into my life, I feel like I've finally woken up."

"Your delivery might need work, cowboy. But the sentiment is spot-on."

Lizzie wrapped her arms around his neck and prepared to hang on for the ride.

Chapter 17

Just as it had that night in her bedroom, the quiet moment between them turned electric in a heartbeat. Ethan marveled at the responsive woman in his arms, as shocked as he was pleased that they could go from a serious discussion to passionately aroused without missing a beat.

Maybe that was what he'd been missing his entire life. A relationship with a woman that wasn't based on bringing the right type of flowers or complimenting the color of a dress, but being able to talk about the important things and still wanting to spend time with each other anyway.

Yes, he wanted her with every ounce of his being. He was a red-blooded man, after all, and Lizzie could turn him on with nothing more than a look.

But it was more than that.

He enjoyed her company. He loved listening to her

and bouncing ideas off her. And he liked pushing her buttons just to see how she'd react. No matter how he looked at it, he just liked being with *her*.

Sweet, sexy Lizzie Conner.

His temptress ran the tip of her tongue down the corded line of his neck and all rational thought fled. He might enjoy spending time with her, but right now, he wanted to brand her with his body.

He stood, pulling her to her feet. Before she could question him, he swung her up in his arms and walked to the stairs and the bedroom that waited at the top of them.

"Ethan. I'm too heavy."

"I've got you."

"But I'm—"

He silenced her protests with his mouth, effectively ending whatever comment she might make about her expanding waistline.

When he finally lifted his lips from hers, he grinned down at her. "That'll teach you to argue with me."

Her eyes were dark in the dim lights of the hallway but he could easily see the desire that lay there, sparked to life by their kiss. "I guess it will."

In moments he had her upstairs and settled on the bed, then lay down beside her. The black material of her dress that fit like a second skin had another benefit—it slid off her as simply as a caress. "This dress ought to be illegal."

"It's perfectly decent."

"It fits you like a glove and it comes off as easily as one." He leaned down and pressed his lips to her belly. "Remind me to thank you for that later."

Before she could stop his probing hands, he had her bra undone, the material following the dress over the side of the bed.

She smiled at him, a goddess reveling in the moment, before her hands wove their way to the front of his shirt. "You're wearing far too much."

"We'll get to it." Ethan filled his hands with her breasts, caught up in the beauty of her body. He bent once more to take her mouth but she was too quick, wiggling so she straddled his waist.

Never in his life had he so enjoyed being at a disadvantage.

"No way, ace. We're doing this together this time."

Even with the teasing tone, her gaze was heavy with desire, and a beautiful blush tinged her chest. He ran one finger across her collarbone, pleased when that blush deepened. "I wasn't planning on going anywhere."

She leaned in and caught his lower lip with her teeth before her clever fingers flipped the button of his dress slacks. "Then you won't mind being naked."

Although she was surprisingly agile despite the roundness of her belly, he had the definite advantage and he acquiesced to her wishes, standing to strip out of his dress shirt, slacks and socks before shucking his briefs last.

"Oh, my."

Those two little words drifted to him from the bed and Ethan turned to see an eager expression on her face that had his self-control rapidly slipping. Anticipation shimmered in her gaze, matching his own.

Had he ever met a woman so responsive? So willing to share the moment with him? She was his goddess, and for tonight, she was all his.

"Roll over so you face away from me."

Lizzie did as he asked, then glanced at him over her shoulder, seduction personified. Ethan nearly lost control right there, the come-hither look in her eyes the embodiment of every fantasy he'd ever had and a few he hadn't even thought of.

"You're beautiful." He murmured the words and rose up on an elbow, pressing a line of kisses to her neck while his free hand played over her breast. The heavy flesh filled his palm, the nipple already erect where he rubbed it between his fingers. She ground against him, the silk of the panties she still wore a torment against his erection, but he pressed on, unwilling to break the moment.

Drifting down over her body, he slid his hand beneath her panties and fought another notch of control vanish as he met the heat at the juncture of her thighs. She opened for him and he slipped his fingers more deeply inside her, lost to the magic of being with her.

Sensation after sensation rocketed through her body, and Lizzie fought to hold on to something as the storm buffeted her with increasing waves. Just as the night in her room, he'd found a way to bring their bodies close despite her increasing size, and the feel of his erection pressed to her bottom made an erotic counterpoint to the increasing pressure of his hands.

Oh, how she wanted him.

And oh, how the man did things to her. Wanton, wicked things that made her feel more alive than she ever had in her life.

A shock of sensation layered over the already-pleasurable tremors that had begun building in her system, and while she'd like nothing more than to surrender once again to Ethan's magical touch, she was determined this time they'd find the magic together.

With a hand over his, she stilled his movements, nearly crying out at the change in pressure when his thick fingers lay firm against her. But she held her ground, determined to have her way. With a turn of the head, she pressed her lips to his cheek. "We go together this time."

She reached behind her and slipped a firm hand around his erection. The hard clench of his body ensured she'd effectively shifted control, and she reveled in the ease with which she could tempt him in return as she worked her fingers over his flesh.

Ethan made her feel powerful and feminine, and she'd never before realized what a potent combination that was.

With a surprising mobility born of urgency, she rolled over into his arms. He freed her of the last constraint of silk against her body, then positioned himself at the entrance he'd just unveiled.

"My Lizzie."

Two words. So simply possessive yet shockingly freeing. Before she could say anything in return, he'd joined them fully, filling her completely. The tight, intimate fit of their bodies shot a wave of pleasure through her, jumbling her thoughts even as one stood out in startling relief.

This was *life*.

The joining of their bodies had created their child, and their rejoining only affirmed the choice they'd both made.

As Ethan moved inside her, Lizzie held on tight, his body the touchstone that held her in place, even as he flung her soul into a million glorious pieces.

He moved, his powerful body straining with hers, his need merging with hers until they were one. Thoughts vanished, replaced with nothing but sensation. Impressions, really, that filled her up.

Joy. Ecstasy. Bliss.

And love.

Always love.

Light filtered through her blinds and Lizzie opened one eye to gauge how early or late it might be. The bright gold indicated morning had well and truly arrived, and she burrowed into Ethan's chest, willing it to go away for a few more hours at least.

The night before had been beyond her imaginings. She'd believed herself indoctrinated into the true depths of pleasure on their first night together, but last night had been…mind-blowing.

There really was no other word for it.

She'd read that her body would be more sensitive to pleasure with the pregnancy and the continuous flood of hormones in her system, but even that couldn't quite explain what she'd dubbed the Ethan Colton Effect. The man was amazing. He seemed to know every place to touch, whether it was to draw out a response or gentle her after the wild rush of orgasm.

He was a sensitive soul. His work with animals had proved that over and over. Was his touch somehow a by-product of that same gift? It was as if he sensed her needs before she could even think them, so in tune was he with her body.

He'd also been a willing recipient. She'd never considered herself all that adept at the extras that came with lovemaking—those teasing touches that gave as much pleasure as the final act of joining—but Ethan gave her confidence that what she was doing to him felt good. He was an encouraging lover who gave praise and confidence as easily as he gave pleasure.

Stretching under the covers and running her hands

over the thick muscles of his stomach, Lizzie had to admit it bordered on unfair. The man was gorgeous. His body was a temple of masculinity. And he seemed to deliver orgasms with as much ease as the mailman delivered the mail.

"Are your thoughts always this noisy in the morning?"

His voice rumbled in his chest and echoed beneath her ear where she lay pressed against him.

"I didn't say a word."

"No, but you've thought an entire opera's worth."

She swatted at his chest as she struggled into a sitting position. He helped her immediately, his strong hands supporting her as she resettled against her headboard.

"And I haven't been up long enough to sing an opera."

"A small aria, then." He shot her a lopsided grin, his eyes still heavy with sleep, before he pulled her close, snuggling her against his chest.

"I'll give you that."

They sat there in silence, both still waking up, and something he'd said the night before took root in her stirring mind.

What would you have done if you hadn't seen me at the rodeo? Would you be here six months later, still alone? Still working your job and making your car payments?

Although she hadn't been insulted—and still wasn't—by the pointed questions, she had to admit his words gave a woman something to think about. Perhaps it was a moot point. They were here and she was having a baby, the very definition of a life-changing event.

But his words still lingered.

"Are you okay?"

"More than okay."

They stayed like that for a long while, the sun steadily warming the room with early morning light.

Ethan showered and shaved, pleased he'd remembered to put his toiletries into his overnight bag. Although he had the house locked up tight, he was ready to get home.

Back on his own turf.

Sam had texted him while he was in the shower and he figured he'd call him from the car. Lizzie had already confirmed she didn't have much to eat in the house and it was an extra reason to get cleaned up and on their way home.

Home.

While he'd thought of the ranch as home ever since he purchased the property, he hadn't fully understood what that meant until Lizzie began living with him. It was a shared space and one that would soon be filled with the laughter and cries of an infant.

He knew he had no right to ask Lizzie to stay permanently—especially if he wasn't willing to give permanence in return—but the thought of her and the baby living an hour away was increasingly a frustrating one. They'd deal with Zane Hardwick, but then what? She'd come back here, to her neatly decorated townhome, and build a life.

They'd share their child, that he already knew, but the time they spent together as a couple would be at an end.

Isn't that what you want?

The question thundered in his mind with the power of a thousand horses, and it pained him that he still had no answer. Instead, his mental gymnastics managed to add a layer of irritation when he should only be feeling the glow of a spectacular night.

Lizzie had made coffee in a large to-go cup and handed it to him along with their bags.

"Sam called me looking for you."

"What did he say?"

"He wants us to call him back from the car, but the cops didn't turn up anything on Zane."

The news delivered another hard spike to his rapidly disintegrating mood, and he took the coffee without another word. In short order, they had the house locked up and were pulling away.

"I'd forgotten how wonderful it is to sleep in my own bed."

"You don't like your accommodations?"

"I—" She stopped and pointedly caught his gaze as he came to a stop at the exit to her neighborhood. "I didn't say that."

"You didn't have to." Ethan reached for his coffee cup, well aware he'd gone from happy to surly in what had to be a personal record.

"Perhaps it was a mistake not to feed you this morning. There's a ring of fast-food places before we get on the highway. Let's stop."

"Are you placating me?"

She pasted on a smile and a sugary-sweet voice that dripped with disdain. "No, I'm hoping you'll shut the hell up."

The phone rang, interrupting the brewing fight, and Ethan hit the on button on his steering wheel. "Sam?"

His brother outlined the same information Lizzie had shared when he'd come down from his shower, adding a few new specifics. "The detective Lizzie's been working with questioned Zane himself. The man's an ass, but unfortunately, there's no crime in that."

Ethan didn't miss Lizzie's pointed stare at Sam's comment, but he deftly ignored the implication. He was being an ass, but he wasn't a stalker or a psycho.

And it only added fuel to his existing ire that the cops had found nothing on Hardwick.

"You find anything when you ran the guy?"

"A DUI right out of college and a reputation for somewhat reckless speeding, but nothing else."

Ethan gritted his teeth. He'd *seen* the man with his own two eyes, for Pete's sake. The lascivious stare and the possessive touch were real, and there had been danger lurking in his laid-back master-of-the-universe attitude. "Hardwick's a slime. And he's the one behind this."

"Maybe he isn't, Ethan."

Lizzie spoke up and Sam jumped on the opening. "If you can come up with anything concrete on him, we can look into it, but I'm inclined to agree with you, Lizzie. The man's got nothing popping."

Ethan promised to swing by later and snapped off the phone. The air hung thick with frustration and disappointment as he pulled near the highway and the promised lineup of greasy take-out joints. "What do you want?"

"I want to know what has you in such a snit this morning."

"I'm not—" Lying about it was only making the problem worse, so he chose to ignore her pointed remark and pulled into the nearest drive-through.

It was only when they pulled back onto the highway, the truck's cab redolent with the smells of greasy goodness, that he finally spoke. "I don't like what's going on, that's all."

"You haven't liked what's been going on for over a week. Neither have I. But it's not what's got you carrying on this morning. What happened between the time we climbed out of bed and the moment you came down for coffee?"

"I—" Again, he broke off, unsure of himself or the right words to tell her how he felt. "It just dawned on me while shaving that you're going to come back here."

"Of course I am. I have a life. And whether it's at the bank or somewhere else, I need to work. Build a future for the baby. Have money to live on."

"Will you put him in day care?"

"Yes. I found a wonderful one about a mile from the house. They're very well respected."

He cut her off, the idea that she'd already begun making plans another toss of salt in an already-oozing wound. "We haven't discussed day care."

"What did you think we were going to do? She can't very well stay in a dresser drawer all day."

"That's not funny."

"Why should it be different than anything else this morning? It still doesn't change the fact that we both need to work and the baby needs to go to good caregivers while we do."

"I won't have a stranger watching my child!"

The words rushed out before he could stop them, full of all the anger and frustration he couldn't put into words. The image of a woman who wasn't Lizzie holding his child close tore him up. And the idea that they'd not sleep under his roof every single night was like a knife to the heart.

"What's the alternative, Ethan? It's not like you've asked me to marry you."

* * *

The urge to slap a hand over her mouth was strong, but Lizzie held her ground. Ethan hadn't asked her to marry him and he had no right to act like a belligerent ass now that he'd finally woken up and figured out she'd be heading home at some point.

Because make no mistake about it, whatever had him riled up this morning had its roots in that simple fact.

"Do you want to marry me?"

"I'm not marrying a man who doesn't want to marry me."

"That wasn't my question."

"Well, that's all the answer you're getting."

She stared out the window, mortified she'd said even that much. She had no interest in fishing for a marriage proposal and even less in being married to someone she felt leg-shackled to. Yes, they were having a child. But that didn't mean they had to order up a marriage to add to the mistake.

Mistake?

The swirling anger of her thoughts vanished, a furious whirlpool that suddenly stopped. Did she really feel that way? Could she honestly say she felt her child was a mistake?

The hand she'd protectively settled over her belly when she got into the car tingled with awareness. Her child lay beneath her palm. Tiny. Vulnerable. And wholly dependent on her.

She'd loved the baby from the moment she knew she was carrying it. He or she wasn't a mistake. The baby was the biggest blessing of her life.

"Come on, Lizzie. Do you want to get married?"

"No."

"You don't?" She didn't miss the surprise that painted

his features as sunlight streamed over the hard, angled planes of his face. "Why not?"

"Because you don't love me. And I won't marry someone out of a sense of duty. I won't consign myself to that life."

"You need protection."

"No, I need a partner. If all I wanted was protection, I'd get a dog."

The words were tart and she knew there was more roiling beneath the surface than Ethan would ever admit, but she had a right to her anger, too.

"I wasn't aware you had such a low opinion of marriage."

The jab was the final straw, and she was done playing nice. "Why do you want to be married to me, Ethan? So you can continue to skate by, avoiding the real hard work of living?"

Despite the speed at which they were moving, he turned to look at her. "What's that supposed to mean?"

"It dawns on me that I'm an easy choice. A childhood friend who already knows your background. Sort of an emotional shorthand, if you will. 'Lizzie already knows me, so I don't need to talk about anything.' Or even better, 'Lizzie knows what a bastard my father is, so she'll give me a free pass.'"

"That's unfair."

"Is it? Why are you so resistant to going to see your father?"

Again, she'd clearly stymied him, and his voice was thick when he finally stammered out, "That's none of your business."

"You say we should consider marriage, yet that's not my business? Isn't that the definition of marriage?"

"It's a personal matter."

"Your brothers and sister aren't exactly leaping for joy to take their turn, but they know they need to. Why should you be exempt?"

"I'm not—"

She barreled right on through his protests, unwilling to listen to one more excuse. "You asked me a question yesterday and it's given me a lot to think about. I have been living a half life, going through the motions and thinking I was happy. But you, Ethan—you haven't been living at all."

Lizzie had never been one to hang on to anger, and it sat uncomfortably on her shoulders when they finally pulled into Ethan's long driveway. She considered apologizing, but one glance at his stoic facade and she admitted they might need a bit more time. She needed to call Cheryl anyway and assure her she was fine.

Ethan grunted out a few words as he carried their bags inside, then stopped and shoved his hands in his pockets. "I need to get a bit of paperwork done."

"I'll see you later, then."

He shifted uncomfortably from foot to foot and the apology was on the tip of her tongue, but Lizzie held back. They had a lot that needed to be said and now wasn't the time to do it.

"See you later."

He turned on his heel and left, and she had the insane urge to sit down and bawl. When had her life gone so far off the rails? And was there any way to get it back on track?

She hated that she and Ethan had exchanged such hurtful words. But even more, she hated that they even needed to be said. She didn't want to fight with him, but there was no way she could even contemplate a life with him—even if he wanted one with her—while his demons continued to haunt him.

For all Ethan's protests that he was fine, Matthew Colton's legacy and life hung like a shadow over his son. And until Ethan chose to do something about that, there'd never be any light in his life.

Her gaze caught on her small overnight bag and she remembered she'd left her cell phone in the cup holder in Ethan's truck. She needed Cheryl's number, so she headed back to the driveway to retrieve the phone.

Her cell was right where she'd left it, and she opened the door and leaned over the seat, stretching to reach the slim rectangle that ruled so much of her life. A small grunt escaped as she pressed on her belly, her fingers just edging over the silver frame.

But it was the hard hand that clamped down over her mouth that had panic leaping through her chest.

Chapter 18

Ethan stared down at a stack of paperwork and fought to remember what information he needed to fill out for an upcoming cattle auction. He'd got as far as his address and that was it. Instead, Lizzie's voice looped through his head as if on autoplay, and he couldn't even concentrate on the most basic of tasks.

I'm an easy choice.

She *was* an easy choice to spend his life with, but not for any of the reasons she'd named. She was an easy choice because he loved her. It was that simple and that complex, all at the same time.

The heavy weight that lodged inside him—that had settled the moment he'd discovered his mother and had never really gone away since—lightened, vanishing like a bird taking wing.

He loved Lizzie. She and the baby she carried meant everything to him, and he loved them both, with everything he was.

Which only made the other question she'd asked that much harder to answer.

Why are you so resistant to going to see your father?

His father was a blight on humanity. A living reminder that people could be the worst version of themselves, wreaking havoc on the lives of every person they touched. While he no longer worried that he carried the same urges, despite carrying the same blood, he didn't want to face the man.

The man who'd deprived him and his siblings of a life with their mother.

Ethan lived with the consequences of his father's actions, as did so many others. He'd once heard a saying about not mourning the dead, that it was the living who needed the kind thoughts. His father had proved that in spades, leaving behind broken families, damaged because he'd so cruelly taken the life of one of their loved ones.

How could he face that?

"Boss!" One of his hands, Rolando, raced into the office, his shouts echoing off the thick wood of the stables. "He's got her! A man's got her!"

Everything in his body went stone-cold still as Ethan took in the words.

"Who?"

"Miz Lizzie. A man's got her. Dragged her away from your truck, plain as day afore I could get to them."

Ethan didn't give another thought; he just moved.

Lizzie tugged against the tight restraints at her wrists and feet as Zane drove over the edge of Ethan's property. She knew she'd slowed him down some, her kicking and clawing in the driveway going a long way toward hindering his escape, but it hadn't been enough. He'd been terribly prepared and even with her fussing had managed to drag her away from the truck, hands and feet tied and tape over her mouth.

He'd removed the tape once they got into the car and the risk of her being able to scream for help faded, but it didn't do a thing to help calm her down.

"What's wrong with you? Why are you doing this?"

"I need a wife or there's no way I'm getting the bank presidency."

"You what?"

Every moment of fear she'd experienced in the past three months coalesced into a ball of white-hot anger. This was about a bank presidency?

"This is about your job and your freaking ego?"

"It's all about taking the next step in my career."

She'd heard him mumble something earlier about there needing to be an "easier way" but had figured he just wasn't prepared for a six-months-pregnant woman to fight him like a she-cat.

"You do realize there are about a million women in the Dallas–Fort Worth area who'd be happy to marry you." *Or might have been willing*, she silently amended. "You've got a good job and a lot of money. Why do you need to kidnap someone to get a wife?"

"You're my edge for the president's job. The bank brass loves you."

Zane leaned forward over the dash, his focus on the ruts in the old dirt road that rimmed Ethan's property, and she had the fleeting thought that he was crazy. It was only as she kept asking questions that she realized something even scarier.

He was lazy and scared, and that was almost as potent a combination as crazy.

"Look. Just take me back. You can't think I'm going

to sit idly by and be okay with this. Are you prepared to kill me?"

The question was a gamble, but one that paid off from the horrified look that crossed his face. "I'm not a murderer."

"Oh, but breaking and entering, kidnapping and scaring the almighty shit out of someone is okay?"

"All I wanted to do was scare you a bit. Once you were upset enough, I could swoop in and offer my protection. You weren't supposed to quit."

She wanted to roll her eyes at the absurdity, yet somewhere she realized he was a billion percent serious. But it was when he continued that she saw the ridiculous plan he'd cooked up in his head.

"You'd fall in love with me and be so happy to have a father for your kid, and then I'd get the position."

When she said nothing, he added, "It's not a bad life, you know. My house is a lot bigger than your shoe box."

"I like my shoe box. My job, too."

"You won't need either. Being a bank president's wife is a full-time job."

"I liked the job I had just fine."

Ethan sent Rolando to rally the team while he raced for his truck. He had to get to her in time. Had to.

There was simply no alternative.

Rolando said the black luxury sedan had headed for the western end of the property, so Ethan went that way. His fingers trembled as he dialed Sam's number.

"So soon? You calling to harangue my as—"

"Lizzie! He's got her."

All teasing laughter fled from his brother's voice. "Ethan? What? Who's got Lizzie?"

"Hardwick. Bastard waltzed right up to my front door."

"How'd he get in?"

"More like she got out. She must have been getting something from my truck. One of my ranch hands saw her being dragged away."

He gave Sam the details and heard his brother already shouting orders as they disconnected the call.

Lizzie. He had to get to Lizzie.

She was his only thought as he flew over the land that was as familiar to him as his own bed.

Images of the past week filled his mind. The danger that had swept Blackthorn County over the Alphabet killings. The possible discovery of his sister. And now this—a hidden threat who'd had his sights set on Lizzie all along.

Each danger had seemed to bleed into the next. But in reality, Hardwick had been the true threat all along.

He turned past a small copse of trees and there in the distance he saw the black luxury sedan Rolando had described, bumping slowly over the ground. With a quick set of instructions over the walkie-talkie he carried, set to the same frequency as the rest of the comms on the ranch, Ethan gave out a set of orders for everyone to join him at the west end of the property.

And as he pushed the truck on as fast as it would move, bouncing ever closer to Lizzie over the pitted and dented earth, Ethan leaned over and grabbed a gun from his glove compartment.

Zane's hard curse sent a shot of hope through Lizzie's chest and she tried to twist in her seat. "This damn farm's hell on my tires."

She ignored the whiny complaint and focused on the safety that awaited her the moment Ethan caught up with the fop beside her.

Ethan had asked her what she saw in her job at the bank and, at that moment, she had to admit not much. Greed had taken an otherwise normal person and turned him into a kidnapper. Worse, his position of power and influence had somehow warped his thinking. It had been only a matter of minutes since Zane had pulled her from Ethan's truck, and in that short time, she'd come to understand how misguided and greedy the man really was.

He probably didn't even realize yet there was no bank presidency in his future.

A gunshot lit up the air and the already-bumpy ride came to a jarring skid over the dirt road, the car's back tire exploding in a blowout. Another string of curses filled the air as Zane slammed the car into Park. Before he could even get out of the car, the driver's-side door was wrenched open. Ethan let out a nearly inhuman growl as he grabbed a fistful of Zane's dress shirt and dragged the man from the car.

Lizzie screamed as she caught sight of a gun in Ethan's other hand. They'd come so far—and were too close to so many wonderful things in their lives—she couldn't let him hurt Zane.

"Ethan!"

Zane's head hit the car door as Ethan threw him bodily away from the sedan, and she screamed once more. "Ethan! No!"

She heard the heavy tread of more tires through the open door and twisted as best she could to see three trucks as large as Ethan's rumbling their way. Pushing herself as hard as she could with her hands tied behind her back, she leaned forward in her seat, scooching her butt as far forward as possible. Ethan's face was a mask of fury, rage twisting his lips into a snarl.

On a deep breath, she summoned up every bit of energy she had as she hollered his name once more. "Don't kill him, Ethan. He's not worth it!"

Whether it was the sound of her voice or the shouts of his men or the simple fact that Zane cowered at Ethan's feet in a tight ball, she didn't know or care. He stilled, the gun shaking in his hand as he stood over her captor.

"Please, Ethan. Don't hurt him."

"Yeah. Listen to her!" Zane whined from where he lay beside the car.

"I'm not going to shoot you." Disgust layered through every syllable as Ethan stared down at the man.

"We've got you, boss." One of his men moved up to take his place, and Lizzie was grateful to see him take the gun from Ethan.

And then Ethan was racing around the front of the car, the door wrenched so hard on its hinges it practically fell off. "Are you okay?"

He fell to his knees beside her, his hands roaming over her face and down her shoulders before coming to rest on her stomach. "Are you both okay?"

"We're fine." She leaned forward to press a kiss to his forehead. "Both of us."

He dragged a knife from a holster at his waist and made quick work of the ties on her hands and feet. Zane continued to scream from outside the door, especially once Sam arrived as backup, but neither of them heard him. Or cared about his whining excuses.

Ethan pulled her from the car and walked them across the small grazing pasture, far away from the drama unfolding with Zane. "I'm sorry. I'm so sorry."

He pressed kisses to her face, his strong hands planted on her shoulders. She kissed him back and tried to tell him everything in her heart in between his fervent shows of affection.

"I love you, Lizzie. I love you so much."

She stilled at that, every thought in her head vanishing as his words filled her heart in a rush.

"You love me?"

"With everything I am. Every breath is yours. Every heartbeat." He pressed a kiss to her head before pulling her close. "My life is yours if you'll have me."

"Yes, Ethan. I'll have you." She pressed his hand to her stomach, covering it with her own. "We'll both have you."

"Does that include marrying me as soon as possible?"

"Absolutely." She lifted up on her toes, pressing her lips to his. "I love you. I think I've always loved you."

"Then that makes me the luckiest of men."

As he wrapped Lizzie tight in his arms, for the first time in longer than he could remember, Ethan could picture his future.

And it held only love.

Epilogue

Ethan walked down the long sterile hallway, escorted by the prison guard. He'd initially suggested Lizzie stay home, but she'd insisted on coming with him to see his father. She'd stayed behind with Sam and Zoe in the car, but something about knowing she was so close gave him an extra shot of strength.

"Colton!" The guard hollered for his father, and in moments, Ethan was seated at a wall of glass booths, a phone handset on either side.

Ethan took his seat, anticipation clenching his gut in a hard knot. Other than TV or newspaper images, he hadn't seen his father in nearly two decades. Not since the day he'd testified in court, offering up the words that had finally—irrevocably—put Matthew Colton away.

So it was with no small measure of shock that he took in the slim man who shuffled toward him, taking a seat on the opposite side of the glass.

"Son."

Ethan chafed at the words, but nodded. "Matthew."

"That's all I get?"

"Do you want me to leave?"

The old man laughed at that, his voice like sand mixed with gravel. "Always were a stubborn little cuss. Even when you were still in diapers, bouncing on my knee, you knew your own mind."

The image his father painted in so few words—of himself as a baby—struck Ethan as unbearably sad. In a matter of months he'd have his own infant child, small and entirely dependent on the care he and Lizzie would provide.

His father had been the same once.

Batting away the odd shot of sympathy, Ethan focused on the matter at hand. "You know why I'm here."

"Figured talk of your mama would get you here. The last wishes of a dying man sure as hell wouldn't have been enough incentive." A hard cough racked his father's body, an odd punctuation to the comment about dying.

It was long moments later, after Matthew wiped his lips, that he focused on Ethan once more through the glass partition. "I was mad at you for a long time. Couldn't believe my own flesh and blood turned on me."

Ethan nodded, well aware his testimony against his father was the family equivalent of a revolt. "You should have left her alone."

"She knew. Figured out what I was up to." Matthew slammed a hand on the counter. "Questioned me and told me she was going to go to the cops."

"So killing her was the better choice?"

"Woman didn't give me a choice."

Matthew stared off into the distance, his unfocused gaze full of old memories. Ethan wanted to be angry—

hell, he'd spent the past five days preparing himself for the rage that he'd thought would inevitably rise up and swamp him at the sight of his father—but nothing materialized.

Instead, all he felt was a strange sort of emptiness. The man opposite him had caused so much grief and pain. And in a matter of months, he'd be gone from this earth, a blight that would be erased quickly with the passage of time.

Matthew Colton had lived his life poorly, and what time he hadn't spent in a cage, he'd instead spent mad at the world. His wife hadn't been able to assuage that anger. Nor had his children.

And he'd die alone because of it.

In that single instant, staring at his father through a lone pane of prison glass, Ethan finally understood the great tragedy of Matthew Colton's life. The man had had everything and had mistakenly believed he had nothing.

Whatever fear—no matter how small—had burned in Ethan's gut that he might end up the same was finally vanquished.

He loved and was loved by another.

And that trumped anything he might have unwittingly inherited from his father.

Ignoring the overwhelming sadness for the man opposite, Ethan focused on the reason he'd come. "Trevor said you'd share a clue. Might as well get on with it."

Matthew nodded, resigned. "Might as well."

Images of his mother rose up in Ethan's mind's eye. Her bright smile and the touch of her fingers as she ran them through his hair. The warmth of her arms when they wrapped around him and the soft, summery scent of her that always lingered on her skin.

The powerful memory had him leaning forward, willing his father to understand the need he carried deep inside. The desperate desire to see his mother properly laid to rest, in a place where her children could visit her.

Could honor her.

"Tell me where she is. *Please.*"

Matthew blinked at the *please*, and for the briefest moment, Ethan thought he'd got through. That he'd finally—*finally*—broken his father down.

But with a shake of Matthew's head, whatever he'd seen in his father's eyes vanished, his decision made.

"Hill."

"That's it?"

"That's my clue and it's all you're going to get."

Ethan knew there'd be no more that day. Nor would he ask again. Without another glance for his father, he stood and turned his back on the old man.

He heard his name shouted, a muted whisper through the thick glass, but he never turned back.

His future waited for him outside the prison.

And he couldn't wait to get started.

* * * * *

Don't miss the next book in
THE COLTONS OF TEXAS *series,*
by Lara Lacombe, available March 2016 from
Mills & Boon Romantic Suspense.

And if you loved this novel, don't miss other
suspenseful titles by Addison Fox:

THE PROFESSIONAL
TEMPTING TARGET
SECRET AGENT BOYFRIEND
SILKEN THREATS
THE MANHATTAN ENCOUNTER

Available now from Romantic Suspense!

MILLS & BOON®

INTRIGUE
Romantic Suspense

A SEDUCTIVE COMBINATION OF DANGER AND DESIRE

A sneak peek at next month's titles...

In stores from 11th February 2016:

- **Navy SEAL Survival** – Elle James *and*
  Stranger in Cold Creek – Paula Graves
- **Gunning for the Groom** – Debra Webb &
  Regan Black *and* **Shotgun Justice** – Angi Morgan
- **Texas Hunt** – Barb Han *and*
  Private Bodyguard – Tyler Anne Snell

Romantic Suspense

- **Cowboy at Arms** – Carla Cassidy
- **Colton Baby Homecoming** – Lara Lacombe

Available at WHSmith, Tesco, Asda, Eason, Amazon and Apple

Just can't wait?
Buy our books online a month before they hit the shops!
visit www.millsandboon.co.uk

These books are also available in eBook format!

MILLS & BOON®
The Sheikhs Collection!

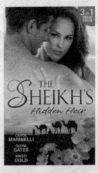

This fabulous 4 book collection features stories from some of our talented writers. The Sheikhs Collection features some of our most tantalising, exotic stories.

Order yours at
www.millsandboon.co.uk/sheikhscollection

0116_MB518

MILLS & BOON®

The Billionaires Collection!

This fabulous 6 book collection features stories from some of our talented writers. Feel the temperature rise with our ultra-sexy and powerful billionaires. Don't miss this great offer – buy the collection today to get two books free!

2 FREE BOOKS!

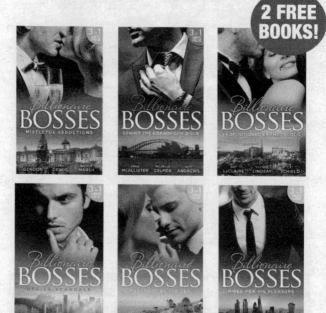

Order yours at
www.millsandboon.co.uk
/billionaires

1215_MB16

MILLS & BOON®

Let us take you back in time with our Medieval Brides...

The Novice Bride – Carol Townend

The Dumont Bride – Terri Brisbin

The Lord's Forced Bride – Anne Herries

The Warrior's Princess Bride – Meriel Fuller

The Overlord's Bride – Margaret Moore

Templar Knight, Forbidden Bride – Lynna Banning

Order yours at
www.millsandboon.co.uk/medievalbrides

MILLS & BOON®

Why shop at millsandboon.co.uk?

Each year, thousands of romance readers find their perfect read at millsandboon.co.uk. That's because we're passionate about bringing you the very best romantic fiction. Here are some of the advantages of shopping at www.millsandboon.co.uk:

✳ **Get new books first**—you'll be able to buy your favourite books one month before they hit the shops

✳ **Get exclusive discounts**—you'll also be able to buy our specially created monthly collections, with up to 50% off the RRP

✳ **Find your favourite authors**—latest news, interviews and new releases for all your favourite authors and series on our website, plus ideas for what to try next

✳ **Join in**—once you've bought your favourite books, don't forget to register with us to rate, review and join in the discussions

Visit **www.millsandboon.co.uk**
for all this and more today!

MILLS_WEB